THE ABERRANT LIVES OF DAMIAN CALLAHAN

Red Grit
Books

RICHARD J. O'BRIEN

There was a further confusion—he was unable to acknowledge the reality of approaching death, and the conflict led to a sense of ubiquitous unreality.

~Carson McCullers, *Clock Without Hands*

All moments, past, present, future, always have existed, always will exist...It is just an illusion we have here on Earth that one moment follows another one, like beads on a string, and that once a moment is gone it is gone forever.

~Kurt Vonnegut, *Slaughterhouse-Five*

The Best Laid Plans or, A Prelude

Damian Callahan was already dead when I intervened on his behalf. Lord knows how much begging and pleading I had to do just to get my case heard. These things happen from time to time. You won't read about them except in books like this one. Ordinarily, we take special care to hide our work.

What forced my hand in Callahan's case was not pity. No, what made me reconsider had to do with my own mistake. I could tell you it is too hard to explain; that the human mind is incapable of handling such a thing. What would be the point of this record if I did that? I can tell you that men and women are imbued with a will separate from our own. It is for this reason that I campaigned for such a sad case as Callahan's, and in doing so enabled him with a second chance.

The truth of the matter is none of this was Callahan's fault. There are times when we play it too close to you; and how I loved to play it close, especially when Callahan was a boy. My trouble is I am not a very good listener. In the distant past there had been some trouble. Some thought that we needed new management; others were content. I stood accused of waiting to see which side prevailed. My sentence, fortunately, was pardoned. After that I vowed to take extra care of my charges; in retrospect, I may have been too careful. However, those troubles are mine. So, I will not bore you, dear reader, with any lengthy discourse about how I came to be the way that I am. It's bad enough I have put pen to paper here.

We are supposed to remain hidden from the world. The directive is an old one; none of us can dispute it. Little children can see us—ditto for the mentally unstable and the dying. Adults are another matter. They become convinced soon enough that we are but the imaginary friends of children or, worse, little more than a figment of the imagination. We have a saying in our sphere: the further from Eden, the weaker the belief. Still, we remain hopeful. In the world there is room enough for science and reason, and faith and mystery. It is not our place, however, to figure it out for humankind.

So why did I risk my reputation and my standing in the organization for the likes of Damian Callahan? Maybe it was because he decided later in his life that perhaps there was some merit to all his fanciful childhood musings. Maybe in the end he took more stock in mystery than in reason. In all, he was a curious creature who nearly blew my cover. I could not, in good faith, allow him to slip from my grasp; not, at least, without a fight. For that, I had to call in a favor.

The curious thing about Damian Callahan's case is that he never quite grasped the powers at play. Despite all prayers and petitions, we prefer no recognition. From the beginning, it was never about us. It was about people like Damian Callahan; those who, despite our best laid plans, often slipped from our grasp. We are an enigmatic bunch, but we are not perfect. Still, we remain loyal to our charges. So, when the opportunity presented itself, the best I could do was to take Callahan back to where possibilities and probabilities were in his favor.

PART ONE: THE DOOM EQUATION

Ariel In Goth Clothing

In the early morning light Serena Moon looks like the Madonna at rest. Damian Callahan wakes up beside her, liquid blurry residue of dreams wreaks havoc on him. When he can focus once more, he knows that Serena is much older than she first let on. The woman lies on her back naked. Her left foot rests against her right leg at the knee; her lower body shaped into a figure 4. Callahan thinks of the tarot Hanged Man but dismisses the thought for fear of some stroke of bad luck on a cosmic level.

There are no blinds or shades in Serena's apartment. Harsh sunlight reveals the downiness of her facial hair. The make-up around her eyes has been rubbed nearly clean. The dark mound of pubic hair is kept trimmed like an undersized Attilio. Callahan sits up slowly so as not to disturb Serena. Leaning forward, he inspects her vaginal lips. They appear to be moist. Callahan attempts to dream up some poetic description of Serena's sexual organ, but he comes up empty. He only knows the hard-sounding words he learned as a young boy; words that most women are never interested in hearing unless they spur a lover on to speak such slang.

Outside the bedroom window in Serena's second floor studio apartment, somewhere along the street below, a car door opens and shuts. A man greets someone: *¿Qué pasa, mi amigo?* A gaggle of school girls passes by. Their banter sounds like gulls over the ocean. Callahan rubs his eyes. He should be in the office today. He should have gone home last night. It takes two attempts to haul himself out of Serena's bed. Aside from the headache, Callahan's balance is off. He goes to the window, cupping his hands in front of his genitals.

Nothing on the street looks familiar. The cab ride from the club to Serena's apartment was a blur. What Callahan remembers now is how Serena's red hair looked like brush fire as she went down on him last night. He feels himself getting hard again. So, he steps to the side of the window. Across the street, in a second-floor apartment, there's a dark-haired woman, older than he, wearing nothing but black stiletto heels as she vacuums her living room. Callahan looks back at the bed. Serena is awake now.

"That's Anna," Serena tells him.

"Who?" Callahan pretends he has not seen the naked woman across the way.

"The vacuuming lady," she replies. Serena cups her breasts in her hands and studies them. "I wish I had her boobs."

"Yours are fine."

"Anna is sixty years old," Serena informs him. "Sometimes she hosts gangbangs up there. I watched her get double-teamed one night by these two Dominican dudes that work in the grocery around the way. We should go one night."

A trash truck makes its way down the street. There's a metallic chunking noise that accompanies it. Light flickers in Callahan's eyes. *Not again*, he thinks. *Not here.* Suddenly, Serena lying there naked in bed blurs and the room goes dark. There's the briefest sensation that Callahan is being pulled inside out.

Now Callahan stands face to face with a voluptuous redheaded beauty with green eyes dressed in black. This is Serena. This much he knows. They haven't left the club yet; the club in which Callahan is the oldest guy in the room. It's a trendy spot somewhere in downtown Philadelphia. Once upon a time it might have been a church, or a warehouse, or a nuclear waste facility. In fifty years all the kids dancing on the dance floor will develop inexplicable forms of cancer. And advertisements on television depicting lawyers who specialize in post-hip-club-cancer lawsuits will encourage the afflicted to call today for a free consultation.

It's hard for Callahan to understand the words Serena's mouth shapes since the techno music is so loud. The more he watches her mouth, the further he suspects that it's not a conversation going on between them so much as Serena reciting some ancient incantation. He doesn't know for sure. And he does not want to shout at her for fear of scaring her off.

"I didn't hear you," Callahan says.

Serena waves her hand in front of her ear. "What?" she screams back.

"Forget it!" he shouts.

She regards him now like some lecher on a crowded subway train, the guy who's just gotten away with grabbing her tit for a feel, and then got caught in the act. Her green eyes roll in quasi-orgasmic abandon (or is it utter disgust?) until she performs an about-face and marches away. Callahan will later tell his friends (what few are left in the world) that Serena was nothing short of a beatific vision dressed in black.

His threadbare hopes dashed upon the rocks of rejection, Callahan, abandoned by reason, moves headlong into the crowd to find her. He avoids the suggestive glances from others in order to show his devotion to a woman about which he knows nothing. Callahan is convinced beyond a doubt that the redheaded seraph in black is the girl the Creator put on Earth for him to meet and mate with, to live and die for; and while he's pretty sure her breath doesn't stink, Callahan cannot help but to wonder if inside her fashionable high-heel shoes she doesn't have webbed feet, or whether a parasitic twin may reside inside a huge mole on her back. Still, in matters of love it's best to be thorough than sorry. Callahan needs to uncover the mystery that is Serena, to covet that which is forbidden.

The mechanized industrial music keeps time with Callahan's beating heart, as well as everyone else's in the club, the 4/4 beat of techno-music the direct descendant of the shaman's drum. For the first time since he's turned thirty-eight years old he understands that some places are not meant for people his age, that at any minute some young Turk surviving on a steady diet of steroids and energy drinks could punch his lights out, grab another drink when it's over, and brag about it to his 'boys' during the drive back to the burbs. At that moment, however, Callahan considers himself a god, at least in his own inebriated mind, a furious trickster who will not be shunned by Ariel in Goth girl disguise. Nothing can come between him and the object of his desire.

No sooner than Callahan's hot pursuit begins his dreams of waking up in a strange bed shatter as a beast of Cthulhu-like evil steps between him and the siren who calls him. The ghoul outweighs her friends by at least eighty pounds. Callahan cannot remember her name. Instead, he tags her by her purpose, referring to her simply as 'COCKBLOCK'. Callahan presses against her mammoth breasts, enraptured by the scintillating scent of equal parts sweat and Chloe perfume that emanate from between Cockblock's cavernous cleavage when she steadies him with a meaty paw adorned with three-day-old henna tattoos.

Strangely enough, Callahan becomes momentarily sidelined by this curious creature. Cockblock's blue eyes and Merlot red hair mesmerize him. She reminds him of a girl from Vanderbilt University he had slept with when he was in the army; his recollection is but fleeting, clouded by the agony of years half-lived in pursuit of career and family.

The rusty tumblers in Callahan's head click and he thinks one of his friends will perhaps run some interference and make small talk with the big girl so that he may continue to follow his dark-clad angel. That dude from accounting with the extensive big tittie porn collection on a flash drive he keeps hidden in his desk drawer beneath his files, what was his name? The guy with the framed photo of his mother on his desk? This woman is perfect for him, Callahan thinks. The realization that follows is delayed somewhat owing to his state of inebriation. Callahan's work buddies abandoned him hours ago, begging off on an early work day the next day, a wife sick at home, children that need them, and a host of other legitimate reasons men their age have for not pretending to be footloose and fancy-free frat boys hell-bent on getting drunk and laid.

The maniacal look on Cockblock's face reiterates what Callahan fears most: that he is alone now and that she can smell the fear on his skin.

Callahan moves to his left to bypass Cockblock. The blue-eyed demon blocks his way. When he moves right, she moves to her left. They perform this ritual a half-dozen times before Callahan feels a sharp pain run its course on the left side of his head. The room tilts for a moment, and then settles itself. He moves once more, but Cockblock is onto his game.

"Wanna dance?" she sneers at him.

The music's bass line comes up through the floor. It turns Callahan's guts in a bad way. As they stand facing each other, the seizure-inducing lights blink faster and faster to the beat, and suddenly the expression on Cockblock's face changes. Callahan's concern with the look on her face wanes now. The four shots of Jägermeister, the six bottles of Beck's beer, and the twenty-some-odd nachos smothered in apparently poisonous cheese product all seek an exit from Callahan's fatigued intestines; since his ass closes up tighter than an oil drum he renders a weak smile; as the putrid liquid works its way up his esophagus he remembers in a vague way his orthodontist, the one his parents insisted on because he was the cheapest, the very one who performed substandard work, making a mockery of Callahan's teeth when the boy was in his early teens, causing him to remain self-conscious about smiling; but, as the color fades from Cockblock's face, there's a certain justice when puke sprays through the gaps left between Callahan's less-than-perfect teeth and through his nose. He bends at the waist and throws up all over Cockblock's designer biker boots. No timid wall flower herself, poor Cockblock of the vomit-soaked boots decides she's offended now and kicks Callahan right in the balls.

The world turns inside out once more as Callahan drops to his knees. Two goons who were raised on York free weights and steroids materialize behind him. They take him by the arms. For an instant Callahan thinks that maybe they are angels sent to whisk him away from this place of pain and suffering, but tonight there will be no promised land. The bouncers bum-rush Callahan through the nearest fire exit, taking body shots on him along the way as they chastise Callahan about puking on Cousin Renee's shoes.

"No," Callahan says, "it was Cockblock. I don't even know Renee."

Out in the cold, the Muscles Marinara twins work over Callahan. Their thick arms do not lend to delivering powerful blows to the body. And for that Callahan is thankful until one of the bouncers punches him in the head. Callahan feels like he's been hit with a brick. The fire exit door slams shut. Left alone, Callahan rolls over in the alley. The building facades warble as they reach toward stars rendered invisible by city lights against the dark sky.

It took him nearly forty years, but Callahan now understands his true purpose; despite being inside the club protected by Cockblock and her short-tempered, juiced-up cousins, Callahan knows that one day soon he will be with Serena. There is, however, work to be done. First, he needs to get past the hangover that will surely plague him by the time he wakes up. Then he will need to explain to his wife the romantic revelation he experienced that night.

Sometime after 2:00 AM Callahan arrives home with a severe pain in his gut and a throbbing headache. His shirt and coat are covered in blood and dried vomit. The left side of his head is swollen; so much so that his wife Jill demands that he goes to the hospital.

"Just let me sleep," Callahan tells her.

"You could die in your sleep," Jill responds. Then, taking a deep breath through her nose, she asks, "what's that smell?"

The seat of Callahan's pants is soiled. He doesn't remember shitting himself, but the way his night has turned out it seems a logical step in the progression of recent events.

"That's not me," he tells his wife.

"Take everything off," says Jill. "I am throwing everything out."

Callahan pulls off his coat. The next item of clothing to go is his shirt. When his wife touches his bruised ribs, he winces. He holds out his hand, attempting to steady himself when he goes to remove his pants (somewhere between home and Philadelphia he's lost his shoes). Jill crosses her arms. Callahan loses his balance. The living room wall abruptly morphs into the living room ceiling. *Well isn't this some shit*, Callahan thinks as he falls over backward. The back of his head hits the oak coffee table, the one Jill insisted they buy from Sheffield Furniture and Interiors in Malvern; a white light fills Callahan's field of vision for an instant before darkness consumes him.

As he loses consciousness for the second time within a three-hour span, the last thing Callahan hears is Jill's voice; even though it sounds as if she's shouting down a long tunnel.

"Oh, fuck you, Damian!" Jill screams. "You cracked the table."

The Einstein-Rosen Coffee Can, An Interlude

A single star shined that night as the sky turned from deep blue to black. None of the other kids in the neighborhood were around as he sat on the front step, waiting for night. That July had been a hot one, one of the hottest on record, and now, as if sent by an old god, a cool breeze blew from the west; the air that night was charged; somewhere thunder rumbled. Out of the burgeoning darkness came a man walking down his street. By the time he saw him the man was already passing the front of the house. He started at the sight of him, preoccupied as he was with the single star overhead and the sound of thunder and the smell of rain on its way and the whole damned universe that waited for him to muster the courage to go back inside and tell his parents he wanted to go for a bike ride; a row would ensue because his mother didn't want him out there on a bike where he could be struck by lightning and his father, aware of the physics of lightning, how electricity came out of the ground and not, as his mother would have everyone believe, from the rain clouds during the storm, his father was convinced that his son was night blind and that no good could come from a night blind boy out riding his bike in the dark when all the other kids in the neighborhood were home where they belonged with their parents; at ten years old he had already moved beyond slamming doors and holding his breath and exhibiting other various forms of protest. Now was the season of logic and reason, for in a short span of time he had come to know longer, more intricate thought patterns; that his parents were afraid of unknown variables, from lightning and night blindness to the inevitable change going within the neighborhood, what with the Kims opening up their dry cleaning store on the Black Horse Pike and the black family, the McNallys, moving in over on 4th Avenue; his father had had a field day when he learned their last names, making jokes about black Irish and all manner of pigheaded statements, that's what his mother always called it whenever his father got on a roll; change was a constant in the universe; he had read that in a book at the local library, that and how matter and energy could never be destroyed; how everything in the universe, from the most complex star systems to atoms buzzing around inside molecules that bounced around making up cells that made up larger systems; yes, there was decay; yes, there was entropy; but nothing ever truly went away; for these reasons and others, the secret knowledge he had gained over the course of that year, as if something inside his head had been cogged and only recently worked itself free to process learning and knowing and understanding because during his frequent trips to the library since spring he had learned this too, that there was a difference between these three things; for these reasons he questioned nearly every decision his parents made on his behalf. At night when he lay in his bed he longed to break free, often plotting how he would run away; but, unlike some of his friends who harbored ridiculous notions about becoming hobos, or joining the circus, or becoming child soldiers in whatever country would have them, he wanted to strike out somewhere farther away. In his readings he had discovered faraway worlds, some in science fiction books, others in fantasy novels; places that existed side by side with the universe he knew; someplace else where perhaps, if he was lucky, he would find a house just like his own; and parents that looked just liked his, only the similarities would end there because his mother and his father in the universe next door would be okay with him going off for bike rides in the dark ahead of a storm; some place where no one ever argued over money, a place where his parallel father didn't complain all the time about the Kims and the McNallys or the Indian couple with their little baby girl whose ears were pierced, the Cheemas, the daughter's name was Paravi which means bird; these are things his father could have learned if he took the time to speak to strangers; when he left the present universe perhaps Paravi could turn into her true form, she could become a bird and guide him to the new; for now, he was stuck.

As he sat watching the single star he had wondered about what secret and magical properties lightning might imbue his bicycle with so that he could escape; for it was only recently that he had leafed through a copy of Omni magazine at the library and read an article about wormholes, and something called the Einstein-Rosen Bridge. He was thinking about wormholes and the theoretical bridge when the stranger walked out of the darkness, stopped in front of his house, his wide shoulders draped in a London Fog overcoat colored gray, long thick dreadlocks like water-logged low-hanging branches atop his head, eyes the color of sweet peppers his father sometimes ate on his sandwiches, eyes that appeared in the darkening night to possess an inner light, and warm dark skin that made the boy embarrassingly aware, in that moment, of his bloodless and pale complexion. The man carried a tin coffee can under his right arm. In his left hand he hefted a walking stick which he presently pointed at the single star just overhead. As soon as the man was about to speak the front door opened and the boy's father appeared, barking orders for his son to get inside before ordering the stranger to move on. The boy got up, took one last look at the star, and kept his back to his father when he asked the man to repeat what he had said. The man shook his stick once, as if saluting the boy, and then banged on the coffee can like a drum. The boy's father told the man to knock it off. The man announced that this was how he created infinite universes and moved on down the street.

A Convergence of Causal Events

This guy must be high, happens to be Matt Tully's first thought when his friend tells him of his plan.

Two weeks after his beating, Callahan is on the mend. He spends another five minutes or so laying down the nuts and bolts of various scenarios by which he can achieve his goal. He can see it in Tully's eyes that his friend doesn't believe him. Or maybe the desperation Callahan detects is something else. Suppose if Tully does believe him? Then the expression his friend wears has less to do with believing him and more to do with the ripple effect his actions will cause.

"You can't be serious, Damian," Tully tells him. "You have children to think about."

"I know plenty of divorced people whose kids survived their parents' divorce," Callahan counters.

"Name one."

"My point is that they are out there. Why should Jean and Jackie be any different?"

Tully breaks down his biggest fear: through some weird osmosis once Callahan is divorced others will soon follow. He talks all kinds of crazy shit that Callahan pays no attention to since his mind vacillates between images of sugarplum pussy and a stable doom equation that might lend credence to Tully's senseless worry:

$RD^1 (inappropriate\ timing) \times (hasty\ action) \geq RE^2$
$[EC^3 = (Fallout \times Misery\ Shared\ by\ Best\ Friend's\ Wife\ When\ Your\ Ex\ Confides\ in\ Her)]$

Ultimately, Damian knows he's doomed. For the time being, however, he's convinced himself that he's in love, only not with his wife. Callahan tells his best friend over coffee at a roadside diner all of this while he studies closely the servers bustling from table to table. *Are they even aware of the cosmic scope involved here?* Callahan pictures oblivious people while envisioning at the same time powers and principalities beyond human understanding that work overtime in several dimensions at once, cramming square pegs into round holes in some instances, for the convergence he so desperately hopes for, a convergence that will set into motion a chain of causal events that will not only affect the people he knows but their children and their grandchildren. It matters little to Callahan now that Tully stood as his best man at his wedding. Tully is a limited visionary; that is to say, he's not a visionary at all, lacking, as he does, the poet's soul that Callahan longs to possess. Is it so unreasonable to implore a friend of limited vision to be reasonable enough to contemplate the birth of a new reality? It depresses him to think that his best friend cannot conceive of the quest he is about to embark upon. For Callahan, if true love exists anywhere it is within the arms of the redheaded black-clad angel from the previous evening.

"Are you sure about this?" Tully inquires. "Maybe you just need some good therapy."

"I don't need therapy, Matt," Callahan tells him. "I need Serena Moon."

"Is that her name?"

"I think so."

---

1 Where RD is Rash Decision

2 Where RE is Ripple Effect

3 Where EC is Ensuing Chaos

"You don't know this woman's name."

"Sure, I do."

"The question, I guess, is does she know you?"

"We have crossed deserts of time to be together."

Tully gives him a look, and tells him, "Jill says you were beat up pretty good. Did you get a CAT scan?"

"I don't need one."

"It will be costly."

"The CAT scan?"

"Divorce," Tully replies.

"It's the right thing to do."

"Jill will take you for everything," Tully warns him. "When you lose your house to her you can't come live with Pam and me."

Callahan pushes his coffee saucer and cup to the middle of the table.

"I will worry about that," he tells Tully.

"Maybe it's just some mid-life crisis thing," his friend says.

"I am thirty-eight years old," replies Callahan. "If it means mid-life crisis then I will be dead by the time I am seventy-six? What kind of life is that? And why would I want to live that long if I am not happy?"

"No one gets to be happy all the time, Damian."

"Matt, I love you," he replies, "but you are out of your element here."

"What's going on in that head of yours? Did you just wake up yesterday and decide this?"

Callahan imagines how the news will go down at the accounting office. The corporate branch where he works in center city Philadelphia is as dull as dull can be (well, maybe not when you throw in that dude with the big tittie porno flash drive and the framed photograph of his mother on his desk). Maybe it's exactly the thing everyone has been waiting for (Was his name Winkler? Is that it?); or it could backfire on Callahan. It could turn him into a pariah among the female staff. In his estimation, women were all wounded birds of the same feather; when one is done wrong they are all done wrong. Men never act like that. (It's got to be Hinckley. No?) Such were the mysteries of the human make-up that Callahan never could figure out.

"No," he lies now. "I have been thinking about it a long time."

"You two never look unhappy," Tully says as he waves off the server making her way toward their table with a fresh pot of coffee.

"The heart has its reasons," Callahan tells him, "which reason doth not understand."

It's a last-ditch effort. Matt Tully slaved through English composition when they were in college together. And while Callahan minored in English literature his friend steered clear of anything to do with the subject unless it was a required course. Quoting Percy Bysshe Shelley in a diner like he was an old college roommate and not some dead poet from centuries past was lame by Callahan's estimation. In college he hated the guys who could memorize Romantic poetry or quote at length from Shakespeare's plays. He saw a few of them now and again over the years. One guy named Jacobs was working at a rest stop gas station along the Atlantic City Expressway. Callahan pulled in with his family in tow a couple of summers ago, and there he was: old Jacobs. He was forty pounds heavier and nearly bald, but it was him. Callahan learned that Jacobs had been in an out of a few mental institutions, was still hashing out the monster of a science fantasy novel he had started writing in college, and was the proud father of a boy, aged 13, who listened to Krokus (of all the shitty bands, Jacobs had remarked). Jacobs told Callahan that his son had made excuses for not wanting to be with him because he thought his father was a loser for living in a studio apartment when his mother and his step-father owned a six-bedroom home in Haddonfield. Callahan had felt sorry for him, and in a strange way envious. He did not doubt that Jacobs probably had to work at least two jobs to keep himself in shelter. And here is Callahan quoting Shelley with all the unchecked pomposity he could muster, thinking about old Jacobs and feeling envious of his former college friend's seemingly bohemian southern New Jersey lifestyle.

"I am serious," Tully is saying now.

He looks frustrated, as if he's the one Callahan is about to dump and not Jill. Tully will always be the beacon of sanity in the sea called Crazy that is Callahan's life.

It occurs to Callahan now, because he's been thinking a lot lately and questioning the reality he has taken for granted for so long, that Matt Tully may not be Matt Tully at all. Instead, he imagines him as some sort of imposter, a doppelganger sent in his best friend's stead to lure Callahan back into the droning, bleary-eyed, half-asleep fold of familial responsibility and all the rubbish society drills into people. It angers Callahan that people still fall into lockstep with hollow expectations, that despite their best efforts to work, to pay taxes, and to raise families—all the while obeying the law—society itself never improves.

"Just let me worry about my own life," Callahan says.

Tully reaches across the table and places his hand on Callahan's arm.

"That's just it, man," he tells him. "You have no idea what your life has become anymore."

Callahan pulls out his wallet. He fishes out a ten-dollar bill and drops it on the table.

"I want to get out of here," he tells his friend.

Tully takes the ten-dollar bill and sits back. He frowns a moment, and says, "You know what I hate most about you?"

"Do tell," says Callahan.

"I know you will go through with this," Tully replies, "no matter how many people get hurt in the process."

Saints, Shit-heels, and Color-coded Terror

"Have you lost your mind?" Jill asks.

Callahan remains silent. He knows what's good for him. It has always been this way, long before the magic of childhood surrendered to the impetus in adulthood that makes adults concentrate all their attention on the here and now, to not ask questions, to go with the flow, to put aside inquiry and wonder and replace them both with something more crooked and weak. Callahan wonders if his wife understands this at all.

Things never work out. So, when Jill hauls off and slaps her soon-to-be ex-husband in the face Callahan stands there and takes it. The report of Jill's slap causes the children to wince. He wishes there could be another way. But if he chose to stay the situation would worsen. What Callahan doesn't want is for his children to hate him. That's all he cares about at that moment.

Callahan focuses on Jill's freckled chest, the portion that remains visible despite her wrapping her housecoat around her body more snuggly now. He had given his wife the housecoat as a gift the previous Christmas. Jill complained all the time about the house being cold. That Christmas had been a good one. Matt Tully and his wife had visited for dinner that night. Callahan felt sorry for Tully's wife Sybil. She was fond of Jackie and Jean, Callahan's children, but he knew that there existed within her a certain sadness; one that came with the ever-relenting prospect of remaining childless. Tully and Sybil had tried for years to have a child together. Callahan knew that there were some merits to not having children, but in Sybil's world that was the ultimate anathema. In her mind there was no other reason to marry. And now, as his gaze focuses on Jill's chest, Callahan understands that the once familiar territory of his wife's body—her freckled breasts, her inverted nipples, the soft swell of her stomach—is now a foreign land. His all-consuming desire to go off and chase a woman at least a decade younger than him, has forced him to turn over his passport to that impressive geography that had been a part of his life for so long.

Despite his newly found passion for another, there had been a time, before Jackie and Jean had come along, when Callahan looked forward to the weekend. In Jill's mind, before she became pregnant with Jackie, weekends were for sex. There was no part of the house that was off-limits; there was no time between Friday afternoons and Sunday nights when they could not keep their hands off one another. They had sex in the garage, sex in the basement doing laundry, and one moonless autumn night they had sex in the backyard. It helped that Jill was already drunk.

After Jackie was born it all changed. Callahan and his wife became celestial bodies created in the fire of the moment, the blast that had brought all things into being, spinning close together and influenced by one another's gravitational pull until another was introduced to the system. As a result, Jill and Callahan moved further apart, little by little each day. That he got her pregnant a second time was by pure chance. It was one of those winter nights when Jill had succumbed to his advances, hoping that Callahan would finish quickly, and he did. Further and further apart they moved after that. Jill's second pregnancy marked the beginning of the end of their physical relationship. New objects and energies were introduced into the equation. Callahan had been bumped out of his original orbit around Jill and left in the cold void to fend for himself. Callahan had stayed awake in his college physics class long enough to learn that A) nothing is permanent and that B) energy is never destroyed. What he struggled with when the children came along, and Jill became more distant from him, was how to redirect his energies so that he still mattered in his wife's life.

"Are you even listening to me?" Jill asks.

Callahan's gaze falls onto his children. He waves them toward the stairs.

"Go to bed," he says.

"Don't tell them what to do," his wife steps close to him. "Don't you *ever* do that again."

"I know it's hard to say good-bye," Callahan tells her. The words coming out of his mouth feel as if someone else is speaking through him. "But every door that closes—"

Jill storms up the stairs leaving her husband alone with Jackie and Jean. Callahan hears the bedroom door slam.

Neither child appears upset. Callahan understands that their silence comes from shock.

Jean will start kindergarten the following year. Callahan's biggest fear regarding his son is not knowing which will get him beat up for his lunch money first: his French name or that fact that Jill had named him after Jeanne D'Arc, the Catholic saint born at Domrémy (Doh Ray Me?) circa January 6, 1412, Jeanne D'Arc who received a mandate from God to expel the English from France, angry God-touched Jeanne D'Arc who pleaded with Charles of Ponthieu (King Charles VII) for an army which was given to her after gaining the approval of the Church scholars at Poitiers in March of 1429, the very same Jeanne D'Arc who commanded an army that lifted the siege of Orléans on May 8, 1429, the woman who captured Jargeau, Meung-sur-Loire, and Beaugency in mid-June; the soldier of God who went on to defeat an English army at Patay on June 18; Jeanne D'Arc who accepted the surrender of the city of Troyes and other towns, and who was granted by Charles VII noble status along with her family on December 29, 1429; Jeanne D'Arc who, upon returning to the field the following year despite predicting her own defeat, was captured at Compiegne on May 23, 1430; she who was transferred to the English, and placed on trial in Rouen by a selected group of pro-English clergy who had to be coerced into voting on a guilty verdict; the Catholic girl who suffered visions, became a warrior turned heretic turned Saint; by Callahan's estimation, it was all a bit much for such a young boy to be burdened with. Jean's name had been retribution, owing to Callahan choosing the name of their daughter who had been born first.

Callahan's daughter Jackie doesn't get the same treatment his son will one day. In their suburban town west of Philadelphia, where prejudice seems more the rule than the exception, where bonus point cards at the local GameStop hold more equity for local youths than a library card, one might question why Callahan named his daughter after an African-American baseball player from Cairo, Georgia. It would always be Jackie-not-Jacquelyn. Callahan would tell the story of how he came to choose his daughter's name when he had been watching a biography on television about Jackie Robinson the night his wife went into labor. During the drive to the hospital and in the delivery room, the life of Robinson gnawed at Callahan. Here was Jackie Robinson, the major league baseball player who broke racial boundaries despite the treatment he had received from shit-heels like Dixie Walker and the entire Philadelphia Phillies team during his rookie year with the Brooklyn Dodgers. In the first grade Jackie was sent home from school with a note that reminded her parents that children should not use profanity in class. It turns out that the children had been asked who they were named after. When it came time for Jackie's turn she told her class all about the famous baseball player. And, recalling how her father told the story, remembered to use the term *shit-heel* during her narrative. That day Jackie became popular among her classmates, and infamous among other teachers at the school. What Callahan doesn't realize now as he looks over the faces of his children is just how prophetic he had been in naming his daughter after Jackie Robinson. For like the famous baseball player, his daughter would eventually be brought up without a father.

"Why do you have to leave?" Jackie leads off the interrogation.

Twenty minutes later the children are crying along with Callahan. Jill appears on the stairs, descending slowly until she reaches the living room. She quickly pries Jackie and Jean from her husband's grip and, amidst a storm of protests, ushers the children to their rooms.

In Callahan's pocket is the address of the rooming house where he will move when he leaves the house. There will be child support and no doubt palimony to pay, and his budget will shrink by fifty percent.

At present, he doesn't care about any of that. Callahan stands on the cusp of something big, something inexplicable. The rooming house is just seven blocks from where he works. He's thrown a couple of suits into a garment bag and other items into a duffle bag. He harbors romantic notions of quitting his accounting job and maybe getting a series of odd jobs around town at places where they will pay him under the table. The prospect of leaving the corporate world nags him. His goal is to find permanent new housing once the divorce settles. Callahan intends to stay in Philadelphia, even if it means renting (and it more than likely will once Jill is through with him). The best laid plans are often pure bullshit.

No sooner than Callahan moves into the rooming house his wife executes her plan of action with her father's financial backing to see to a speedy and exquisitely painful divorce. The judge at the hearing will look on lethargically as Jill catalogs all the injustices she has suffered over the years, including the brief affair her husband carried on in college with another man. Callahan will plead that an experimental phase in his life before he met his wife has no bearing on their current situation. And it will be of no use. The odds will be stacked against Callahan. The judge will turn out to be a card-carrying member of the John Birch Society, an anti-Semite (Callahan's not Jewish, of course; but his nose may lead those less-than-informed individuals like the judge to think otherwise), and, based on his hardline Christian values, a vehement opponent of same-sex relationships regardless of how short-term and experimental they may be. Callahan will be in a state of shock when the judge literally throws *the book* at him (a King James Bible, hardback naturally since it's more lethal). Callahan will suffer a deep cut to his forehead. He will be transported to an emergency room and through a glitch in the filing system at the hospital it will be months before he learns that stitches were the least of his worries. He will attempt to sue the judge, and when that fails he will take to hanging around the town hall with the hope of catching the bible-throwing fascist alone. Callahan will even make a pass at him waving a tire iron, looking a lot like that prehistoric man in the beginning of *2001: A Space Odyssey* waving around a thigh bone and smashing animal skulls, but he'll never get close enough to do any real harm. The local police will arrest him, and ultimately Callahan will receive a suspended sentence for threatening a judge after Callahan is diagnosed with primary brain cancer now that the hospital has finally tracked down the CAT scan and some zealous brain specialist gave it a second look.

Brain cancer will scare the hell out of him, at first. As time goes on, Callahan will recall how he worked summers at a chemical manufacturing plant while pursuing his college degree. The doctors will mention *vinyl chloride*, *genetic mutations*, and *deletions of suppressor genes*, and when they tell him about *Tuberous sclerosis* Callahan will pause a moment and decide that it was something brewing within him for a long time. His options will be the standard fare for brain cancer treatment. They will ask him if he's exhibited any irrational behavior, but Callahan will evade such questioning. None of the treatment will work, of course; the doctors will inform him that mutations on the genetic level will run rampant as his tumor suppressor genes become more and more altered, and that this chaos will go on until the end. Callahan will not survive long enough to hear that one of his children has graduated college. Jean will continue his higher education at the graduate level and be recruited by the National Security Agency for his graduate thesis on bit technology and chaotic number sequence. Even if Callahan lived through the cancer he would have no idea of what the hell his son's thesis entailed (as most others will not except for his thesis mentor who is actually an NSA man and some folks at NSA who, once the recruiting process is complete, never existed in the first place). Jean will never receive the letter.

As for Jackie, she will quit college after her second year and travel to South America where she will join a cult in Brazil. From there she will wander into the Amazon Basin and natives will tell of brilliant lights and star people. Callahan's daughter will never be heard from again. None of the aforementioned future events Callahan knows while he presently listens to his wife soothe the children's fears behind a closed bedroom door. He waits five maybe ten minutes, knocks on the door, and receives no answer. He is itchy to get to the rooming house in Philadelphia before it's too late.

At the last second, the bedroom door opens a crack. Jackie stares at Callahan, her eyes red and tear-filled. Jean is another story. He nudges his way in front of his sister. He offers his father no tears. Instead, he looks at his father as if he were a stranger on the front steps of the house looking to sell crap that no household needs.

"Get back," Jill instructs the children.

"I...," Callahan cannot articulate the words he wants to say.

"What?" the venom in his wife's voice could stop a charging rhinoceros.

"I want to leave my car here," Callahan says. "Could you give me a ride to the train station?"

What follows is a tantrum on Jill's part worthy of an Oscar. Callahan does his best to duck objects thrown at him; most of the projectiles are not lethal: socks rolled up military-style, a hairbrush, and other assorted bedroom sundries. When his wife realizes the absurdity of such weapons, she steps over the threshold into the hall. There she rains blows down upon Callahan with closed fists. All the while the children are crying, and Jill screams unintelligible nonsense that calls to mind for Callahan snake-charming ministers from backwater Southern churches. And then, as abruptly as she commenced her assault, Jill makes a bee-line for the bathroom and slams the door.

THE ABERRANT LIVES OF DAMIAN CALLAHAN

Callahan attempts to console his children, but Jackie and Jean render blank Village of the Damned stares. He can hear Jill as she weeps in the bathroom. Callahan coaxes his children onto the bed in his room as he packs clothes and shoes into an old army duffle bag. His plan is to exit the house before Jill can emerge from the bathroom, but his plan becomes thwarted when his wife reappears with bits of tissue paper stuck to her upper lip from a nose-blowing episode. There is etched on her face now a look of utter compassion.

For Callahan it is a mistake to let his guard down. Still, he sees a day in the future when the ugliness of divorce is behind them both, a day when they can do what is best for the children. It turns out to be the opening Jill is looking for as Callahan takes two cautious steps toward her. She opens her arms as if to accept one last hug from her soon-to-be ex-husband. Callahan glances at his children a moment, and it proves to be a mistake. Jill drives her left knee into his groin with all her might. Callahan crumbles to the floor like a marionette doll whose strings have been severed.

"Jackie, Jean," says Jill. "Get your overnight bags. We're going to grandma's house."

Minutes later, Callahan sits on the floor with his back propped against the side of the bed. The front door slams shut. Jill and the children are gone. Slowly, Callahan gets up and makes his way into the bathroom. In the harsh light there he discovers what he had suspected after his wife kneed him in the groin. His scrotum has turned a nasty shade of black and blue and deep green where hundreds if not thousands of capillaries have burst.

The pain in Callahan's lower abdomen does not diminish as he makes his way down the street with his duffle and garment bags thrown over his shoulder; if anything, walking seems to aggravate the wound Jill inflicted. At the first cross street he turns left. Three blocks down is where Route 1 cuts through town. Callahan shuffles along until he reaches his destination. There is a bus stop across Route 1. He's already plotted out what bus number to take that will leave him at the 69th Street

23

Station in Upper Darby. From there he will take a train to Suburban Station in Philadelphia.

At the bus stop there's a bench with some graffiti on it. To pass the time Callahan studies the graffiti closely, realizing that years and years of Magic Marker and carvings have turned the pressure-treated wood into a mosaic of carnal musings and crude sexual pictographs. Here's a man with an enormous erection wearing a crossing guard vest and cap. There's a woman with breasts that look like two basketballs in a burlap sack.

Not far from where Callahan grew up, across the Delaware River in New Jersey, there was a similar bus stop bench. He remembers that hot summer afternoon when four overweight, sweaty, lethargic men from the town public works department, each one with a balding head and scabs on his knuckles, took hours to assemble the bench and anchor it into place. On that day, the bench looked pristine. Callahan was only ten years old. Back then he thought he'd grow up and live in a moon colony or some giant steel and glass satellite orbiting a dying Earth. Instead, twenty-eight years have passed, and Callahan has moved only thirty miles from the place where he had grown up.

Several blocks from his parents' house there was a little league field where Callahan went one night when he was fourteen years old. He was never any good at baseball (a shortcoming for which his father never forgave him). Sure, he could throw a ball and catch it, but, as his father liked to point out, monkeys could sling their own feces from time to time. Callahan was on his way home from his friend Toby Clarkson's house. Along the way he ran into Marcella Drummond, a girl Callahan knew from high school; a girl who had kissed him during a game of 'Spin the Bottle' at Toby's house that previous weekend. It was a big stink at school because Marcella was sort of going steady with Guglielmo "Ugly Moe" Valero, a gargantuan fifteen-year-old sophomore who looked like an extra from an old gangster movie. Ugly Moe had a thick forehead, one that cast a shadow over his dark eyes, and big catcher mitt hands. No one ever called Guglielmo "Ugly Moe" to his face. He preferred to be called Moe, to distance himself from his immigrant parents and his staunch Italian Roman Catholic upbringing. So, there was young Callahan standing beneath a streetlight with Marcella when he noticed she'd been crying. He and she got to talking about how much of a douchebag Ugly Moe was; though, to be fair, Callahan did most of the listening. Marcella admitted that she was afraid to break up with the ogre. She also told Callahan that she was glad she got to make out with him the previous weekend. Marcella and Callahan started walking after that with no destination in mind. When they ended up at the ballfield Marcella took Callahan's hand in hers and led him to a dugout, so they could talk some more in private. The talk part lasted only long enough for Marcella to confess that she had a crush on Callahan. They kissed after that. It wasn't long before his hands slipped beneath Marcella's Jethro Tull Stormwatch Tour tee shirt, and felt her pert little nipples harden. When she lay back, Callahan pushed her shirt up around her neck, exposing her breasts. Marcella reached down into Callahan's jeans; her slim fingers cool on his cock. He wanted to feel her mouth on him, but she gave him a quick handjob instead. No sooner did Callahan ejaculate all over Marcella's slender hand the moment was over when headlights cut through the dark baseball field, illuminating the dugout for a moment before the car backed up and drove away.

Once the coast was clear Callahan walked Marcella home. The encounter turned out to be a one-time thing. Autumn that year gave way to winter, and Marcella and Callahan barely spoke in school. When the Christmas break arrived, two events occurred that turned Callahan's life from bad to worse.

The first event involved Ugly Moe Valero who had left Callahan alone during football season that year, even though he knew all about his tryst with Marcella. When football season ended, and he was a free agent again, Ugly Moe took his time kicking Callahan's ass on the eve of Christmas break. There were at least fifty spectators, including Marcella who rooted for Ugly Moe; most of them lost interest after Moe knocked out Callahan the first time. But Ugly Moe was not satisfied with how quickly things went down. So, he revived Callahan by slapping him across the face several times; only to knock him out a second time with a series of savage blows that left Callahan face down in a mud puddle. Had it not been two other freshmen from the AV Club who rescued Callahan from a slow and embarrassing drowning, Callahan may have died that afternoon.

The other event happened over that winter break. Two days after Christmas Marcella showed up at Callahan's door and told him that she and her family were moving to Texas after the New Year. Callahan looked a mess; his eyes were bloodshot, and the side of his face still swollen (his parents had refused to bring him to a hospital because the mindset back then was that 'boys will be boys' and there was no cause for an emergency room visit). When Marcella delivered the news, he felt like he had just gotten his ass kicked all over again.

After Marcella was gone Callahan's life took a shitty turn. Sophomore and junior year were marked by fights with his parents about Callahan's failing grades and his penchant for heavy metal music. Judas Priest had become the boy's new god as well as Queen. During the summer between tenth and eleventh grade Callahan got drunk in the woods with friends where all the local kids went to get high and drink. The topic of conversation soon turned to Hobbits, as everyone in school that year had become enamored with all things Tolkien.

Ugly Moe eventually showed up, lugging a fifth of bourbon he had stolen from a liquor store. Callahan rushed him from behind and beat Moe bloody. He failed to knock him out, however; something that would sit with him for years to come. It would have been just another fight in the woods between two teenagers. But as the fight wound down Ugly Moe fell off a foot bridge after he lost his balance wind-milling punches at Callahan who stepped aside to avoid being clobbered. Moe fell twenty feet, landed on the rocks below, and cracked his skull.

Later, Callahan saw Ugly Moe from time to time. The one-time scourge of the school, the guy voted most likely to exact revenge on Callahan, took to skulking around and withdrawing into himself. And while Ugly Moe did not suffer any real brain damage because of his fall something within him had definitely broken. When high school ended and most of the people Callahan knew were going off to college, Ugly Moe flitted from odd job to odd job.

It would not be until Callahan was in his twenties when he learned that Ugly Moe Valero took his own life. Moe's method of exit had been a fourteen-inch-long butcher knife festooned with rust and germs. Several self-inflicted stab wounds to his neck left Moe's jugular vein intact. His father carted him off to the hospital, but the damage had already been done. An infection followed, turning Moe's brain into mush. Everyone from the old neighborhood except for Callahan attended Moe's funeral. Rumor had it that even Marcella came back to New Jersey to see her abuser laid to rest. It bothered young Callahan that so many people had shown up at the funeral of a royal asshole like Guglielmo Valero; another shred of proof that something was inherently wrong with the world.

When he looks back, Callahan remains forever envious of Ugly Moe Valero. His former nemesis had won the cosmic lottery. Marking time in a small town after college graduation meant slow death. And after Callahan completed his studies he had to move back to his parents' house in New Jersey. As suburban towns go, Runnemede was like any other. He ended up that summer working in a warehouse.

By the time autumn arrived, he managed to get a part-time job with H&R Block in his neighborhood. It was an easy gig, even during tax season. His boss was named Sloane. Besides Sloane and Callahan, there was one receptionist that worked in the storefront office. Her name was Barbara Mills. Between the boss and the receptionist, Callahan nearly went crazy from boredom. When they had no clients, usually during the day when everyone else was at work, Sloane spent his time standing by the window that faced the Black Horse Pike. There he would play a silly game in which he guessed the weight of passersby; men and women alike became the unknowing participants in Sloane's game. And when he grew bored of guessing people's body weight Sloane would summon Callahan to the window to gaze upon girls walking down the pike on their way home from school. At times, the boss would be quite vocal about his approval, letting loose with a simple *woo-woo* like a monkey in the zoo who had just scored a fresh batch of ripe bananas. Meanwhile, oblivious to Sloane's antics, Barbara busied herself by stuffing envelopes with tax return forms. Callahan did not care to talk to Barbara because she had a rare affliction, one that had caused her to grind and click her teeth before muttering a word. Her conversations on the telephone were disastrous at best, but Sloane kept Barbara on as a favor to a family friend. Some afternoons Sloane would be at the window, eyeing teenage girls as they passed, muttering his 'woo-woo' at them from behind the glass, and Barbara would be on the phone with either her sister Claire who was her roommate or a client, clicking her teeth away. Barbara and Sloane, each making their respective noises, often fell into a syncopated rhythm, a metronome of the absurd.

It was by a sheer stroke of luck that Callahan had ended up landing a job with a big accounting firm in Philadelphia. He joined the rank and file commuters who drove to train stations like Haddonfield or Woodcrest and stood on the platform without fail Monday through Friday to make the journey from the suburbs into the city. On the train he divided his time between reading the newspaper, or a cheap badly written paperback, and eyeballing women in polyester skirts and sneakers who wore more make-up than the troupe from the Cirque du Soleil. By the mid-1990s the boom that was the 1980s was a memory and that meant longer hours. Little by little, Callahan and the rest of his fellow commuters went from being nine to five zombies and turning into eight to six zombies.

Life went on like that for Callahan. In September 2001, a band of Islamic fundamentalist cocksuckers (his father's words) flew airplanes into the World Trade Center towers and the Pentagon. A third plane went down in Bum-fuck, Pennsylvania (also his father's words); and the whole country went on lockdown. Callahan went on cruise-control, driving to the Haddonfield train station and enduring a McCarthy-esque nightmare dreamscape of color-coded terror alerts until he became, like so many other Americans, desensitized to it all. After he had landed his full-time gig Callahan had convinced his parents to let him remain at home, so he could save up to buy his own house. Despite his best efforts to sell his parents on the logic of his plan, his father was convinced that his son was *shitting* him; and feared that he would never move out.

"You're going to be one of those bastards who lives in the basement and plays video games until you're forty," his father decreed one evening.

In Jack Callahan's worldview, there were *bastards* who mooched and milked the system, bleeding it dry in the process; and there were *cocksuckers* who meant to do America harm; this last categorization was meant for enemies of the state both foreign (jihadists, communists, and socialists) and domestic (hippies, anarchists who, by Jack Callahan's estimation, had resurfaced after decades of being underground, and anyone else who fit his mold of Democrats and Lefties alike). On rare occasions when he was growing up, Callahan had heard his father accuse some individuals of being both: a *bastard cocksucker*. The downfall of the Callahan family had been the advent of cable television; more specifically, the birth of FOX News Network. Jack Callahan was proud to tell anyone foolish enough to listen that *those other bastard cocksucker new stations spin nothing but lies.*

Just when Callahan began harboring second thoughts about his decision to remain at home, he met Jill. Within three months he moved out of his parents' house and took an apartment in Philadelphia. A year later, he married Jill. Their wedding present from Jill's parents (*them rich bastards*, as Jack Callahan had often referred to them on the sly) was a house in Drexel Hill.

For Callahan it was both a boon and a blessing. His father continued to retreat into his paranoid conservative cocoon, watching the war on two fronts in Iraq and Afghanistan as if it were the Super Bowl and the World Series being simulcast at once. Callahan worried about his mother, but he knew that she would never attempt to change her husband. When his father's lunatic ravings about the liberal agenda became too much, Callahan's mother Aubrey assured him that everything was going to be fine; for Callahan's mother would have much rather had her husband home when he was not working, even if he spent nearly every evening ranting about the social decay of the country and the world at large, instead of becoming one of those men who spent his free time in bars chasing *unstable women* (his mother's words) who were ripe with sexually transmitted diseases.

More than his parents and their respective extremist views, Callahan feared dying on a commuter rail train on a Friday afternoon, courtesy a stroke or a heart attack. He worried that he would not be found until the weekend was almost over when some security guard on a routine patrol, checking the train cars in the rail yard, discovered Callahan's dead body forty-eight hours after he had expired. No, if any man needed to be married and cared for it was Callahan. Marriage would not save him from taking a SEPTA train once he and Jill had moved into their Drexel Hill home, but at least there would be one person in the world who cared about him enough to make some inquiries if he failed to come home after work one night.

Callahan looks up now and watches as his bus arrives. After the door opens he climbs the steps and the bus driver, a tall, lanky man with a full beard and a kufi on his head, lowers his mirror shade sunglasses, and gives him a look like he's keeping score of the wrongs suffered by his people at the hands of white people like Callahan everywhere. Callahan nods at him, deposits his token, and walks to the back of the bus. He sits down next to a boy dressed in black listening to an iPod. He smiles at the kid, perhaps a little too lecherously, and as the bus pulls away he looks out the window. The worst of the day is over. And for that Callahan is thankful. His mirth is short-lived, however; by the time he reaches the 69th Street Terminal, Callahan realizes that he left his duffle and garment bags back at the bus stop bench.

Claire (like Dane) and ze Sex Zirkus

The first night Callahan spends in the rooming house called The Winston Hotel is the longest of his adult life. There was only one other night he could remember that came close, and that was at Harmony Church Fort Benning, GA when he had joined the army. He slept that first night in basic training in a rickety old bunk in an open bay barracks facility that wailed like a banshee each time the wind blew. Callahan hated the army, but the GI Bill had paid for his entire college education; so, there was never much use in complaining about his time in the service. As he stands in the lobby of the rooming house now, he knows that Harmony Church has nothing on the dump he picked at random from the yellow pages. Prior to setting his plan into motion, the one in which he would pursue the woman of his dreams, Callahan had read Charles Bukowski's *Factotum* and Henry Miller's *Tropic of Cancer*. Between the two books he carries a false sense of romanticism about living a bohemian life in places like the Winston Hotel. Mostly, he's become accustomed to a decent house and a routine schedule; plus, Callahan makes no illusion about ever becoming a writer—his world is one of numbers and arithmetic. As he waits for the proprietor to greet him, Callahan counts seven cockroaches, one after the other, as they scurry across the white tile floor.

Mrs. Winston, the rooming house proprietor, looks to be nearly one hundred years old. Her chalky skin calls to mind the age-old wraps on a mummy, and her demeanor makes the drill sergeant Callahan had in basic training seem like Mother Theresa.

"No telephone in the room," Mrs. Winston announces. "I take cash only. And I will need your driver's license."

Callahan forks over two weeks' worth of rent. He fishes his license out of his wallet, and before he can hand it to her Mrs. Winston snatches it from him.

"Wait here," she instructs him.

Mrs. Winston unlocks a door marked 'office' and closes the door behind her.

Callahan smells mildew. The walls are wood and in the dim lobby light they appear moist.

When the proprietor reappears, she hands him back his license and a hand-written receipt.

"You're good for two weeks," she tells him. "I let rooms out for the week Sunday through Saturday. You leave on a Wednesday; you get no money back. Understood?"

Callahan nods.

"Payment for the upcoming week is due on Friday night," says Mrs. Winston. "I am in the office here between six and eight. If you don't show and turn over your rent, you're out on your ass."

"Friday," Callahan says, "between six and eight."

"And no girls. You wanna get your wick wet go find a massage parlor. If you need help with that I can accommodate you."

"Getting my wick wet?"

"Don't be a boob," Mrs. Winston leers at him. "I don't mess around with my tenants."

Callahan doesn't know what is more frightening: that Mrs. Winston knows the address of an accommodating massage parlor, or the fact that despite her not diddling her tenants, she may elsewhere lead, at her advanced age, an active sex life.

"I won't be bringing any girls to my room," he tells her, realizing too late the folly of that statement.

"Same rules go if you're queer," Mrs. Winston proclaims. "I am as progressive as the next gal, but if I hear any rough-riding going on in your room you'll be out on your ass. You got me?"

Room 603 is the one assigned to Callahan. On the sixth floor, he discovers that, after negotiating a lift that runs as if it was installed before the Great War, there are only six rooms on the floor. Room 603 is next to the lift. When he unlocks the door, he finds a closet of a room that smells as if it has not been cleaned since V-J Day. Worse, the mattress on its rusted metal single bed frame looks like a bas relief of images taken by the Viking and Voyager missions to Mars. Dark red rings, brown craters, and raw sienna streaks pepper the surface of the ragged mattress not unlike the craters, crevices, and volcanoes on the red planet. For a couple of hundred bucks it seems like a reasonable sum to part with to be free of this collapsing culvert of a rooming house. Callahan weighs the possibility of it, just walking out and going back to his house in Drexel Hill; another thought occurs now, one in which focuses his attention on the soiled mattress. There is the chance that the other side may appear cleaner than the side facing him. A quick glance proves otherwise. He leaves the mattress alone.

Any further thoughts of the room (and its hidden occupants of the insect and rodent variety) fall away soon after that as hunger sets in and Callahan considers his options. There's another ride on the lift that takes nearly two minutes to descend six floors.

In the lobby, the office door is open. Mrs. Winston is there, staring into the space just ahead of the spot where Callahan steps as he makes his way to the door. She holds a rock glass half-filled with some amber liquid. Callahan wonders if by the time he returns the old woman will have passed out in her chair or, perhaps the liquor is a ruse and she will venture to his room with a master key to rummage through his things; only, the joke will be on her since Callahan has left his bags behind. On the way out, there's a queer sense that Mrs. Winston studies his every step until he reaches the vestibule, scanning him and deciphering from his gait the sins he's committed to bring him into her lair.

Out on the street he doesn't feel much better. Callahan knows Philadelphia well, but tonight it looks like a foreign city to him. It's only been a few weeks since he had accompanied his coworkers to the club where he met Serena Moon. Some of the haunts around center city that he used to know are boarded up; others have been torn down and empty lots filled with trash stand in their place. There's a weird fog that obscures the tops of the tallest buildings, and it seems to be making its way down to street level. No one else is out; an occasional car passes him, but otherwise he is alone.

Around the corner from the rooming house Callahan finds a cozy bar with low lighting, dark wood and brass fixtures, and a shitty jukebox. Behind the bar stands a man who looks alarmingly like Robert Smith from The Cure. His hair is teased out and colored black, and he wears what looks to be a long white fur coat. When Callahan sits down to order a beer he also asks for a menu.

"No menus," Robert informs him. He produces a stick of ruby red lipstick and applies a massive amount to his lips.

"No kitchen?" Callahan asks.

"We have a kitchen," the bartender replies, and then he smacks his lips together. "What do you want?"

"Burger?"

"Are you asking me? Or telling me?"

"What are you?" Callahan asks. "Some sort of English teacher?"

"You're good. That's my day job, in fact. What are you drinking?"

Callahan leans forward to get a better look at Robert's get-up. What he took to be a fur coat turns out to be a full-length polar bear costume.

"Beck's beer," he tells the bartender. "And I will have a burger and fries."

Robert fixes his gaze upon Callahan for a good thirty seconds before he lumbers off to retrieve his beer. Then he walks to the other end of the bar where there's a small window that provides a miniature glimpse of the kitchen.

"What the fuck do you want?" A man shouts from somewhere in the kitchen.

"A hamburger. And use the good meat."

"What's the gag?" Callahan asks when Robert returns and stands in front of him.

"80's Night," Robert performs a little dance in his polar bear outfit.

Callahan looks around the bar. The place is empty.

"You should advertise more," he tells Robert.

"Why? I hate people," the bartender tells him.

Before Callahan can say anything, Robert produces a remote control and aims it at the jukebox. The opening bars of 'Why Can't I Be You?' by The Cure sends Robert into an ecstatic and frenzied dance.

The cook's wide and bitter face looms into view at the small window at the other end of the bar.

"Turn down the volume, motherfucker!" The cook screams. "Turn it down or so help me Jesus I will kill you!"

Robert remains oblivious to the cook's death threats and keeps on dancing; even when the mad man in the kitchen rings the bell, signaling that there's an order up.

Callahan eats his burger in a fashion typical of any starving man; he refuses to savor the taste and washes the burger down with beer. When he's nearly finished a young couple walks into the bar; each one is dressed in black leather. Callahan decides that they must be German, and, from the looks of them, into kinky hard sex. No sooner than he's made the baseless assumption the young guy opens his mouth to speak, and his accent is a bona fide southern one.

"Well, I say there, barkeep, what's a boy have to do to get a mint julep around here anyway?" the young man asks.

The woman at his side giggles and snorts...a lot. Every time she does Callahan steals a look at her ample cleavage as her large pale breasts jiggle inside her leather vest.

Twenty minutes later, Callahan introduces himself when Claire (like Dane) and Val (like Kilmer) invite him to sit with them at the other end of the bar. They tell Callahan that they live in a big old house (Val like Kilmer's description) around the corner. They are both lonely, and they want company. At some point Val excuses himself to go to the men's room. He gives him a come-hither look that creeps out Callahan. Claire gives him the cold shoulder until Val returns.

"Do you get high?" Val wants to know when he returns from the restroom.

"Oh Valance," says Claire. "I don't think our friend here embraces the culture."

"Sure, I get high," Callahan tells them.

"I was referring, of course, to an alternative lifestyle," she offers.

"Do you party, sir?" Val presses the issue, sounding like he's challenging Callahan to a duel.

"For a writer," Claire says, "you really don't know how to get your point across." She leans close to Callahan and whispers, "I end up rewriting all his stories."

"That's a bald-faced lie, woman!"

"Oh hush. So, what about you?"

"Me?" Callahan asks. "I'm no writer."

Claire rolls her eyes.

"Thank Heaven for small favors," she exclaims. "No, what I am talking about, my dear man, is do you consider yourself a libertine?"

"They want to know if you take it up the ass?" a cry sounds from the kitchen.

"Hush, Hector," Robert stirs to life now. "Let my customers be."

"Is that mink?" Claire asks.

"This old thing?" he asks as he rubs the faux fur on his arms. "No, it's synthetic."

"Where was I?"

"Libertines," Callahan reminds her.

"Sodomites!" Hector screams from the kitchen.

"Yes," she says as she takes hold of Callahan's collar, pulling him off the bar stool like a child about to be spanked. "Let's go."

Claire and Val's big old house turns out to be a tiny trinity built, from the looks of its exterior, after the end of the Revolutionary War and before the last of the five yellow fever epidemics that swept through Philadelphia. The rooms inside are quite small. Claire and Val instruct Callahan to go up to the third floor and wait for them there.

The third floor is one room. A light switch by the door turns on track lighting along the ceiling. The ceiling fixture throws about as much light as candles in an empty church at night. The windows in the front and the back are blacked out. A large television sits on a stand in one corner of the room along with a DVD player. Callahan peruses the movies on a shelf to the left of the television, an even mix of horror films and German porn. Against one wall there is a sofa. Two beanbag chairs, one colored blue and the other black, are heaped one on top of the other against the other wall.

Callahan's having second thoughts now. And just as he's about to make his exit along come Claire and Val. They have lost some of their leather clothing. In her right hand, Claire holds a leather riding crop. She's changed her leather vest for a bustier that appears to be a few sizes too small for her ample breasts. Next to her Val stands shirtless. His leather pants have somehow become chaps and his cock and balls are visible. Val holds three pewter chalices in one hand and a jug of red wine in the other. Tucked under his left arm is a wood box.

Inside the box is hashish that Val swears is fresh from Turkey. Callahan gets high with the couple after Claire puts on a porn DVD. He doesn't understand the language at all but, judging from the aerial sexual acrobatics, Callahan gathers that the loose storyline here centers around a circus where everyone is doing everyone. At some point a goblet of wine ends up in Callahan's hands. He drinks and watches Claire straddle Val and tease him. After a few minutes of this display they move to the floor. And that's when everything starts to get hazy. Callahan can barely keep his eyes open, despite the German porn actors shouting at each other on screen and Claire going down on Val. The room tilts one way and then the other; before long, despite every effort to remain awake, Callahan loses consciousness.

The Hipster Exodus

Callahan wakes up in his little room. He's not sure of the time. Going to work is out of the question. His stomach performs numerous somersaults, and his head feels as if someone just buried a hatchet in it. Worse, Callahan's sphincter hurts. He can taste latex in his mouth; maybe the ball gag was just a dream. Vague memories of various couplings with Claire and Val push forward now, but he cannot put together an exact sequence of events. It's all too hazy, and Callahan would be just fine if those memories remained foggy forever.

Fortunately, the shower across the hall is empty. Callahan strips in the bathroom and examines his boxer shorts closely; there's no sign of blood, not even after he wipes himself with toilet paper. Once he's in the shower he breaks down and has a good cry.

As the hot water pours from the shower head, random sequences come back to him from the previous evening. What Callahan wants to do is get on a train and find his way back to Drexel Hill. What he does not know is that at that very moment Jill sits at a lawyer's desk dressed in a smart blazer and a short skirt, reading over the divorce decree that will be served to Callahan as soon as anyone can track him down.

After Callahan showers and dresses, he goes down to the lobby in search of Mrs. Winston. An intricate game of niceties and bribery takes place between them so that he can use a phone to call out sick at the office. In the end, he's five dollars poorer for the local call.

"One more thing, Mr. Callahan," the proprietor pronounces. "Last night your door was ajar."

"That's odd," he replies.

"And quite dangerous," says Mrs. Winston. "My night watchman reported it to me this morning. There are all sorts of sexual deviants, misfits, thieves, buggerers, and other nefarious types who stay here, Mr. Callahan."

Buggerers? Did Mrs. Winston know something she's not letting on?

"I am not proud that The Winston Hotel is reduced to such fare," she informs him now, "but you must remain ever vigilant. That is, of course, until your station improves."

Callahan offers her a humble apology. He worries, having stayed only one night at the rooming house, that standing up to Mrs. Winston in any way could mean expulsion. Confrontation is something he wants to avoid. So, he leaves the building in search of breakfast. All the while he cannot stop thinking about Mrs. Winston's night watchman. Who is he? Does he live in the building?

After breakfast, Callahan's head becomes clouded with even more questions. He knows that his actions do not appear rational; especially, to his wife Jill. Worse, he knows that at some point he will have to go out and buy some clothes and a new cell phone since he had left his bags on the bus stop bench back in Drexel Hill. Of course, when he leaves the small diner on 17th Street none of the stores are open yet, so he walks back to the rooming house. Along the way he passes a small shop that sells cheap bed linens. Callahan pops in, purchases two sets of sheets, a mattress liner, and a pillow. He barely pays attention to the clerk when he pays for his goods; his head brims with questions about all the blank spaces in his memory concerning the previous evening.

Back at the rooming house Mrs. Winston sits inside her tiny office. She pays Callahan no mind as he climbs into the lift and begins the slow ascent to the sixth floor.

In his room Callahan makes his bed. He turns over the old mattress and discovers that it looks worse than the side facing him; as if perhaps someone may have been murdered on it, judging by the dark brown stains all over that side of the mattress and the faint odor of iron. When he's satisfied that the bed is suitable to lie down on he does so and falls in and out of a light sleep for the remainder of the morning.

By noon he's ready to commit suicide. He curses himself for purchasing disposable twin-blade razors instead of a good old-fashioned straight razor. His next consideration is suicide by hanging, but there's nowhere in his room to secure his belt. When suicide no longer seems a viable option, mostly because he can think only of the irreparable damage it would do to his children, Callahan once more considers going home with his tail between his legs and begging for Jill's forgiveness.

The following day, looking much worse for the wear, Callahan goes back to work. His boss takes one look at him and drags him to the Human Resources office. Jill's been in touch with Callahan's boss. After twenty minutes of deliberation, it is agreed by all parties that perhaps Callahan should take a week's vacation and attempt to straighten himself out. It's not a question so much as it is an order.

Over the next few days Callahan has every intention of calling his wife. But as those hours pass he begins to enjoy his new-found freedom. He misses his children; yet, despite that sadness, he cannot bring himself to call home.

On Monday Callahan wakes up feeling hungry again. It is well past noon by the time he's ambulatory. He returns to the little diner on 17th Street that he visits twice a day now for his meals. After he finishes his lunch he stops at a few stores along Walnut Street to buy some clothes and fresh underwear and socks. Sooner or later, he'll have to make the pilgrimage back to Drexel Hill to gather some more things. For now, he will be ok. After his clothing purchase, Callahan buys a throw-away cell phone and two hundred minutes of talk time from a store on 15th Street near Chestnut. He returns to the rooming house where he showers, shaves, and dresses again.

A little later in the afternoon, downstairs in the lobby, there's a big hullabaloo over one of the tenants who's just been ejected from the rooming house. Two police officers struggle to handcuff a man named Roy Harper, the poet who lives on the fourth floor. Amidst the confusion Callahan learns that Harper has sent a copy of his latest poem, *Life, Liberty, and Lynching*, to the mayor's office at City Hall.

"What's so bad about sending a poem to city hall?" Callahan asks Mrs. Winston during the scuffle.

"It appears Mr. Harper calls for hanging the mayor and members of city council from street lamps," she replies.

Later, Callahan will read in the newspaper an excerpt from Harper's poem that reads:

> *Rise up! Rise up, you downtrodden!*
> *Rise up and bring your rope to City Hall!*
> *There's going to be a magnificent party*
> *and we will hang them all!*

In the end Harper will be charged with a host of crimes that includes conspiring to commit murder against a public official, but the charge that will send him to jail will be breaking and entering. The night before Harper's arrest the poet managed to sneak past a host of police officers milling about City Hall after-hours and break into the mayor's office where he left a G.I. Joe doll dressed in a suit hanging from a ceiling fan. Pinned to the doll's suit jacket is a note with the four lines from the poem. Harper's mistake, then, was sending a copy of the full poem to the mayor's office with his signature and address on it (later Harper would admit in an interview that he had mailed the wrong copy) along with a letter warning the mayor and city council members to step down *or else*.

The struggle between Harper and the police turn into a performance art spectacle of sorts, with Harper running around in circles, slapping his face like Curly Howard, barking at the officers, and screaming *WOOP, WOOP, WOOP, WOOP, WOOP, WOOP, WOOP, NYUK, NYUK, NYUK!* repeatedly until one police officer realizes that his shift may go into overtime if the situation does not improve. So, he cracks Harper over the head with his nightstick. The poet collapses on the dirty tile floor just a few feet from Mrs. Winston's office. The show comes to an end. The police officers handcuff the unconscious Roy Harper, drag him out of the rooming house lobby, and toss him like a sack of horse feed into a waiting police van outside.

Several tenants mill about inside the lobby and on the sidewalk outside. There's talk of organizing a march. There's talk of putting money together to bail Roy Harper out of jail. As Callahan witnesses the spectacle of so many people talking at once he feels thankful that he's not half as crazy as some of the other tenants. There's Bertrand Russo, a willow wisp of an old man and a retired philosophy professor whose long sparse curls of white hair calls to mind seed heads on a dandelion. Russo is rumored to possess a penchant for transvestite hookers; though the transvestite hookers, so the story goes, aren't so fond of the Professor and his long lectures on the phenomenology of the mind; but money is money so whenever the Professor puts the call out a half-dozen or more would trickle into the building, one at a time, so as not to arouse the suspicion of Mrs. Winston, and proceed to the Professor's room where he kept old-fashioned wrought-iron and wood desks. Of the many prostitutes who answered the Professor's call, only one had ever questioned the sprite of an old man. The transvestite's name was Tiny. *Don't you want to fuck?* Tiny had asked the Professor one night. The other prostitutes drew a collective breath; none of them, for as long as they had been coming around for the Professor's class, ever considered the possibility of physical contact with such an old man; not that any of them were strangers to the perversions of men (and not a few women) in their golden years; no, the aging philosopher seemed so frail a creature that the prostitutes had all assumed that his plumbing no longer worked. *Pay attention, Tiny,* the Professor scolded him. *It's your money,* said Tiny. *Keep on talking. An hour is an hour.* For such insolence professor emeritus Russo forbade Tiny to sit in on his lecture ever again.

Another inhabitant of the rooming house is Colonel (Ret.) Hammond Dietrich. The Colonel wears a khaki-colored linen suit and white shirt (no tie, with the collar open). He is rarely seen without his sidekick—a lithe, young Cambodian man who goes by the name of Günter. Callahan's pretty sure that the Colonel and Günter occupy the same room on the fifth floor. For all of her tough talk about rough-riding and bringing prostitutes into the building, Mrs. Winston allows both the Colonel and the Professor their indulgences.

"Damian," the Colonel calls out from the crowd packed into the lobby. "It's splendid to see you, old boy."

Callahan's never talked to the Colonel. He's lived at the rooming house for less than a week when Roy Harper gets arrested. How the Colonel knows his name is a mystery. Odder still is that the khaki-clad man sounds British. When Callahan had first heard about him and his Cambodian sidekick he had assumed that the Colonel was an American.

"Good evening, Colonel," Callahan shakes his hand.

As usual, Günter stands at the Colonel's side. Tonight, he's dressed in white jeans and a lavender mesh tank top that shows off his six-pack abs.

"Say hello, Günter," the Colonel instructs his partner.

The young man offers a nod. He's more interested in the Colonel's neck which he softly blows on as his eyes remain locked on Callahan.

"Where are you going?" the Colonel asks as he shoos Günter away.

His sidekick stomps off like an SS Officer on the march, and plants himself on the steps outside the lobby. Callahan and the Colonel watch as Günter crosses one leg over the other, checks out his fingernails, and yells *Hey, girl* to someone across the street.

"Well?" the Colonel asks.

Callahan shrugs. "Out," he tells him. "Just out."

"Günter and I are on the way to the Air Command on 12th Street."

"Nice place?" Callahan asks.

"Karaoke night," the Colonel informs him. "Günter loves to sing. Though, I must admit, he's not very good at it."

"It takes practice."

"You are a singer?"

"No. Not at all."

"It's a pity," says the Colonel. "You have to hand it to the Japanese, what? We bombed the hell out of them in the Second World War, and what do they do? They pay us back with their infernal music machines."

Günter leaves his perch on the steps and returns to the lobby.

"I am hungry," he says and sighs.

The Colonel leans in close to Callahan.

"Can't keep him waiting," he whispers. "Günter is so much more manageable on a full stomach. It's like I used to tell the chaps in Burma. Feed a prisoner and he'll talk all day long. The other chaps I served with were short-sighted that way. Some of the brutality I witnessed there could have been easily avoided. We were officers and gentlemen, but something about the heat there—"

"You don't say," Callahan offers.

"Well, enough waxing nostalgic for now," the Colonel says as he allows Günter to wrap his arm around his. "We're off for some fish. It's good for the glands if you know what I mean."

Callahan stares at them as Günter leans close to the Colonel and whispers something. Then he looks away.

"Well," says Callahan, "I will be on my way."

As the two men head for the door, the Colonel stops. He opens the door for Günter.

"Damian," the Colonel calls after Callahan who steps into the antiquated lift. "Günter likes you. And I like what Günter likes. Do drop by room 503 some night and visit us."

Callahan's meal later that evening consists of the typical Philly fair: a cheese steak sandwich coupled with cheese fries. When he places the order, he eyeballs a cooler filled with pints of milk, and purchases one to go along with his dinner. The expiration dates on the cartons all appear to have been deliberately smudged. Callahan remains undeterred. The milk smells fine when he drinks it.

The street outside the steak shop is filled with people, most of them college students. The night air gives Callahan a second wind. He walks down Pine Street, past Pennsylvania Hospital. Along the way he passes old brownstone buildings converted into apartments. On some of the steps of each building young men and women sit in small groups. As he passes them, Callahan becomes acutely aware that, at thirty-eight years old, he is nowhere near close to the age of those who occupy the steps, much less able to understand their dialect, even if it sounds remotely English.

On one corner, at 7th and Pine Street, a woman sits looking pensive with paintings propped up against the side of an apartment building.

"Hey man," the woman says as he passes by. "You want to buy a painting?"

"Not in the market right now," Callahan replies. "But thanks all the same."

"Yuppie asshole," she declares. "Go back to the suburbs."

"You should channel that anger into your work."

"Go fuck yourself."

Callahan's about to ramp up the verbal exchange when he spots a gargantuan man, Māori by the looks of him, emerging from the apartment building.

"What's up, babe?" the giant asks as he embraces the artist in his enormous tattoo-riddled arms.

"My friend here doesn't want to buy a painting," the woman answers.

"You got something against art?" the Māori giant asks.

Callahan tips an imaginary hat and goes on his way. At 5th Street he turns right and walks until he reaches South Street.

THE ABERRANT LIVES OF DAMIAN CALLAHAN

Once upon a time, Grendel's Lair stood at the corner right across from The Book Trader. Now there's a T-Mobile store where the famous club had been. And the space where the Book Trader once stood is a clothing store. The further along Callahan walks, the more evident the corporate virus infection up and down the street where the hippies used to meet. Just before he reaches 3rd and South, he discovers at least one main stay from his college days. J.C. Dobbs, the legendary bar, is still there. The façade looks different now, but a sign outside still boasts 'The Original J.C. Dobbs' so Callahan walks up to the door. A lackluster bouncer demands eight dollars. Callahan hands him a ten-dollar bill. The bouncer makes a face. He fishes eight quarters out of his pocket and hands them to Callahan.

It doesn't take Callahan long to realize he's out of his element once he steps inside. Gone are the leather-jacket-blue-jean-Doc-Marten-boot-wearing alt rockers he knew from his college days. They have been replaced by young homogenous hipster types, dressed in tight khaki pants, Hush Puppy shoes, thick-framed glasses, and expensive flannel shirts made to look second-hand. Surrounded by such people, it's easy to loathe the crowd. They would not know a good guitar lick or lyric if it hit them right between the eyes with the force of a mike stand hurled by a coked-out singer who, on his opening number, decides that he can't pay the rent, that he can't fuck anymore, that there's no God, and that his parents wished they had gone through with the abortion they discussed all those years ago, lashing out at an indifferent audience who, in another era, would have perceived the mike stand turned weapon as a metaphor for the encroaching corporate takeover of the street itself; but not this current crowd. No, they are less interested in rock and roll in the making (for J.C. Dobbs had been the kind of place where lightning did strike with regard to musical greatness) and more interested in attending Tea Party rallies and preaching the benefits of small government, in trying desperately to reduce their carbon footprint, in growing beards (the men at least) so as not to flood landfills with disposable razors, in cutting out a unique niche for themselves, going beyond the tipping point that pushes them into bland obscurity, and in making every attempt to eschew the notion that they are, at heart, no different than any other semi-autonomous peasantry in history; only, in the hipsters' collective case, farming their lord's land has been replaced by working in technology-related fields owned and operated by the very corporate conglomerates they view as the enemy.

The staff working the bar appears to be cookie-cutter weekend-warrior rock-and-roll wannabes who don't know The Cult from The Clash. Callahan's attire makes him look out of place. The bartenders eye him with suspicion, unable to decide if he's a narcotics detective or some do-gooder with a chip on his shoulder from the liquor control board.

Five hipsters take the stage as Callahan attempts to flag down the bartender. The first number the band plays sounds like a Grateful Dead rip-off; the crowd is too busy monitoring social media websites on their cell phones to notice.

"What do you want, buddy?" the bartender asks.

"A bullet to the head," Callahan shouts at him.

"Never heard of it."

"Give me a Beck's."

"No Beck's."

"Surprise me."

The bartender produces a bottle of beer with a colorful label on it.

"Six bucks!" he yells.

Callahan pays the bartender with a ten-dollar bill and tells him to keep the change. A few hipsters standing close to Callahan give him a look.

The beer is awful, a combination of apple, cinnamon, and orange flavoring that turns Callahan's stomach. He sets the beer down on the bar after one sip. As he contemplates leaving he catches a glimpse of long, curly red locks descending the stairs. Serena Moon cuts through the crowd with ease.

Callahan stands up straighter as she makes her way toward him. Serena is only five or six paces away when suddenly the whole bar goes dark. The band stops playing. The singer curses up a storm.

Possessed of not even the most rudimentary understanding of electricity's essential role in playing electric guitars, in powering microphones, speakers, and amplifiers, some less than intelligent hipster girl, no doubt inebriated beyond the legal limit, stands up on a bar stool and shouts, "Keep playing!"

Callahan becomes trapped as a contingent of hipsters press toward the door. One of them mentions terrorists as he bee-lines for the exit. In the confusion, Callahan stays put at the bar. The emergency lighting system casts but a candle's glow. Someone grabs his crotch as they go by. He can't tell if it was a guy or a girl.

The lights come back on. There's an awful squeal of feedback from the stage that sends the singer into a renewed frenzy. Callahan turns his attention toward the door. As the hipster exodus continues, he spots his redheaded siren, the love of his life whose name he dreams now. Serena remains visible only for a moment at the door before she's gone.

The Lesser Angels of Déjà Vu

Callahan follows Serena Moon. As he moves west up South Street, he watches as the beatific vision meets up with a pack of women clad in denim and leather. Callahan smells her perfume, or he imagines he can, over the stink of the street. He pauses in front of the Theater of Living Arts, fearful that he will be spotted before he can make his move.

All the way up the street Callahan tracks the gorgeous crown of red hair. There is the strange sensation that his feet no longer touch the pavement. Soon, his body leaves the ground. He dodges thin tree branches as he floats ever skyward. Before long, the siren's sweet laughter reaches him as he leisurely floats a few stories overhead. Somewhere in the night a trumpet sounds. Callahan expects an onslaught of heavenly hosts, invisible and winged, to swoop down on Serena Moon and carry her off before he can reach her. A second time, the trumpet blasts.

Suddenly, Callahan finds himself standing on 5th Street and staring down a taxi cab inside which the driver lays on his horn several more times. He dives out of the way when the taxi lurches forward. Two metal trash cans on the curb break his fall. The taxi driver curses at him as he speeds past. Two uniformed police officers make their way toward Callahan who stands both garbage cans upright. One of the officers looks like Ichabod Crane; the other is a short heavyset Latina with way too much make-up for a cop walking the beat.

"Hey!" Ichabod Crane shouts.

"Stop right there," the Latina cop instructs him.

Callahan's pretty sure he can outrun the woman, but Crane is another story. By now, Serena Moon is nowhere in sight. Callahan dashes up South Street toward 6th. As he passes Manny Brown's Pub a dozen Brits in rugby jerseys pour out of the bar singing a song just as Callahan slips by. Ichabod Crane and the Latina are blocked from any further pursuit of the lovesick one. Callahan stops at Randolph Street, jumping up and down to see if he can catch a glimpse of Serena Moon's red hair. He looks back, thinking that perhaps she ducked into Manny Brown's. Going back there is out of the question. The rugby jerseys are squaring off against Crane and his partner. Another four police officers cross South Street to lend their support. The Brits point fingers at the police; the cops produce nightsticks and start walloping the Brits on their heads. When this action does not produce the desired results; for by now at least three of the Brits are wrestling with the cops; the remaining police officers swing their nightsticks low, hitting the men in their legs until they buckle and fall to the sidewalk.

Before long two police vans turn onto South Street. A cadre of additional police officers disembarks from the two vans and joins the melee. Onlookers jockey for position along the street to get a better look at the action. At one point, the Latina officer climbs out from beneath a pile of bloodied Brits. She's lost her hat and her make-up is smeared. For a moment, the Latina cop gives Callahan a funny look; as if to say *this is all your fault, cabrón*, just before one of the Brits sucker-punches her. The female officer collapses to the sidewalk like candy from a busted piñata.

Frustrated at having lost sight of Serena Moon, and bored with the fracas outside Manny Brown's Pub, Callahan turns left into the parking lot that borders Randolph Street. Cars line the parking spaces there. When he reaches Kater Street, a narrow side street that runs parallel to South, the noise of South Street dies down.

Kater Street is dark when he crosses. Keys jingle somewhere to his left. A large figure cloaked in shadows lumbers toward him. Callahan can smell the guy before he gets close. The big man passes beneath a lone street light. A large ring of skeletal keys attached to the man's leather belt becomes visible. The belt is fastened around the man's army surplus overcoat. The man stands a foot taller than Callahan. He's clean-shaven, and the skin on his face is so pale it appears to be almost translucent; his hair is a mess of wild dreadlocks colored gray.

"The Watchman," a voice announces in a rich Patwa. "Him out early tonight."

Callahan looks down and sees a homeless man sitting with his back against the wall. Like the Watchman, the homeless man sports long dreads. He wears a long gray overcoat. And to his left sits an old coffee can. The scar on the man's face, running along the length of his forehead, down the right side of his face around his eye, over his nose where it quits at his upper lip, lends to the illusion that two faces are staring at the passerby. Callahan's already heard of the scar-faced specimen back at the rooming house. The other tenants call him *The One*.

"Who's the Watchman?" Callahan asks.

"The one who maintains all the locks on all the doors for me," the One says.

Callahan is still bummed out about losing sight of Serena Moon, but he senses that he's stumbled upon some new secret; mysterious shapes known only to the initiated that traipse through the night among the shadows like wraiths over a moonlit moor only to vanish at dawn.

In a sad way Callahan feels for the man they call The One. He reaches into his pocket to retrieve a dollar and stands over the coffee can on the sidewalk. Looking down, he gets a good look inside the can; the moment he does, he wishes he had not.

The coffee can spell doesn't last long.

The One leads Callahan now into a separate realm. Along the way, he tells him of the Watchmen.

"The Watchmen came eons ago," the One informs him.

Callahan can no longer see the Watchman on Kater Street, but he can still hear the jingling of the skeletal keys.

"Does everyone see them?" Callahan asks.

"No," the One replies. "Each one is charged with maintaining the locks between places. Some locks are hidden in plain sight; others revealed by intricate incantations, variants of the original Word."

"Who are they?"

"Lesser angels, the forgotten."

"How come I can see them?"

"See who?"

"The Watchmen."

"Who are the Watchmen?"

"I see what you're doing," says Callahan. "Very funny. You like fucking with people?"

The One looks at him.

"More than you know, boy," he tells him. "More than you can ever know. Now how about giving me a dollar?"

Callahan turns his back on him, experiencing a strong sense of déjà vu. The sensation leaves him feeling empty inside.

By the time he reaches Bainbridge Street, the déjà vu recedes, making way for a memory of when Callahan was ten years old. He had gone to mass with his parents on a Sunday morning. At the end of the service, the priest asked everyone to bow their heads and pray for God's blessing. Everyone did; everyone except for young Callahan. He held his head high. As the priest raised his hands in supplication, his own head bowed, Callahan saw a second man cross the altar from left to right. He was tall, thin, long-haired, bearded, and dressed in white linens. Accompanying the second man was a woman wearing blue and white robes. The air all around Callahan smelled like hot sand. Then, as quickly as the two appeared, they vanished.

When Callahan told his parents of the vision he had experienced at mass, they reacted with the typical aplomb that most educated parents would. Once a week for nearly a year his father drove him to a therapist to find out if his son was crazy.

The therapist, a chunky Jewish woman who preferred to be called by her first name Lilith, remained silent at the beginning of each visit, waiting for the boy to speak. But Callahan knew he was not crazy. For the first seven sessions Lilith and the boy sat staring at one another until the hour was up. During the eighth session, there was a breakthrough when young Callahan voiced his concerns about his therapist's qualifications.

"Whatever do you mean?" Lilith asked.

"You're Jewish," Callahan told her. "My dad says you don't believe in Christ."

"Do you mean to say you have never met someone who is Jewish?"

"I mean to say that I cannot possibly convince you of what I saw in my church if you think Jesus didn't exist."

"My personal beliefs are hardly relevant to our purpose here."

"My dad wants you to say I am crazy," he told her. "And my mom wants to believe in the miracle. As you can see, it's quite a pickle."

"And what miracle would that be?" Lilith asked.

"A bona fide vision of Jesus and the Virgin Mary," he replied.

"You're quite sure of yourself."

"And you think I am delusional."

"How do you know that word, Damian?"

"I know a lot of things," he said.

"Yes," his therapist agreed. "I am sure you are quite an intelligent young man."

"Smart enough to know that you are not qualified to make a judgment call on my vision."

"So, it's a vision now?"

"Do you get paid for this?"

"Yes, Damian. I do."

"My father thinks this is a racket."

"Therapy?"

"Yes," he replied.

Young Callahan didn't have the heart to tell her about how his father really felt about psychiatry, or Jews for that matter.

"Then why are you here, Damian?" Lilith asked.

"I told you," he replied. "My dad thinks I am crazy. He doesn't want a son who's seeing things."

"Do you think you are seeing things, Damian?"

"Stop saying my name."

"Well, do you?"

"What I saw was real," said the boy. "Do you want to talk about masturbation instead?"

"If you like."

"I don't."

"You don't want to talk about it?"

"I don't masturbate. My mom thinks it's a sin. And so do the priests."

"Do you believe in God, Damian?"

"No," he confessed. "Not really. And that makes me worried about seeing Jesus and his mom in my church. Are you going to have me shipped off to the funny farm?"

"Why would I have you institutionalized?" Lilith asked. "You seem like a sane boy to me."

"Why don't you tell my dad that I am not crazy?"

"Let's just continue talking."

"You do think I am crazy."

"Tell me more about what you saw in the church," Lilith said.

"I already told you."

"Do you see other things?"

"You mean like a three-legged deer with inflatable spheres for feet?"

"Honestly, Damian. Do you think I haven't read Kurt Vonnegut?"

"Maybe we should talk about school," young Callahan told her.

"What about it?"

"I don't trust the nuns."

"Why is that? Are they mean to you?"

"No, they are nice. And that's why I don't trust them."

"Do you find it hard trusting people?"

"Just people like my father who think I am crazy because I said I saw Jesus and Mary in my church."

"You mentioned Salo from Vonnegut's Sirens of Titan," Lilith said. "What else do you read?"

"Science fiction, mostly. Every time I see some cool world on a book cover I want to move there."

"Why is that?"

"Alien worlds probably don't have nuns."

"Some of those worlds may not have oxygen. And your parents would not be there."

"Good point."

"You would miss your parents?"

"I couldn't live without oxygen."

"Time's up, Damian. I will see you next week."

An hour passes as Callahan walks the streets of Philadelphia thinking back to those days when his father dragged him to Lilith's office every week. Before long, he ends up in the Old City section.

On 3rd Street Callahan joins the line in front of a Gothic nightclub that had formerly been a church. Once a place of worship, it now caters to black clad morose young people. The unimaginative name of Lugosi's flashes in bright blue neon light. The line measures twenty or thirty people deep. Callahan sticks out because he's the only one there not wearing black. He glimpses a full head of curly red hair by the door; his siren of the night exchanges words with a gargantuan doorman before she and her friends enter the club single file like an infantry squad on patrol. And who's this pulling tail-end Charlie duty but none other than Cockblock, the one who had thwarted Callahan's most recent efforts to get near Serena Moon some weeks ago. Callahan waves to her, even though he's half-way down the block, waiting among the disaffected and pretend undead. Cockblock returns the greeting by saluting him with her middle finger.

Ten minutes pass before Callahan makes it up the steps where he meets four doormen; each one dressed in black suits and black turtleneck shirts, sporting dyed black hair and silver hoop earrings. Callahan expects them to have thick Transylvanian accents. When the first doorman opens his mouth, Callahan feels disappointed to discover that the doorman is not an immortal bloodsucker. He's just another juiced up goombah from South Philly.

"Ten bucks, cuz," the doorman presses a beefy hairy hand into Callahan's chest. "And I'll need to see your driver's license."

Five minutes later, and ten bucks poorer, Callahan orders a fluorescent blue drink from a bartender who looks like a cadaverous crack whore. He has no idea what a Cobalt Libre is, but everyone around him drinks the same thing. There's not a beer bottle among them. Callahan hands the bartender a twenty-dollar bill. When she hands him back eight dollars it feels as if someone has just kicked him in the gut. Callahan leaves her a dollar tip.

"Hey!" a voice calls out as Callahan turns away from the bar.

The bartender waves the single dollar in the air as if it is covered with cooties. The Goths occupying space around the bar give Callahan the once-over. A plump dark-skinned girl whispers into the ear of a pale blonde standing next to her as she points at Callahan's shoes. The two girls crack up over some private joke and walk away.

"I'm talking to you!" the bartender screams at Callahan.

"What's the problem?" he asks.

"I think you need this more than me," she tells him as she waves the dollar bill.

"Keep it. Go buy yourself some rock."

"Asshole."

"Fuck you."

Callahan skirts the bar and weaves a serpentine path through the crowded dance floor. He looks back a few times, expecting to see the Gothic Italian-American bruiser from the front door bearing down on him; but, given how packed the place is, the odds seem to be in his favor. His paranoia soon dissolves as he takes one look around the dance floor. To Callahan's left and right his gaze takes in more powdered cleavage than that which had populated the 18th century court of France.

The music is another matter; a heavy metal tinged industrial beat dubbed over what Callahan can only guess is a loop of a trash truck's refuse packer crushing garbage. The vocals sound as if someone had stuffed Ozzy Osbourne and Trent Reznor into a burlap bag, doused the bag with flammable liquid, and set it on fire.

Raising his glass to his lips, Callahan takes a sip of his drink. He's just spent twelve dollars on a vodka and orange juice with a blue glow stick sunk into it. The glow stick hits his front teeth. Callahan takes the chemical light between his teeth now, extracts it from the glass, and spits it aside. Left with a dull screwdriver in a drab frosted Tom Collins glass, he saunters to a far wall where it is dark.

Amidst the many pale faces that bob up and down at the edge of the dance floor Callahan hopes to spot the Goth goddess who stole his heart. It's odd to him that so many pretty girls could be in one place. In his experience, before he had married Jill, the law of averages decreed otherwise; yet, here in this former house of worship, the women are all young and beautiful. Such an anomaly might go unnoticed by lesser men, but not by Callahan. It's the peculiarity of the situation that makes him feel uneasy. In what he witnesses there exists something unfair and unnatural. His sudden revelation turns sour as a familiar face approaches him.

It's Cockblock in the flesh, and she's lost her leather coat that she was wearing when Callahan first spotted her outside the club. Cockblock appears to be almost smiling; such an expression, amidst all the sneering vampire-wannabes, disconcerts Callahan. He imagines it's the same look the female Chinese mantis gives her mate just before she devours him. There's nowhere to hide. Callahan stands his ground. To avoid eye contact, he studies the shape of her body; and for reasons he would never tell Cockblock he guesses her measurements: 44DD, 36, 42. Another month will pass, and Callahan will learn that he was off by two inches all around. It turns out that Cockblock is close friends with Claire Not Danes and Val Not Kilmer. By the time the present moment happens at Lugosi's, Claire Not Danes has told Cockblock all about the encounter that Callahan still cannot recall.

They will run into each other at the TLA video store on Locust Street after Callahan rents a studio apartment on Spruce. Since Cockblock and Callahan are both in the adult movie section they ignore each other at first. And then, just like in the opening of some bad porn movie, they both reach for the same DVD.

"I think it's the only one left," says Cockblock.

"Maybe there's another," Callahan offers.

At the counter, a clerk with more piercings in his face than Pinhead from Hellraiser informs them both what Cockblock already suspects.

Callahan plays it cool. "Take it," he says.

"No," Cockblock replies. "You were here first."

Pinhead's expression allows for a sardonic smile.

"Why don't you both just go watch it together?" he asks.

Cockblock gets a look in her eye; half-way between *sure, let's do this* and *I just know this guy is an axe murderer.*

"Watching a porn movie with a stranger," Cockblock muses. "How novel."

Pinhead groans and pretends to look at the computer when Callahan looks his way.

Cockblock agrees to the arrangement, but she wants Callahan to rent the movie.

"We can go to my place and watch it," she tells him.

The encounter turns out to be disastrous. Cockblock owns seven cats, each one filthier than the next, and each one triggers Callahan's allergies. Of course, the reaction does not kick in until they are both naked and fucking. So, when the sneezing starts it all feels a little too weird the way Cockblock gets turned on by all the sputtering and snot spraying everywhere. Eventually, Callahan pulls himself together long enough to pull out, shoot his load on Cockblock's snot-spattered breasts, and calls it a night.

On the way back to his new apartment he stops at a 24-hour pharmacy and stocks up on Benadryl. He has no interest in seeing Cockblock or her filthy cats again. And that's when he remembers that he's left the movie he rented. Worse, he experiences a mounting paranoia over how Cockblock will use their liaison as leverage against him when it comes to Serena Moon.

For now, however, in the deeper recesses of Lugosi's, Cockblock remains immune to Callahan's charms. It doesn't take long for Callahan to realize that her only intent is to further thwart his efforts to get close to Serena, rejecting access to the siren like an angel charged with guarding the gates of Eden after the expulsion. Callahan steps to the left, attempting to dodge her, and Cockblock's right there. When he steps to his right she blocks him once more. Pressing her hand against his chest, she pushes him against a stone pillar.

"Why are you doing this?" she asks.

"What's her name?" he asks.

"Who?"

"Her," Callahan points at Serena Moon who stands not far away.

Cockblock turns to look. When she does Callahan seizes the opportunity and the moment he steps forward he understands what a mistake he's made. A well-placed boot, courtesy Cockblock herself, sends him tripping across the dance floor. Callahan collides with a large bald man with a sigil tattooed to his forehead. The bald man punches him hard in the gut. As his knees buckle, Callahan gives the man mad props. No one punches like that unless they have had some training.

The pain in Callahan's gut subsides, but he's got bigger problems. A wave of nausea hits him. Worse, the bad milk he had consumed earlier that evening has decided that it needs to exit Callahan's body. He clenches his asshole tight, but the diarrhea has other ideas as Callahan high-tails it for the men's room. Within seconds it becomes apparent to him that there are no 'his' and 'hers' facilities at Lugosi's. The restrooms are all marked *unisex*. At last, Callahan spots a door and charges through it. In the process, he knocks a petite Asian-American woman to the floor.

"Asshole," the woman says as she attempts to punch him in the balls and misses.

Callahan spots a doorless empty stall. He hurdles the woman on the floor as she adjusts her short skirt. After he steps into the stall, he wishes there were a door; a modicum of privacy would do well in that moment. It's too late to worry about that. It's time to get down to business. Callahan barely gets his pants down around his ankles when the storm hits.

Minutes later, feeling like he's on the losing end of a bout with malaria, Callahan looks up. A jet of gas escapes his ass, heralding what's to come. When it does, he sees the redheaded siren fill the doorway of the unisex restroom. The smell coming out of him is unbearable. Serena Moon waves a slender hand beneath her nose and backs out of the room.

It feels like hours have passed by the time Callahan's intestines have purged themselves of the poisons he's consumed earlier that evening. Upon exiting the restroom, at last, he's not surprised to discover that the siren of his desire has vacated the club along with her entourage.

Callahan heads for the exit. That's when he spots the cadaverous bartender conversing with the four doormen of the Apocalypse. The most menacing of the four looks at Callahan. He points a meaty finger at him and mouths the words *come here*. Callahan smiles and nods. Then he bolts for the nearest exit. The doormen move as one unit, crashing through a small crowd gathered as they attempt to cut him off. Callahan nearly reaches the door, but he's not fast enough.

"Nobody," one of the goons says as he snatches Callahan by his collar, "says 'fuck you' to my wife."

The next thing Callahan knows he's in a headlock. Two more doormen grab his legs and lift him up. The bartender blows Callahan a kiss. A short run through the front of the club leads to a fire exit door. Callahan's head slams into the door once before one of the men opens the egress. A strange feeling of déjà vu follows as they dump Callahan into an alley. He hits the concrete hard. The four doormen take turns working him over. When they get tired of using their fists they let go of Callahan and push him to the ground. And that's when they start kicking him in the head and the chest. The bartender's husband whips out his dick and pisses on him. One last swift kick to the face knocks Callahan out.

Mysterious Mechanics, An Interlude

Human frailty is the cost of free will. The One Who Creates All, it turns out, possesses a sick sense of humor. We toe the line, answering to His beckon call without ever questioning His motives. This is our nature, and our fate.

You, dear reader, and others like you, are faced with providence different than ours. Here's something that you may not know. People die every day, but not in the way most believe. Take for instance my ward Damian Callahan in the alley beside Lugosi's, lying there dead as the buried in the Old Pine Church Cemetery just a few blocks away. The list of injuries that brought about his end are blunt force trauma to the head (many of us lobbied once upon a time for a better design system for the brain's protection, but The Boss wouldn't hear of it) and multiple broken ribs, one of which pierced his left lung causing it to collapse. Marrow leaked from a broken leg and a miniscule bone shard that pierced an artery both converged on his heart, causing it to quit between beats. Not a fitting end; even for the likes of Damian Callahan who abandoned his family in pursuit of a woman borne from some dream.

It's a pain in the ass for my kind to have to report back to The Office that one of our charges met a grisly end. There are endless inquiries and, if we're lucky, some time spent beyond the sphere of His grace. But there is in all this a loophole; one that I learned to exploit long ago. For Callahan was not my first charge, nor will he be my last. In my line of work, one learns to see a situation not for what is, but for what it could be. And what it could be is based on probability.

Here's another secret: right now, dear reader, you are living multiple lives at once in multiple places in multiple dimensions. It may sound like fringe science to you but take it from someone who was around to see Him create Light. In simple terms if you can imagine a tree with numerous limbs that break off into smaller branches and those branches separating into smaller twigs, then you can understand just how many lives are being led at once.

Fortunately for my charge Damian Callahan, I have learned to prune the tree for other lives to flourish. Yes, he's a lost cause, but there remains another Damian Callahan, one who meets an even more grisly end than the skull-crushing ass-kicking you just witnessed in the alley, and still yet another and another, etc.

So, while it may be true that no dimension exists devoid of violence, traumatic events in one dimension quite often seed the betterment of multiple lives in other places. Suffice it to say that when someone like me becomes attached to a soul like Damian Callahan's one should play the law of probabilities. Along with probabilities in multiple dimensions come several constants; one of which is entropy: things fall apart. This is where the system's exploitation comes into play. No energy (read: soul) can ever truly be destroyed.

Rather than bore you with the mysterious mechanics beyond known laws of physics, I will confess that, despite common misgivings, the soul itself may not be as local as one believes it to be. This notion, as well as all esoterica when you get down to it, is highly controversial. Still, it works to my advantage where exploiting the system is concerned. There are times, after all, when God turns a blind eye, and right now, dear reader, this is one of those times. Now, if you will excuse me, it's time I prune the proverbial tree.

PART TWO: LAB WOUND

Satanas – Venire!

A white noise draws Callahan from a deep sleep. When he opens his eyes there's nothing but light all around him. Death and alien abduction come to mind, but he's far off the mark. The antiseptic smell that assails his nostrils now tells him he is conscious again. The simple act of opening his eyes becomes nearly unbearable. Fearful that the afterlife stinks like industrial-grade cleaning solutions, Callahan readies himself for the worst. The light overhead has nothing to do with the next world; nor does it belong to some fantastic extraterrestrial vessel. It turns out to be a simple fluorescent light.

So far, so good.

Aside from the odor in the room, there's another hint that gives away his current surroundings. Something on the crown of Callahan's head presses down like a knit hat that is too small. He reaches up and feels bandages around the top of his head, down either side of his face, and beneath his chin as well. The first time he speaks his voice sounds funny; the words become trapped between his clenched teeth. Callahan's jaw is wired shut. His left leg is in a cast and his torso is tightly bandaged as well.

Shadows move in his periphery: a tall figure accompanied by two smaller ones.

"Daddy?" Jackie cries out.

She's in mid-air already when her mother catches her and pulls her back.

Callahan's son Jean is reluctant to approach. He remains, as ever, the apple to his father's tree. Callahan never much liked seeing people in hospitals; most of all, his own father after his first open-heart surgery. After that things got progressively worse for Callahan's father. The old man complained one afternoon of lower back pain. Months later, Callahan would return to the same hospital to visit his father again. His father's internal organs were riddled with cancer. The chances for survival were nil. The doctors had told Callahan's mother that it would take a miracle; and barring the aforementioned miracle, wife and son should prepare for the worst. Toward the end, just days before his father at last gave up the ghost, Callahan went to see him in the hospital. He was twenty years old during his second year in the army, a soldier granted emergency leave to return home. And here's Jean now, his own son, rendering the same expression Callahan imagines he did all those years ago when he looked upon the ashen wraith that was his father; back when he had been too scared to approach his father's bedside. By the time he mustered the courage, it was already too late.

"Come on, son," Callahan beckons Jean. "I'm okay."

Jill grunts, expressing her discontent. In the beginning, when they had first started dating, Callahan recognized this trait; but, owing to how in love he was supposed to be with her, he chose to ignore it. The grunting increased over the years. Callahan takes in the sight of his wife as she stands there. Jill looks different. She looks good.

"Daddy," Jackie whispers in Callahan's ear. "When are you coming home?"

His daughter's words are bad enough, the way they weaken Callahan; but it is the look on Jean's face that concerns him most. His son's expression has shifted from overall revulsion at the sight of Callahan in his hospital bed to one of hate. Callahan doesn't know it today, nor does his young son for that matter, but it will be the last time that Jean ever looks his father directly in the eye.

"Fighting in a nightclub?" Jill asks.

"Mugged," Callahan replies.

"Bullshit. You don't think I don't know what's going on?"

"Really? We're going to do this in front of Jackie and Jean?"

"Kids, go wait in the hall. Mommy has to talk to daddy."

"But you said he's not our daddy anymore," Jean tells his mother.

"Shut up, Jean," says Jackie and punches him in the arm.

"You see?" Jill asks as she ushers the children out of the room.

It isn't long before Jill returns, alone.

"Jackie and Jean wanted to see you," she reveals. "But we're sort of pressed for time."

"Going somewhere?"

"The Bahamas, as a matter of fact," Jill informs Callahan.

"You hate traveling."

"Do you remember George Hawthorne?"

"Should I?"

"He's an attorney."

"Are we divorced? Already?"

"Technically, no," Jill answers. "And George is a corporate lawyer. He doesn't handle family law."

"Jesus Christ, you work fast."

"That's quite an indictment coming from you," Jill counters. "It's been nearly a year since you left. And did you bother coming out to see your kids? No."

"A year?" Callahan asks. "But it's only been—"

"Too busy chasing that goddess of yours?" Jill cuts him off.

Callahan closes his eyes. Every part of him hurts. The way Jill digs too deep when she means to wound him only exasperates the way he feels. He knows he deserves it, but now he fears that with the advent of George Hawthorne in her life it will be only a matter of time before his children despise him. Jill will press Hawthorne into a corner, perhaps become pregnant, and the lawyer will be left with no choice but to marry her.

Hawthorne had been a classmate of Jill's during their undergraduate days together. Callahan never got used to how Jill's mother always brought up Hawthorne whenever Callahan was in her company. Even after they had been married for a few years the damned Hawthorne campaign continued unabated thanks to Jennie Moyers, Jill's mother. And Jill's father Derek was no help. By the time Callahan entered Jill's life Derek Moyers was already a broken man. Callahan felt sorry for him. Not long into their marriage Callahan figured out that Jill operated much the same way her mother did. It was no wonder he chose to leave. Some nights he lay awake in the dark next his wife, unable to sleep, and he wondered how long it would take for his shoulders to slump forward the way Derek Moyer's did when he shuffled about, or at what point in his life he would avoid eye contact with others the way Jill's father did. Perhaps it was best that his wife latch on to George Hawthorne. The bastard had been sending Christmas cards to Jill for years. In them he wrote coded messages that made Jill laugh. And when Callahan asked what the joke was his wife never shared the secret.

Jackie and Jean step close to the bed to say good-bye. The pain meds make Callahan feel as if he's on the trip of a lifetime; his children's approach, then, appears ephemeral; as if a sequence from a dream.

Before long he falls asleep. His drug-induced dreams consist of various scenes in which a faceless George Hawthorne charms his children by day and makes crazy, acrobatic love to Jill. At one point, Callahan awakens covered in sweat. When he falls asleep again the same dreams continue uninterrupted.

It's already past four in the afternoon when he opens his eyes. Two nurses stand at his bedside along with a gaunt middle-aged balding doctor who looks like he hasn't slept since graduating medical school. The nurses ask empty questions about how Callahan feels as they take his vitals. They make small talk about the weather as they draw numerous blood samples from their patient. And when Callahan attempts to flirt with them through his wired teeth both nurses laugh in rehearsed unison.

The doctor is another story. He stands there like the angel of death waiting to make his move; unlike the nurses, he's immunized himself long ago against simple nonsensical human interaction. He stands by patiently until the nurses finish their work, holding a file in his hand. The nurses vacate the room. When the doctor finally does speak Callahan expects a cloud of locusts or killer bees to come pouring out of his mouth.

"My name is Dr. Stanton," he tells Callahan. "I am the chief pathologist."

In the patient's ears, *pathologist* sounds like *apologist*.

"What are you here to defend?" Callahan asks.

"Pathologist," Stanton repeats the word in a voice usually reserved for patients who are hard of hearing or foreign. "Is your wife here?"

"No. Why? Is she sick?"

Stanton moves closer to the bed and opens the file.

"Dr. Ehya, your attending physician, asked me to come to speak to you, he says, about your options."

"I have insurance."

"That's not my department," Dr. Stanton reminds him. "No, I am afraid I need to talk to you about the results of your CAT scans."

Callahan wonders what kind of hospital would scan a cat. He chuckles at his own joke, but the doctor isn't laughing.

"Let me put it to you straight, Mr. Callahan," Stanton tells him. "You were involved in an altercation. Your injuries were quite severe. When they brought you in you were unconscious. It's common practice to run CAT scans on patients with head injuries."

"Do I have a concussion?" Callahan asks.

"You may have. But it's your occipital lobe I want to talk to you about, Mr. Callahan. You have a primary cancerous growth there."

"Am I dying?"

"The lesion is quite advanced, I am afraid. Can you recall any radical behavior within the past year? Perhaps you may have suffered from hallucinations?"

"You mean like pink elephants and giant bunnies?"

"The hallucinations can be minor at times," replies Dr. Stanton. "Other times, not so much. In extremely rare cases, hallucinations can be so vivid as to be perceived as real as this world."

"No," Callahan lies. "Nothing like that."

"What about feelings of paranoia? Or perhaps you have experienced memory loss as well?"

Callahan shakes his head. Then he asks, "How long have I been here?"

"A few weeks," he informs him. "There was some swelling of the brain, so we induced a coma. We found the lesion on a subsequent CAT scan. It didn't show on the preliminary scan, owing to the swelling. You're quite lucky to be alive, Mr. Callahan."

"What are my options?"

"Surgery coupled with chemo and radiation therapy—"

"I am sorry, doc. I am a little fucked up from the pain meds."

"You're not on pain meds, Mr. Callahan."

"I have brain cancer?"

"For some time now, I am afraid. I have a questionnaire I would like you to fill out. It's imperative that you be as honest as possible when you answer."

"I need a minute," Callahan tells him.

Dr. Stanton fishes out a five-page questionnaire and places it on the table beside Callahan's bed. He offers Callahan a nod and exits the room.

A minute passes as Callahan begins to sort out the enormity of his situation. After ten minutes, and more than a few tears, he realizes that Dr. Stanton may never return. Callahan retrieves the questionnaire beside his bed and reads the questions. None of the questions are designed to help him get better. Without a fighting chance, he's become a statistic. His answers will be fed into a database and his life will be reduced to percentages in comparison with other patients who have suffered a similar fate. Callahan tosses the questionnaire with his good hand. The stapled papers flutter in the air and drop to the floor.

At 5:00 PM a food service worker named Rhonda brings in a tray bearing a large cup with a lid and a straw. Rhonda's not one for idle conversation, owing to how many meals she must deliver on his floor.

"Good news, Mr. Callahan," Rhonda reveals.

It's the most she's said to him all week. Whenever Callahan previously attempted to engage her in conversation Rhonda's stock responses were *mmm-hmm* and *Lord yes.*

"Dr. Stanton was wrong?" Callahan asks.

"You don't know when to stop playing," she tells him.

"What's the good news?"

"Tomorrow afternoon you will be on semi-solids," she says. "You're getting your wires off."

"No more shit shakes?"

"Mr. Callahan, you are a trip," replies Rhonda. "That shake has everything that does a body good. Now drink up. And have a blessed evening."

And with that Rhonda is out of Callahan's life once more. The milkshake tastes like chalk, owing to the protein powder in it. Callahan drinks it, anyway, thinking about Rhonda and how people like her can be so secure in their relationship with God. It's the kind of personality aspect that had always eluded him; the delusion of faith, when he considers it, being equal to or greater than faith itself.

By the time he's finished his milkshake, he feels tired again. Lulled by the steady buzz of the fluorescent lights overhead, Callahan drifts back to sleep.

As his eyes close, he glimpses a small four-legged mass of black passes in the hall just outside the door. *Strutter*, he whispers. It was the name he bestowed upon a black Labrador he had found mortally wounded in the woods near his house when he was eleven years old. A long gash ran the length of the dog's belly. Her legs twitched as she lay beneath a Blackhaw tree. Flies gathered on the Lab's wound. It was a humid day and the odor coming off the dog's exposed intestines sent young Callahan into a fit of dry heaves. Still, he couldn't bring himself to leave the dying dog alone. So, he pulled a thin branch off an oak tree nearby and set about fanning the dog to keep the flies at bay. *You're going to be okay, Strutter,* he told her over and over again. The name he gave her came from a song by Kiss. It was stupid. He didn't even like Kiss, but the song had been on the radio in his room before he left the house that afternoon. And no matter how many other songs he thought of while riding his bike, young Callahan couldn't shake the Kiss tune. The black Labrador wore no collar. Callahan did not remember seeing her around the neighborhood before he discovered her wounded in the woods. He stayed with Strutter until nearly nightfall. At one point, he reached out slowly to stroke her head, but the dog loosed a low growl; so, he kept his hands to himself. Shadows stretched long through the woods as the sun set. Strutter eyed the boy, licked her bloodied teeth one last time, and exhaled a slow gurgle. Who might do such damage to a dog? Or did she suffer the wound jumping over a fence? After the dog died Callahan used an old branch he found on the ground behind the Blackhaw tree to dig a shallow grave. Once he broke through the top soil the earth became hard. The grave was only two feet deep. Callahan dragged the black Labrador by its hind legs and deposited her in her final resting place. When he finished filling in the grave, he offered a prayer for Strutter. Afterward, as storm clouds stretched out overhead, Callahan used the two sticks and the laces from his Chuck Taylor All-Stars to fashion a cross. He found a rock and pounded the cross into the dirt at the head of the grave. The first raindrops fell as he covered the grave with old leaves and dead vines.

Callahan made it home just as the storm began. Torrential rains lashed the neighborhood all night. The next morning, he took his bike back to the woods. He had fitful dreams about Strutter's grave being disturbed. When he returned to the woods he could not find the cross he had made. The ground surrounding the Blackhaw tree was under several inches of water. From somewhere deep in the woods a dog's yap sounded. Young Callahan trudged through the flooded woodland searching for Strutter, but he never found her.

When he returned to where his bike stood young Callahan discovered the cross he had made dangling from the handlebars. Seated on her hind quarters in front of his bike was Strutter; where her pale abdomen should have been a hole from which jagged rib bones jutted over the open space. The memory is no longer a memory, but a dream now. Callahan draws a deep breath as he wakes up in his hospital bed. His room is dark. And in the lit hallway past the threshold he spots Strutter padding her way past the open door.

A few days later there's talk of releasing Callahan. His jaw has healed, as well as the lacerations on his scalp. Likewise, his broken ribs, having been stapled together shortly after he landed in the emergency room, are healing well. He will have to wear a brace for a few more weeks, but at least the stitches were removed earlier that morning where the incision had been made to staple his ribs. Callahan's broken leg is another matter. The cast will remain. When his attending physician mentions physical therapy following the removal of the leg cast Callahan laughs at him.

"What's so funny?" Dr. Ehya asks.

He's a small man wound tightly with a nervous energy that makes Callahan uncomfortable.

"I am going to strengthen my leg," Callahan replies, "so I can die healthy?"

"Studies have shown that a fatalistic attitude—"

"Save it, doc," he tells him.

Dr. Ehya exits without saying another word.

Minutes later, the morning food services technician rolls a cart into the room. Her name is Brianna. She puts down a tray in front of Callahan that consists of oatmeal, non-fat milk, scrambled eggs (powdered, no doubt), and the smallest cup of orange juice Callahan has ever seen.

Brianna is another staff member who never gets Callahan's name right. He forgives her because of the light that shines all around her; not a visible light, but one capable all the same of making anyone in its radius feel as if they do not have a care in the world. People like Brianna should be doctors, Callahan muses, but instead the world offers the callous and the nervous like Drs. Stanton and Ehya. What Callahan likes most about Brianna is her green eyes. Since his hospital stay began, he's attempted to guess Brianna's age. The problem for him is that she appears to be both young and old. Her caramel skin Callahan imagines is quite soft, though he's never had the occasion to touch her. Brianna carries herself like a divine saint among lowly sinners. Callahan decides that morning that he loves her the way Virgin Mary devotees love the Mother of Christ. It is a pure love, an adoration unfettered by a desire to ply his flesh against hers; a devotion that endures long after she's moved on to the next room to serve another patient's breakfast.

"How are you this morning?" Brianna asks.

"Is this a trick question?" Callahan replies.

"No need to be fresh," she warns him. In her eyes he can see the catalog of hearts she's broken over the years. "I might be old," Brianna tells him, "but I am not too old to whip your ass."

"Do you talk dirty to all your patients?"

"Eat your breakfast," she instructs him. "I spent all morning whipping it up."

"No, you didn't."

Brianna smiles at Callahan. Her eyes shine with the light of unconditional love. For the moment, Callahan wants to forget about Serena Moon. He wants to know more about Brianna. But he imagines her life as one far more grounded than the life he leads. Women like Brianna are capable of sidestepping fucked up guys like him without much effort.

"Enjoy," she tells him. "I can tell you're not that sick."

"You've had this gift your whole life?" Callahan asks. "Or is this the result of some puberty-related trauma?"

"Don't be fresh. Besides, you have things to do before you go."

"How much can I do here in the hospital?"

"No," Brianna replies, "I mean *before you go.*"

After midnight, chaos descends upon the nurses' station just outside Callahan's door. He climbs off his bed, a little unsteady at first because of the cast on his leg, but he manages well enough on his crutches. Callahan cracks his door open, and peers into the hall. Two nurses at the station have their hands raised, more in a defensive posture than one that says *fine, we surrender.*

"Three hours!" a man shouts. The perpetrator of the ensuing melee remains beyond Callahan's field of vision. "Three hours ago, I rang you to empty my piss pot!"

"Do not," one of the nurses warns the unseen patient, "throw that container."

"Fuck you, white bitch!"

An arc of urine fills the air right outside of Callahan's room. He opens his door a little wider now to get a better glimpse. The piss splashes against the other nurse's face.

"Call security," another voice demands.

Callahan watches as the third nurse joins the other two.

"Mr. Jasper, for your own safety," the third nurse declares, "please go back to your room now."

"I wish I had a bucket of shit to throw at you," Jasper says as he steps into view. That's when he catches sight of Callahan on his crutches. "What the fuck are you looking at?"

"Mr. Jasper," the second nurse chimes in, "I just called security. If you don't go back to your room you will be transferred to the psych evaluation unit."

The nurse who received the golden facial courtesy Jasper washes her face in a sink behind the nurse's station.

"He's going to psych evaluation," she says as she wipes her face dry with a paper towel. "No doubt about that."

An elevator bell chimes. Callahan shuffles into the hallway. Other patients emerge from their rooms as well. Everyone is tuned in on the same wavelength. They are all there to watch the spectacle unfold further with the arrival of four hospital security officers wearing black uniforms. Each of the guards is a study in sleep deprivation, illicit bodybuilding substances, and too many hours of overtime. They are hungry for a fight. When Jasper makes his move, striking a contorted kung fu pose, the guards' wishes are granted. What follows is an intricate ballet between Jasper and the team of hospital security officers, accentuated by a few high-flying kicks Jasper executes along with numerous karate chops and a carefully choreographed display of baton use courtesy the four security guards. It takes less than thirty seconds for the four men to beat Jasper into submission.

"No, not the stomach," the victim of the pee toss shouts when one of the guards hits Jasper in the gut with his baton.

"Help me! Murder!" Jasper cries as he clutches his stomach.

"He just had his appendix removed," the first nurse informs the guards.

"Today?" one of the men asks.

"You motherfuckers!" Jasper screams as the others haul him to his feet handcuffed. "I'll kill you! I'll kill you and I'll kill your families!"

"Don't make me muzzle you, Mr. Jasper," a different guard informs him.

"And you!" the patient lunges toward the nurse he had doused with his urine. "I am going to cut you!"

The elevator chimes again.

"Going up to seven," another guard announces.

"I'll let the psychiatrist on-call know you're coming up," the third nurse informs the guards.

"I'm not crazy!" Jasper jumps up and down as the guards usher him to the waiting elevator. "Hey, my man. Come on, take these cuffs off. I was just kidding around. A little piss never hurt nobody."

"You created a biohazard," another guard says.

"Man, fuck you!" Jasper shouts. "Ain't nobody talking to you, step-and-fetch!"

Callahan shuffles further out into the hallway to get a better view. Jasper commences to spitting as the elevator door shuts. Banging sounds like distant thunder from inside the elevator are accompanied by the muffled threats of Jasper. Callahan can only imagine the close-quarter beating the hospital security officers administer to Jasper on the way to the seventh floor.

When the spectacle ends, Callahan returns to his room. Sleep is out of the question. So, he rings the nurses' station, hoping to score some painkiller or another that will render him unconscious. No one answers. Callahan rings the nurses' station five more times over the next hour. He climbs out of bed, finds his crutches, and shuffles back out into the hallway.

"Excuse me," he says to the nurse behind the desk.

Callahan doesn't recognize her. Her name tag reads: Magdalena. On her left forearm, a tattoo of a red heart with a blue knife through it. A furled, fancy banner about a half-inch wide and one inch long over the heart bears the phrase *Sin Amor*.

Magdalena does not look up at Callahan; immersed, she is, in a James Patterson paperback. She raises her left hand, sticks her index finger into her ear, and wiggles it. When she pulls her finger out a chunk of wax sticks to her fingertip. Magdalena wipes the mess on the underside of the desk. When she at last looks up and sees Callahan standing there she's startled.

"What are you doing up?" Magdalena asks.

"Is there a doctor on call?" Callahan inquires. "Maybe there's someone on the overnight shift?"

"The doctors will be back on Monday."

"What day is it?"

"Saturday," she answers. "Well, actually it's Sunday now."

"May I ask you something?"

"Sure, go ahead."

"Did you just start your shift before midnight?"

"Yes," Magdalena tells him.

"You've been working this shift long?" he asks.

"Four years now," she responds. "Why?"

"Did you ever see a dog up here?" Callahan asks.

"You mean like a service dog?"

"No, I mean like a black Labrador."

"Did you see it tonight?"

"Never mind," he shifts gears now. "Will you make a note for the attending physician? I am sure one will be by tomorrow even though it's Sunday."

"What's the message?"

"I'd like to be released as early as possible on Monday morning," Callahan informs her. "I am afraid my landlady might kick me out."

"You can't be evicted for being admitted to the hospital, sir."

"You don't know my landlady."

"I had a cousin. Hector was his name. He got into a car accident. And his rent was due. See, in my neighborhood we always had to hand-deliver our rent because the mail was no good," Magdalena says. "So, Hector was in the hospital on the day his rent was due, and he was still there a week after that, and his landlord put all his stuff on the street. That's when the jackals came out and picked my cousin's stuff clean."

"That's a sad story," Callahan tells her, though he doesn't give a shit about what happened to Magdalena's cousin.

"It is. And we all felt so bad."

"What happened after that? Did he get his stuff back?"

"No," Magdalena tells him. "But he did go see his landlord when he got better. Hector was mad. That's when he died."

"Right in front of the landlord?"

"After Hector's landlord shot him. He sure did."

"That's terrible."

"Hector had it coming. He tried to stab the landlord's wife."

"Why did he do that?"

"Hector was sleeping with her," Magdalena looks left and right before she finishes her story, as if it is a tale for only

Callahan to hear. "And then while Hector was in the hospital the landlord's old lady started doing it with some Asian dude. It was a slap in Hector's face. Latin men don't do well with infidelity, especially when a side piece cheats."

"So, the landlord's wife sleeps with Hector and then cheats on your cousin?"

"Yeah, it was all messed up. Anyway, you better get back to your room before we wake up the other patients."

The weekend at the hospital passes without further incident. By Monday morning, something in Callahan snaps. He's sick of the cast on his leg. The forced smiles on overworked nurses appear more insincere than normal. Worse, the hospital admits a guy into his room who divides his time between snoring in his sleep and praying in Latin when he's awake. The antiseptic smell within the room causes Callahan to consider just what pathogens in their microbial hidden world have evolved to the point where they are immune to industrial-grade disinfectants; super-pathogens that are plotting a reshuffle of the biological order of things; an assault with a particular endgame in mind, a relentless offensive that means the end of Homo sapiens by any means necessary.

To pass the time, Callahan begins fumbling with the cast on his leg. If he had a real knife he'd cut through the plaster, but he has to improvise with a plastic one he kept after Brianna delivered his breakfast. Callahan diligently works at the top of his cast as the patient in the next bed quits snoring and sits up. It's the first time Callahan gets a good look at him. The guy is thin, pale, and bald. He has no eyebrows and a Van Dyke beard dyed jet black. The patient looks at him and begins his Latin prayer again. It's the same one the guy's been chanting ever since the attendants wheeled him into the room.

"Sanctus Satanas, Sanctus
Dominus Diabolus Sabaoth.
Satanas – venire!

Satanas – venire!
Ave, Satanas, ave Satanas.
Tui sunt caeli,
Tua est terra,
Ave Satanas!"

"Hey buddy," Callahan quits working on his leg cast and points his plastic knife at the other patient. "Why don't you knock that shit off?"

The patient stops his dark litany and stares at Callahan. He makes several signs at him, mumbling unintelligible words. When he realizes that none of the sigils he draws in the air are working the goateed patient resumes his prayer.

"Sanctus Satanas, Sanctus
Dominus Diabolus Sabaoth.
Satanas – venire!
Satanas – venire!
Ave, Satanas, ave Satanas.
Tui sunt caeli,
Tua est—"

Callahan, when he relates the story at some future date, never remembers which came first: the temperature drop within the room or the appearance of the sharply dressed young man standing in the doorway.

"Enough," the young man tells the other patient.

The first thing Callahan notices about the stranger is the charcoal suit he's wearing accented by a crisp white shirt and silver-gray tie. The stranger has long dark hair swept back behind his ears. He looks ordinary enough except for the oblong shadows where his eyes should be.

"Master," the patient whispers.

"Tell me, Robert, what do you seek?" the stranger asks.

"You know me?" the patient Robert asks.

"I know every human's name," he replies.

The stranger turns his attention to Callahan now.

"You want to get out of here?" he asks.

"No, I am good," Callahan tells him as he pulls his covers up to his neck.

"I am your faithful servant, Lord," Robert announces.

"What are you here for?" the stranger asks.

"Appendectomy."

"Here's how it works, son. I need good agents in the field, not with me in the home office. Understand?"

"But—"

The stranger points a finger at Callahan. His hand is long and slender, his fingernails perfectly manicured.

"I know you," he tells him.

"Not me," Callahan replies. "I don't think we've ever met."

"Never?"

"I don't think so."

"I swear I know you from somewhere."

"Are you—?"

"Shush," he replies and holds his index finger to his lips.

Robert balls up the edge of his bed cover in his fists. Tears run from his eyes as he looks at the stranger in utter admiration.

"No, Master," he says. "It's me you want."

"And what would you have me do?" the stranger asks Robert. "Drag you back to Hell?"

"I have devoted my life to you!"

The stranger purses his delicate lips and shakes his head as he jerks a thumb at Robert.

"Rookies," he tells Callahan.

"I could give you guys some privacy," Callahan tells him. "Just hand me my crutches there."

"Is your leg broken?"

"It is."

"Master," Robert interjects.

The stranger holds up his hand to quiet him.

"In a minute," he announces. To Callahan, he says, "how did it happen?"

"I got jumped by some bouncers outside a club," Callahan informs him.

"Well," the stranger spreads his hands out now, "no matter. You're all better now."

"Master, I have devoted my life to you," Robert raises his voice now. "I have made sacrifices. I have followed all the dark books."

"Excuse me," the stranger tells Callahan. He turns to face Robert. "What books? Did I write them? Honestly, I spent the better part of human history trying to convince you people that I do not exist."

"I beg your pardon?"

"As you should."

"I don't belong here," Robert confesses. "I want to be with you. I want to serve you for all eternity. I want—"

Suddenly, Robert's body goes rigid. Callahan's no doctor, but he's certain the man's suffering a massive coronary. The cardiac event monitor next to Robert's bed confirms Callahan's suspicions when the lines on display turn straight and the numbers all drop to zero.

"Do you know what the problem with blind worship is?" the stranger asks.

Callahan shakes his head slowly.

"Blind worship lacks conviction. It is meaningless. And that, my friend, is the world's pain."

"If you say so," Callahan replies.

"People always blame me," the stranger informs him as he stands up and adjusts his tie. "The devil made me do it! The devil made me do it! It's Satan's fault! It's Satan's fault! Human beings need only to look within the depths of their own hearts to realize free will itself gives rise to the evil that men do. In effect, it's not me who is responsible for sin."

"To be honest," Callahan tells him, "I don't know anyone who believes in you anymore."

"That's just it," the visitor replies. "I was *the* angel once, loved by Him above all others. So, I got a little big for my britches. Where's the harm in wanting a little shake-up in the power structure?"

"I never heard it that way."

"History is written by the victors."

The stranger sits down on the end of Callahan's bed, fussing with the crease in his pant leg.

Three nurses and a doctor rush into the room. They go about trying to revive the patient named Robert.

"Look at them," the stranger says to Callahan. "Wasting their time trying to save that piece of shit."

"Can they—"

"Not this one, I am afraid."

"I was going to say can they hear you?"

"Good question," the stranger replies. Then he launches into a rather decent rendition of *Hello My Baby*.

One nurse rolls the curtain shut around Robert, as if the dead needed privacy.

"You're not real," Callahan whispers.

The stranger stands up and offers a flourishing bow.

"My work here," he responds, "is finished. Seriously, though. Think about my offer."

"What offer?"

The stranger smoothes out his sleeves and adjusts his tie once more.

"I said I need good men in the field," he reminds Callahan. "What do you say?"

"I don't think it will work out well for me," he declares.

"I can make you rich and famous."

"And spend eternity next to Robert over there after I am dead?"

"That buffoon? Shit. I have a special circle for moronic devotees like him. Are you sure you won't reconsider?"

"I'd like you to leave now."

"What about that precious wife of yours?" he inquires. "I could square things between you and Jill and the kids?"

"That's none of your business."

The stranger snaps his fingers. "Of course," he exclaims. "The other tart. Serena is her name. Serena Moon. What if I told you how to win her? What if I help you with that and arrange it so you two end up in some posh apartment overlooking Rittenhouse Square?"

"We'd have to stay in Philly?"

"I can put you in Manhattan. Or how about a nice loft overlooking the Seine?"

"Please leave."

"It's not that simple, Damian. The guy who called me here is dead."

"And you killed him."

"Details, baby. Details. What do you say I hook you up with the girl of your dreams?"

"You're relentless."

The stranger's expression turns sour.

"You have no idea," he tells Callahan.

"Jesus—"

"No—"

"—Christ," Callahan cries out.

"—don't!"

The stranger's last word lingers for a moment after he vanishes.

Minutes later, the curtain around Robert's bed remains in place. Callahan feels exhausted, but there's work to be done. He produces his plastic knife and gets back to work on his cast.

"Please don't do that," a nurse tells him as she approaches his bed.

"My leg is fine," Callahan informs her.

"Your leg is broken."

"Not anymore."

"It's the cast."

Callahan climbs out of his bed. He marches to the door and back to his bed several times without his crutches.

"Satisfied?" he asks. "Now, if you'd be kind enough to schedule me another x-ray I would be much obliged."

The nurse wrinkles her nose and asks, "What makes you think your leg is healed?"

"The devil told me so."

"Mr. Callahan. You're not making much sense."

"Get me a doctor."

Callahan's leg is indeed healed courtesy Lucifer's dark miracle. What he doesn't know is that the cancer in his head continues to gather strength.

"Wait here," the nurse informs him.

Ninety minutes later, an x-ray proves that Callahan's leg has mysteriously healed. Back in his room, the patient is relieved to discover that Robert the Satan worshiper is gone. Callahan takes a sponge bath in the bathroom, scrubbing at the dead skin on his leg where the cast has been removed. After he finishes, he gets dressed in the bloodied clothes he wore on the night he was first admitted.

"Hello," Callahan says to one of the nurses at the duty station outside his room. "I'd like to leave."

"Sir," the nurse eyes him suspiciously.

"Look, I know there's a form I can sign," he tells her. "And I know my rights. I'd like to go home now."

"Wait right there, Mr. Callahan," the nurse says.

It occurs to Callahan that the response may come in the form of four or more of the hospital security staff who will want to take him to the psych evaluation unit. Several minutes pass and Callahan wonders if the nurse has forgotten about him. When she eventually returns the nurse walks side by side with an old lady holding a clipboard.

"This is Mrs. Gryon," the nurse informs him. "She's a transition specialist."

"Please, Mr. Callahan," Mrs. Gryon says. "Have a seat."

Callahan does what he's told. The nurse leaves him alone with Mrs. Gryon who proceeds over the next twenty minutes to fill Callahan's head with reasons why he should complete his stay. He's resistant of course, but when the old woman launches into the meat of her purpose he feels scared. There's the next phase of his treatment, the one to do with *the* cancer (Mrs. Gryon uses the article preceding the word cancer to emphasize the illness). Some of the aspects Callahan will encounter will be radiation (yes, Mrs. Gryon informs him, his hair will fall out), chemotherapy (some of the drugs have been known to hinder sexual prowess; this last bit of news from Mrs. Gryon compels Callahan to chuckle), and the implementation of some *experimental* therapy of which Mrs. Gryon's explanation concerning it is vague at best. In all, the old lady's extemporaneous pitch is in fact well-rehearsed; a skill she's honed over several years by conversing with numerous cancer patients who passed through the hospital's rigorous treatment program only to die anyway. Callahan feels sorry for her. He's able to sift through all the bullshit, but it bothers him that Mrs. Gryon truly believes in the system; despite that the system exists, in Callahan's opinion, for hospitals to gain a sizable profit and for patients and their respective insurance companies to fork over large amounts of money to pharmaceutical giants. Callahan would rather drop dead than become a statistic in some research journal or, worse, a footnote in some medical trade publication. Mrs. Gryon senses that Callahan has become incensed. She's gotten quite good at reading patients' body language in the long years she's worked as a transition specialist. So, without offering any further argument in favor of the patient remaining at the hospital, Mrs. Gryon offers Callahan two forms to sign. The first one contains the regular legal jargon recapping the talk they've just had. The second form, longer than the first, is a Release Against Doctor's Orders (RADO) summary. Callahan reads over both forms; though the one containing the legalese may as well have been written in Cuneiform; and signs them both. Mrs. Gryon excuses herself and a minute later she returns to present Callahan with a copy of the RADO form.

"You are free to go, Mr. Callahan," Mrs. Gryon informs him. "Please seek help with the cancer somewhere, if not here. Great strides have been made—"

"Save it," he tells her.

Ten minutes later, Callahan is on the street. The air is warmer. A westerly wind hints at rain, but the storm is far from the city. He barely makes it past the hospital grounds when movement against the wrought iron fence bordering the parking lot catches his eye. Upon first seeing the homeless man with his dreads colored black and gray, Callahan takes him for The One. But the homeless man is smaller in stature and empty-handed. Callahan rubs his eyes and gets a better look as the man enters the hospital through the Emergency Room entrance. When the doors slide closed he loses sight of him and continues on his way.

Tricks of the late afternoon light are not finished with Callahan. A block from the hospital as he moves north along 18th Street, Callahan stops and waits for the traffic light to change at Lombard. The sun's rays coming from the west dowse his eyes. The familiar city corner turns into an ethereal space graced with white light everywhere, a paradisiacal boulevard where pedestrians appear as meandering angels and building exteriors look as if they are trimmed in gold. A tall angel with fire for hair steps out of a woman's clothing store. Of all the strange faces on the street, this angel Callahan knows. Just then an errant cloud blocks out the sun, casting shadows all over the intersection. The traffic light changes colors. Callahan gives chase to Serena Moon for a couple of blocks. The elusive angel ditches him when the cloud passes as she turns right down Delancey Place; a white gold bath of sunlight consumes her. Callahan shields his eyes for a moment. Sadness overcomes him the way it might a boy who has walked the length of a long field, searching for the rainbow that has appeared after a storm, only to find that the rainbow's end vanishes in the woods that border the field.

A distant memory of boyhood comes to mind, but the recollection is cut short for Callahan when he hears a jingle of keys behind him. Less than an arm's length away the Watchman passes by. The skeletal keys on their big round ring sparkle in the afternoon sunlight. The Watchman walks west up Spruce Street. Before long, the daylight envelopes him and he vanishes. A sharp pain courses through Callahan's head. Lightheaded and nauseous, he sinks to his knees. People on the street no longer resemble benevolent angels; their faces turn back into the angry indifferent visages that populate the city. In that moment, Callahan considers his insistence on leaving the hospital; that it may not have been the best-laid plan when he feels a set of hands on each of his arms.

Two medical students dressed in lab coats help Callahan to his feet. They offer to buy Callahan dinner at a small eatery a few doors down from where they stand. The medical students are curious about Callahan's leg, having heard about his miraculous healing. When he attempts to explain what happened, Callahan stops. No one would believe that the devil had performed the miracle; least of all, two first-year medical students. After thirty minutes of eating grilled chicken and baked potatoes served with cheddar cheese and sour cream, Callahan's had enough of the small talk. He drains the cup of water in front of him, thanks the students, and exits the establishment.

Outside, there's a coolness in the air that reminds Callahan of autumn. The west wind continues to blow. Everyone around him goes running helter-skelter when lightning flashes and the first lashing rains begin to fall. Callahan walks through the pouring rain now as thunderclaps reverberate between buildings and lightning flashes turn the faces of strangers into demons ready to torment the unsuspecting. *This can't be happening*, he thinks. *It must be the cancer.* Regardless, he runs at a brisk pace now all the way back to Mrs. Winston's rooming house.

The Physics of Erotic Acrobatics

The moment Callahan enters the building, happy to be sheltered from the rain, Mrs. Winston corners him.

"I'd like to speak to you," she tells him.

In her brown and blue peasant dress with its high white collar, Mrs. Winston looks like the wife in Grant Wood's American Gothic painting. And that's not all. Her face looks different; her features softer than Callahan remembered them.

"I was in the hospital," Callahan tells her. He presents his patient wristband for good measure.

Mrs. Winston exudes only mild interest when she remarks, "nothing serious, I hope?"

"Not at all, thanks."

There's no sense in getting into the dirty details with her. Her features may look softer now, but the emptiness in her eyes, the callous air about her, tells Callahan more about the conceit that lies within her soul than any words could describe. Mrs. Winston wants him to mention what ails him just so she can trump his condition with some malady of her own.

"What were you in for?" she asks Callahan.

"Like I said," he replies, "nothing serious."

It's a lie; to be sure. Callahan doesn't go in for the bait. Mrs. Winston's jaw sets as she grinds her teeth a moment.

"Do you recall our lease agreement?"

"Of course," he tells her. Callahan produces the form from the hospital. "And I have these if—"

"I don't like to do this," she ignores his paperwork. "An emergency has come up and I need your room."

"But I really was in the hospital," he tells her. Visions of homelessness fill his head now. *You're dying,* he tells himself, *get a grip.*

Mrs. Winston produces an envelope and hands it to him.

"That's your month's rent," she informs him. "I have a family member in a bad way. Since you're the newest tenant, I am afraid this disadvantage falls to you. I am very sorry. If you need help finding accommodations—"

"No, not at all," Callahan counters.

"I will wait here while you go upstairs and gather your things," says Mrs. Winston. "And I've left you some luggage upstairs. I saw you were without, so I took the liberty of providing for you. No charge."

Upstairs, the room looks smaller and dingier than when Callahan last left it. A coat of thick dust covers everything, including a cardboard suitcase lying on his bed. The suitcase reminds Callahan of the type he was issued in Catholic school when he and his classmates were charged with selling candy and small toys to raise money for the needy. As a child, Callahan was a terrible salesperson. He used to talk his neighbors out of buying the candy and toys he sold, even when those adults offered to make a purchase from him anyway. He opens the old cardboard suitcase now, expecting to find stale candy and toxic toys inside, and packs his things.

"Work," Callahan exclaims before he exits the room. "Shit."

He would understand if they thought he was dead. The last thing he had counted on was for his ex-wife to telephone his job and tell them of his situation. Callahan dials his boss's cell phone number.

"Wow," his boss Krantz says when he realizes it's Callahan on the line. "This is awkward."

"I was in the hospital," Callahan explains. "I have paperwork—"

"Yeah, about that," Krantz interrupts. "You didn't call or show. I had to start the paperwork on our end. I thought you had quit."

"I got mugged," another lie but the boss doesn't need to know all the details. "And then I ended up in the hospital. They put me in a coma."

"The guy who beat you up?"

"Guys. Plural. And no," Callahan clarifies. "It was the doctors that did it. The coma, I mean. They worried about brain swelling."

"Tough break, but it's out of my hands. Corporate is all over it."

"I'd like to come back—"

"It's not just that," Krantz cuts him off. "There was a list, Damian. We're downsizing. Either way you were going to be called out and let go."

"Is there a severance package?"

"Can you come by tomorrow? I can pass you off to O'Hara in Human Resources. She will know what to do. And bring your paperwork from the hospital."

No sooner than Callahan hangs up the hairs on his neck rise as if there's a static charge in the air. Gunter stands in the doorway. He's dressed in a pair of gym shorts that would make Richard Simmons envious and his signature mesh tank-top shirt. Callahan avoids staring at the bulge in Gunter's shorts for too long. It bothers him that he can't decide if Gunter stuffs his shorts or if he's carrying around a real package that big.

"Tough business, old boy," Colonel Dietrich appears now in the doorway behind Gunter, "this getting kicked out by the hag."

"It's time to move on," Callahan tells him.

"That's the spirit, chap. In one door and out the other one."

Gunter chuckles at some private joke. The little Asian likes toying with Callahan. It's not flirtation, not by any means. No, Gunter knows secrets that Callahan does not; it shows in his eyes. The outer shell, the flamboyant gay man, is a front. Gunter, Callahan realizes, aside from possessing inside jokes and private innuendos, has that look of a man who's been to Hell and back; and if not, he's at least gotten as far as the suburbs of the Infernal City and lived to tell about it. Gunter is a man, and more; an avatar, Callahan decides, of an ancient and wise free spirit; one that meddles in the lives of men but holds no value to them; a trickster god hiding in plain sight.

"I heard you were in the hospital," the Colonel is saying now.

He pushes his partner aside and steps into the room. Between the bed and the wood chair, the Colonel chooses the bed and sits down. Gunter slips into the room and plants himself beside the Colonel.

"Terrible," the Colonel says, "just terrible."

"I will be fine," Callahan assures him.

"Even so, life is strange," the old man declares.

He pats Gunter on his thigh, a little too close to the Asian man's crotch for Callahan's comfort. Callahan tries to look cool, hoping the uneasiness he feels doesn't register on his face.

"I agree," Callahan says.

"It's the one constant that is at once so fragile and yet so full of vibrant energy," says the Colonel.

For the next ten minutes, Callahan endures a soliloquy by the Colonel that sounds like a cross between Carlos Castaneda and a hodge-podge of Gnostic faith accentuated by Jewish mysticism. This pious potpourri peppered with the Colonel's own mystic experiences, segues into the origins of an ancient alien race, one that controls reality, an extraterrestrial tribe that dated all the way back, the Colonel quickly points out, to Eden where these jealous aliens entombed life energy forces into human bodies modeled after their own. The Colonel's musings offer just the right amount of paranoia and authority to have the makings of a bad cult. The Colonel presses on, offering a detailed explanation now of how a Merkabah, constructed out of divine light, allows one to ignore universal laws of physics. As Callahan listens to the old man, a revelation strikes him. Despite the bad news at the hospital, he will survive cancer in his brain; if only long enough to pick up a newspaper and read about how an elderly retired British army officer duped a thousand morons who lacked the wherewithal to think for themselves, and led them deep into the Amazon Rainforest with the Colonel's promise that there, among the ancient trees and indigenous peoples, they would meet the aliens who created man; how, once in the rainforest, they would conduct a Q&A before boarding alien ships of light to travel into the Nth dimension; how no one among the many cult members would question why ships of light disguised themselves as death through malarial fever and starvation; how indigenous people would tell the tale at night of the ailing British colonel who survived his followers and wandered into the rainforest where he was captured by members of a rival village; how Colonel Hammond Dietrich's whereabouts would remain a mystery, leaving some to speculate that people from the sky came and took him away; while still others from the region would surmise that the poor Colonel was mistaken as the vanguard of an illegal logging operation, and met his end at the hands of an as-yet uncontacted people.

Callahan cannot believe that the Colonel is still laying down his rap about the aliens and the forgotten knowledge of indigenous peoples. Working in the corporate world for many years, not to mention his college education beforehand, has taught him to nod, grunt, and look interested even if the words coming out of the old man's mouth sound like white noise. Callahan wants to get out of there, but he makes no sudden movements; mostly because the Colonel's enthusiasm and that of Gunter beside him, borders on the maniacal.

"You are a prophet," the little Asian man tells the Colonel when he completes his dissertation. "I should know. I've met enough madmen in my life."

"It's too bad you are going," the Colonel offers his hand to Callahan. "I could loan you my manifesto."

"I'm not much of a reader," Callahan explains.

"No matter," the old man replies. "Well, it was good knowing you."

Callahan feels like the Colonel's words are a jibe, a cryptic pun on Callahan's recent diagnosis. Or perhaps it serves as an ominous warning. What if he plans to remove himself from the alien-controlled equation? The thought depresses Callahan.

"We're going to the Wing Command," Gunter announces. "You should come along."

When the little man shimmies off the bed and stands up Callahan looks away after he notices that the bulge in his little shorts has grown bigger. And judging by the way the Colonel is licking his lips, Callahan isn't the only one who notices.

"I'll leave you two alone," says Callahan. "Maybe we will see each other around town."

He doesn't wait for a reply. Half-way down the hallway Gunter's giggles follow him.

The small manual elevator is out of the question. The last thing Callahan wants is for little Gunter or the Colonel to emerge from his old room, catch him before he can close the elevator door, and engage him in further conversation as the old elevator descends to the lobby at a sloth's pace. He heads for the stairs. Now here's something disconcerting that Callahan did not know.

The stairs aren't the typical fair with a landing between sets of steps. Instead, they are spiral and even though Callahan's former room was on the sixth floor the spiral stairs extend a considerable distance downward before they vanish into shadows. He loses count of the steps as he traverses the winding stairs.

Callahan reaches a landing with a door that is marked with the number 5 in faded red paint. It occurs to him that it might be easier to walk the hallway of the fifth floor to the ancient lift; only the door there is locked. By the time he reaches the first floor he's relieved to find out that the ground floor door is unlocked. Callahan cranes his neck to get a good look at the winding stairwell as it snakes its way up until the stairs and the darkness merge as one.

In the lobby Callahan pauses a moment so his eyes can adjust to the light there. Mrs. Winston is nowhere in sight.

There's a note taped to the office door that reads:

> **Mr. Callahan:**
> **There are rooms available at the Chesterfield over on Juniper Street near 13th. I am sure you will find the staff there quite accommodating. Please accept my apologies for this inconvenience.**
> **Sincerely,**
> **Mrs. Winston**

Callahan knocks on the office door. There's no answer. He wraps on the door once more and turns the doorknob. The office is unlocked. Callahan grabs a pencil and a message pad from the narrow desk just inside the door. After he writes his name and *Room 603* on the message pad he tears off the top page, tapes his key to the message, and places the note and the key on the edge of the desk just before he closes the office door.

It's still raining when Callahan exits the rooming house. Somewhere on the street the now familiar sound of jangling skeletal keys can be heard. Callahan looks up and down the street. The Watchman, if he's nearby, remains concealed. Right now, Callahan's got bigger problems than the frequency with which he's heard those keys clanging against The Watchman's hip. The rain is already doing a number on his cardboard suitcase.

Callahan makes a run for it, clasping the flimsy suitcase in his arms. When he reaches 13th Street he doesn't wait for the traffic light. Dodging a taxi, he crosses to the other side of the street where at the last moment he performs a limbo dance to avoid clothes-lining himself on a metal support cable that runs on a forty-five-degree angle from its anchor in the curb up to a telephone pole situated to Callahan's right. He nearly loses his cardboard suitcase in the process, but he manages to stay on his feet. By the time he reaches Juniper Street his suitcase looks more like a wet paper bag wrapped around the clothes inside.

Judging from its exterior, Chesterfield Apartments on Juniper Street looks to be another dump. In the street and on the sidewalk in front of the apartment building there are dark marks, made from cooking grease was Callahan's guess, that had been there for years. The air on Juniper Street is heavy and close; even the rain barely penetrates the atmosphere there. Fans and air conditioning units on buildings across the street from the Chesterfield Apartments blow non-stop; an urban white noise that leaves Callahan feeling disoriented. A heavy dark-stained oak door emblazoned with faded golden lettering spells out *Chesterfield*. On the wall next to the door is a painted wood sign advertising *1 Bdrm Avail.*

Callahan finds no sign of controlled entry. He depresses a latch on the door handle and discovers that the door is unlocked. The lobby is dreary—white tile floors and paneled walls, but it is larger than Mrs. Winton's rooming house lobby. There's no one about, and across the lobby a single metal door painted dull gray, the words *Do Not Enter* stenciled on it in black. Callahan shuffles through the lobby, clutching his soggy suitcase to his chest. A partition that initially blocked his view as he first entered hides a tall desk with a wood stool behind it. And just beyond the desk is an elevator. The 'up' arrow on the wall above the elevator door lights up as a bell chimes. An elderly woman dressed in a plush velvet powder blue warm-up suit steps out of the elevator when the door slides open. She grips her purse at her side as she passes Callahan without paying him any mind.

"Excuse me," says Callahan. "Do you live here?"

The woman turns on him with a wild look in her eye.

"Leave me alone," she warns him. "I am not going to let you rob me!"

Callahan ducks out of the way just as the old woman pulls a can of mace from her purse and sprays a pungent stream directly over his head. It's hard to move. His leg hurts. What's worse is the sullen realization that his life has come to this: dodging the chemical attack of an elderly woman who clearly is not in her right mind. Callahan backs up, dropping his sodden suitcase and covering his face with his hands as the old lady points the can at him. The lobby already smells like a basic training gas chamber. Slowly now, he spreads his fingers to get a look. The lobby door out onto the street swings shut. His attacker has fled, leaving him alone.

The door marked 'Do Not Enter' swings open with a bang. Callahan flinches. A fat, old, bearded man with hair the color of cumulus clouds steps into the lobby. The bearded man is dressed in a security uniform complete with a shiny badge. He shuffles past Callahan, offering a knowing nod, and props open the doors that lead out to Juniper Street. Next, the security guard pulls out the tall desk from behind the partition. Then he does the same with the stool. Once more he shuffles past Callahan, offering him the same nod, and opens the 'Do Not Enter' door. The guard emerges with a bag of rock salt. He tosses handfuls of it all over the floor where the old woman had loosed her mace spray. After he puts the rock salt back into the small room behind the 'Do Not Enter' door, the guard sprays the entire lobby with a pungent air freshener that smells of cinnamon and clove. At last, having put away the can of air freshener, the heavyset bearded man perches himself atop the high stool behind his tall desk.

"Visiting?" he asks, impervious to the faint odor of mace that still lingers in the lobby.

The guard's bulbous nose is laced with ruptured capillaries. His chubby cheeks above his beard are ruby red.

"I am here about the apartment," Callahan informs him. He gathers up his sorry excuse for a suitcase and clutches it to his chest.

The guard gives him a quizzical look, as if Callahan's just spoken in a foreign language he does not comprehend.

"We have an apartment for rent?" the guard asks.

"There's a sign on the building," Callahan replies.

He leans close to get a look at the man's name tag over the badge. *Cringle*, the name tag reads.

"The sign's always there," says Cringle. "It's been there for a decade or more."

"So, is there one available? Or is there someone I can speak to?"

"Let me find out for sure."

He depresses a panel in the wall beside him. A small door springs open. Cringle lifts a receiver there and smiles at Callahan as he waits for someone on the other end to answer the call.

"There is a gentleman here," says Cringle when his party picks up, "about the apartment. Yes...yes, I suppose so. Oh, Mrs. Conti sprayed mace again...Yes...Yes, of course I will." The guard smiles at Callahan as he hangs up the phone. "You're in luck," he tells him. "The manager will just be a minute."

The elevator closes. Callahan excuses himself and steps out of the lobby to draw a few deep breaths. When he steps back into the lobby Cringle is busy at his tall desk, filling out a timesheet. The elevator bell rings. After the elevator door opens, a pale woman in a gray dress steps into the lobby carrying a leather folder. She wears cat-eye black frame glasses. Her eyes, when she steps up to Callahan and offers her hand for him to shake, are big and green. The woman's salt and pepper hair is pulled back in a tight bun. Callahan notices she's not wearing any rings, engagement solitaire, wedding band, or otherwise. When he shakes her hand with his right, using his left arm to hold onto his cardboard suitcase, he's surprised to find that it is warm. Callahan wants to kick himself for surveying her for any signs of attachment. He blames the woman's full figure, the shape of which cannot be concealed by the gray dress. Callahan's always had a thing for women in glasses. When he was a teen he had a crush on a local librarian, Ms. Rothstein, and by the time he turned sixteen he had memorized her work schedule just so he could visit the town library when she was there.

"It's very nice to meet you," the woman says. "Mr...?"

"Callahan," he replies. "Damian Callahan."

"You can let go of my hand now."

"Sorry."

"It's quite all-right," she tells him. "My name is Annabelle Conti. I manage the Chesterfield."

"There's a sign outside—"

"Traveling light?"

"My things will follow when I have adequate accommodations," he tells her, acutely aware of the slowly disintegrating cardboard suitcase under one arm.

"Of course, Mr. Callahan."

Annabelle pulls a blank application from her leather folder and hands it to Callahan. He fills out the application and passes it back to her along with his driver's license. Annabelle excuses herself and steps into the little office behind the 'Do Not Enter' door. A few minutes later she returns to the lobby and gives him back his license.

"Everything seems to be in order," Annabelle tells him. "As for rental fees, we accept only money orders. You can leave it with one of the watchmen."

"What did you say?" Callahan asks, just to make sure he heard her correctly.

"The watchmen? You know. One of the guards?"

"You have a guard around the clock?"

"Three shifts. Isn't that right, Chris?"

"Yes, Ms. Conti."

"Did you meet Mr. Cringle?" Annabelle inquires.

"Tough break," Callahan tells Cringle when he shakes his hand. "I bet you heard all the jokes by now?"

"I am not sure I follow you, sir?" Chris Cringle replies with a confused look on his face.

"Come along, Mr. Callahan," Annabelle takes hold of Callahan's arm. "I will show you your new home."

The elevator rocks slightly from side to side. The car is small and not well-lit. Callahan can smell Annabelle's perfume. It's the same scent his mother used to wear—Jean Naté. He crosses her off the fantasy-fuck list; librarian look or not, any sexual interest he had in her dissolved the moment he realized Annabelle smelled like his mother; and yet, as the elevator car rocks ever so slightly, and the floor number lights flash Callahan can't help the sudden hard-on that he hopes Annabelle doesn't notice.

"Are you ready to get off?" she asks.

The 6th floor button on the panel beside the door lights up. The elevator grinds to a halt.

"I met one of your tenants in the lobby earlier," Callahan offers as the door slides open.

"How nice," replies Annabelle.

"An old woman, white hair pulled back in a bun like yours."

"Blue warm-up suit?" she asks as she leads Callahan down a narrow hall.

"And a can of mace," he tells her.

"She's not a tenant," Annabelle informs him. "That's my step-mother, Maria. She thinks she owns the building. It belonged to my father, but he's gone over now."

"Won't we all?" Callahan responds.

"Sooner or later, I suppose. Here we are!"

They stop in front of a door marked 6-C.

"I didn't mean to frighten her," says Callahan.

"You probably didn't," Annabelle slips a key into the door lock. "My step-mother is crazy."

The door opens with relative ease.

"It's hard," Callahan says.

Annabelle turns and gives him an inquisitive look. The expression lands her back on the fantasy-fuck list.

"When people get old," he goes on to explain, "suddenly, everyone seems out to harm you."

"Oh bullshit!" Annabelle exclaims. "She's been crazy ever since she weaseled her way into daddy's life. But that's none of your concern. I think you will like living here."

The unit turns out to be an efficiency model with two windows that face the back of another building. It's roomier and cleaner than the room he rented from Mrs. Winston. Annabelle insists on showing Callahan the small bedroom located to the left of the kitchen. Callahan can't help but to stare at her bare legs and her black high heels. He reruns in his head a few different porn movies in which a real estate deal turns into a full-on raunchy fuck-fest of the highest order; an erotic symmetry of acrobatics, penetration, sweat, and bad acting. When Annabelle shows him the small bathroom on the other side of the wet wall in the kitchen, Callahan feels lightheaded. The shower is a stand-up stall, barely enough room for him inside. He imagines himself crammed into the compact space with Annabelle, steam in the air from the hot water, soap suds coursing over her pale magnificent breasts and—

"Mr. Callahan? Are you feeling all-right?"

"I haven't eaten lately," he says and backs out of the bathroom.

"There are some rules," Annabelle announces.

"No girls?"

"What? No," she replies. "I mean, of course. I mean, look at me. I am blushing. What you do here is your own business. If you have someone choose to move in with you it's an extra one hundred dollars a month."

Annabelle goes into full landlord mode after that, informing Callahan of the building's amenities (not many) including directions to the basement via the elevator and a set of stairs that lead to the laundry facilities.

"I can show you the way, if you'd like," she tells Callahan.

"No, that's cool."

"Will you have a bed? Some furniture?"

"A few things," he answers. "Not much."

"I am sorry about the view," Annabelle says. "I am just three stories above you on the ninth floor. I don't worry about people seeing me when I wake up naked. Is that too much? I am sorry. That's so unprofessional of me. I should be spanked."

Callahan's erection comes back to life. Annabelle's green eyes scan him from head to toe.

"I should get to the bank," Callahan tells her as he turns toward the front door.

"Of course," Annabelle agrees and clears her throat.

"They're no doubt closed by now."

"Well, I am not opposed to cash. I can write you a receipt."

When they return to the lobby, Annabelle and Callahan work out the further particulars of payment. Chris Cringle looks as if he's hypnotized by the crossword puzzle he's doing in the Philadelphia Daily News.

"So, if I give you cash I can move in today?" Callahan asks.

"The month is already half-over," Annabelle replies. "I'm sorry. All leases start on the first of the month."

"I can pay half a month now."

"Well, I prefer a whole month," she tells him. "So, if you are willing to do the next two weeks I will need a month and a half."

"That's fine."

"It's no reflection on you," says Annabelle. "But we don't rent week to week."

"I will get some cash from an ATM and return shortly," Callahan tells her. "In the meantime, may I put my suitcase up in my room?"

"Chris can keep an eye on it."

As Callahan exits the building empty-handed now he keeps a watchful eye out for Maria Conti and her can of mace. Outside the rain has stopped, and there's no sign of Annabelle's stepmother.

Callahan discovers that the bank is still open. He waits for a customer service representative to acknowledge him. There are four of them seated at desks in front of their computers. Callahan is familiar with the tactic: pull up a document and stare intently at it hoping the customer will go away. Everyone has performed this trick at some time or another; on a grand scale, it isn't any wonder that any commerce gets done in the world.

"Busy?" Callahan approaches a desk where one of the reps contemplates his next move as he plays blackjack online.

"No," the young guy answers. He minimizes the game to the toolbar. From the looks of him, he's in for quite a bit. "How may I be of service?"

THE ABERRANT LIVES OF DAMIAN CALLAHAN

Callahan closes out his secret savings account that he's had ever since he got engaged to Jill. He doesn't know if his soon-to-be ex-wife ever knew about it. And it's not important if she did. What is important is that Callahan's built up quite a little war chest for dire times such as now. He could not retire on the money he's squirreled away, nor could he buy a house. At best, he will be able to set himself up in a nice apartment with decent furniture and have enough left over to last him a few months before he needs to find another job.

The prospect of finding new work irritates Callahan. Across the street from the old bank there's a credit union. Callahan forgets about his pending termination (he possesses little faith in his inept boss to undo the domino effect that Callahan began when he ended up in the hospital). At the credit union, much to the chagrin of the customer representative there, Callahan opens a new account. He keeps a thousand dollars in cash for himself. After he opens the account, Callahan purchases two money orders, enough to cover his rent at the Chesterfield for a few months. At the last minute, he considers walking around Philadelphia with a thousand dollars in his pocket and thinks better of it. Callahan approaches one of the tellers to make a deposit. Once he finishes this final transaction he turns to depart and sees a familiar face in line behind him.

Cockblock acts as if she doesn't know Callahan when he approaches her. She's dressed in a service uniform of some sort. Callahan can't decide if it's a legitimate housekeeping or candy striper outfit, or if Cockblock is on her way to turn a trick.

"How have you been?" Callahan asks.

"Do I know you?" Cockblock's on the defensive.

"On your dinner break?" Callahan stoops so that he's eye level with the name tag on her left breast. "Renee?"

"Yes," she answers.

Callahan allows his eyes to linger long enough on Renee Cockblock's polyester-clad breasts to make her feel uncomfortable.

"I'll see you around," he tells her.

Cockblock breathes a sigh of relief when the teller calls her forward.

Callahan exits the credit union. He repeats the name of the hotel where Cockblock works several times, so he can commit it to memory. Heading back to the Chesterfield, he gets caught in another downpour.

At the End of Hell

Annabelle Conti stands at the podium desk in the lobby with Chris Cringle, the security guard. As Callahan approaches, the two conduct a heated discussion about Annabelle's mother. From what Callahan can gather, having arrived half-way into the conversation, it appears Annabelle's mother had fled the premises stark naked, but was returned by a Philadelphia police officer. The old woman is convinced, Cringle divulges to his boss, that reptilian aliens have positioned a vessel (invisible to everyone, of course, except Maria Conti) on the roof of the building where the aliens feed Annabelle's step-mother subliminal information. Annabelle gives Cringle strict orders to watch Maria and ensure that she never leaves the building alone again.

"I'll do what I can," Cringle tells her.

"And pass the word on to the other guards," Annabelle says. "This is getting out of control."

"I should think so," Cringle replies. "There must be some sort of city ordinance against parking invisible alien spacecraft on rooftops."

"Mr. Callahan," Annabelle ignores Cringle for the moment.

Cringle returns to his comics in the daily newspaper. His lips move as he reads the little balloons carrying the comic characters' voices. He pauses, scratches his head as he looks up and stares at the empty space over Callahan's head, then chuckles.

"I have the money order," says Callahan.

"Mr. Callahan, I am so sorry," Annabelle tells him. "In your absence there seems to have been some water damage to your room. Do you have a cell phone number where I can reach you?"

"I was hoping to move in soon. In fact, today would be good."

The smile on Annabelle's face vanishes as she looks him over head to toe.

"But it's the middle of the month," she informs him.

"I know. I thought we agreed that I would pay you a month and a half today?"

"Do you have money?"

"Before I left we went through this," Callahan reminds her.

His head hurts. In the periphery of his vision tiny points of light perform chaotic arcs and circles.

"I would be amenable to that arrangement," Annabelle tells him. "However, the fact remains that there's water damage to the apartment."

"From the storm?" Callahan asks.

"A plumbing issue," she answers. "It will be addressed and then the apartment will be readied for lease. There's a portion of the ceiling that will need to be replaced. And then painted."

"How long?"

"A week. Maybe ten days."

"Fine," Callahan says.

"I know an inexpensive hotel nearby," Annabelle informs him. "You can work out a deal if you stay an entire week there."

Some rational part of Callahan urges him to seek a home elsewhere. With his job in jeopardy, he entertains the idea, at least for the moment amidst the points of light still performing their anarchic ritual in his periphery, that he will write a novel, maybe a memoir, a testament of his last days. With luck, some unsuspecting literary nut might find his manuscript after he's dead and his name might live on forever.

Chris Cringle's idiotic laughter reels Callahan in from his reverie of posthumous literary recognition. He holds up the funny pages to show Annabelle a comic strip, but she pays no interest. Cringle looks hurt. He plops the paper down on the podium and excuses himself so that he can retreat to a small bathroom behind a wood door in the corner of the lobby.

"Where is the hotel you mentioned?" Callahan asks.

He hands her two money orders. One for a half-month's rent; the other for a full month. Annabelle signs the application.

"Why pay for the next two weeks?" she asks. "That wouldn't be right."

"Of course," Callahan takes back one of the money orders. "Look, I am extremely tired. I just go out of—"

"Yes, the hotel," Annabelle interrupts him. "When you exit the lobby, turn right. It's actually connected to this building."

Callahan picks up his disintegrating cardboard suitcase that lay next to the podium. He wants to thank Cringle for keeping an eye on the suitcase, but the guard remains out of sight.

"I will check in with you in a couple of days," Callahan announces, "and see how the room is coming along."

"Fair enough," Annabelle replies. "And I am truly sorry about the inconvenience."

Around the block, Callahan carries his battered suitcase into the Double-Cross Hotel. An elderly Sikh seated behind the front desk appears statuesque until he leans forward as Callahan approaches him. In the dingy lobby with its poor lighting, the old man's skin appears pale blue. The clerk listens to Callahan as he explains his situation. When the wayward traveler gets as far as Annabelle Conti's name the old man beams as he smiles and nods.

"Yes, yes," he says. "Lovely, lovely." He produces a registration card and a pen and presents them to Callahan. "Please, please. Fill in. Thank you."

Before Callahan writes anything on the registration card he spends the next five minutes negotiating a fair price for a five-night stay.

A yellowed brochure on the desk catches his attention. The brochure boasts such amenities as laundry service and shoe shine. But it's the description on the back of the brochure that causes Callahan to laugh.

> *A charming, old-world, stylish lodge close to all modern modes of transportation, including the 12th Street Trolley and the new Broad Street Subway*

"Is this for real?" Callahan asks.

"Kunda," the man says, patting himself on the chest. He gestures at his guest.

Callahan tells him his name. Then, "The Broad Street Subway opened before The Great Depression—"

"Damian," Kunda repeats Callahan's first name. "Day-me-ahn!"

"That's me."

"Kunda. That is me."

"Yeah, right. I got that."

Callahan waves the old brochure in Kunda's face.

"I asked you if this is real?"

"What is real, Damian?"

"I am asking you."

"Exactly. But are you really asking? Am I going to answer? Or perhaps you know the answer already."

Callahan forks over the money order in his pocket. It's more than enough to cover his five-night stay. Kunda hands him a hand-written receipt.

"Room 515," the old man tells him.

Callahan hugs his ruined suitcase to his chest and takes hold of the key.

Kunda gestures to the elevator: a turn-of-the-century death trap with a flexible steel cage door that, when Callahan steps inside, does not close.

"Push, push," Kunda instructs him.

"Where?" Callahan shouts. "What button?"

"Push the bar," he tells him. "On the floor."

Callahan looks around inside the cramped space. Beneath the control panel is a bar on the wall by his feet. He steps on the bar like a clutch, presses the button for the 5th floor, and the steel cage door slides shut.

It takes 30 seconds for the elevator to ascend to the fifth floor. When the car comes to a halt, Callahan steps on the bar again. The door slides open. The hallway smells of mothballs and cigarettes.

Room 515 is a simple space with a single iron-frame bed, and a large armoire. In the corner of the room is a sink with a single faucet. Over the sink, a sign rife with typos reads:

Toilet faculties are located

at the end of hell.

Be courteous and floss.

Thank you.

The typos on the sign are a portent. Callahan is sure of it.

A single window near the bed provides a view of the rear of the Chesterfield Apartments. A brick structure, single-storied with a tar pitch roof, runs between the hotel and the apartment building. Callahan drops his suitcase on the floor when he realizes he's been had. Crazy Mary and her alluring step-daughter have taken his money for the second time in one day.

Until the Devil Healed Me

The Saint Helprin Hotel located on JFK Boulevard near 15 Street looks promising as Callahan approaches; promising, that is, until the doorman gives him the once-over, paying particular attention to his damaged cardboard suitcase. Upon viewing his accommodations at The Double-Cross Hotel, Callahan had demanded his money back from Kunda. Now, armed with his money order and some extra cash, Callahan asks about available rooms. The doorman opens the lobby door and gestures toward the front desk.

"You're in room 515," the receptionist informs Callahan after he registers.

Her name tag reads: Clarissa. Her accent sounds like New England.

"Thank you," says Callahan.

Weird, he thinks now. *That was the same room number Kunda checked me into at The Double-Cross.*

Callahan cannot put it together, but whatever is going on is certainly beyond coincidence.

"Would you like a bellman to help you with your bags?" Clarissa asks.

"That won't be necessary," Callahan holds up his cardboard suitcase. His words go unheeded.

Clarissa nods at a bellman standing nearby. The bellman nods at Callahan, offering the same rehearsed smile that Clarissa offered as Callahan approached the front desk, and executes an about-face. He walks through a dark-stained wood door, the same somber color as the walls in the lobby and vanishes.

Callahan walks to the lobby elevator. When the doors slide open two couples, younger than him by at least ten years, give him a wide berth as they exit the elevator. Callahan stands inside and presses the button marked '5.'

Room 515 is much larger than Callahan expected. Once he unpacks his clothes he places them in a plastic laundry bag. Next, he fills out a form and writes 11:00 AM on the laundry slip. Callahan opens his room door, hangs the bag on the doorknob along with a DO NOT DISTURB sign, and shuts the door. After he draws the heavy curtains shut, Callahan lies down on his bed. The alarm clock on the nightstand reads: 5:24 PM. That's the last thing he remembers, the odd combination of numbers that correlate to his room number somehow, before he falls asleep.

Four hours later, Callahan awakens feeling refreshed and hungry. He showers, changes his clothes, and goes down to the lobby where he eats a steak dinner in the hotel restaurant. Before long, he's standing on the front drive.

"Where to, sir?" the doorman asks.

A taxi pulls onto the drive and stops. Callahan climbs into the back of the vehicle and shuts the door.

"Old City," Callahan replies.

"Anywhere in particular?" The driver asks.

"Lugosi's."

"Never heard of it."

"It's a former church on 3rd Street," Callahan tells him. "Near Market Street."

The cabbie looks at Callahan in the rearview mirror. An odd sense of déjà vu turns Callahan's stomach. Something in the cabbie's lascivious smile unearths a memory long dormant. Callahan recalls what Dr. Stanton had told him at the hospital about memory loss. In some respects, losing one's memory may not be a bad thing. The stale odor of cigarettes fills the cab. The scent helps Callahan to recall what it is now that he had buried for so long. A man in a car when he was a boy. Or is it his memory at all? He's struck by the impulse to contact the hospital and see if Dr. Stanton is still there. Of course, if Callahan were to suggest he had somehow tapped into someone else's memories, perhaps some as yet undiscovered side effect of his particular form of brain cancer, there was no telling if Dr. Stanton would want to have him committed. And wouldn't that be just the leverage his wife would be looking for with regard to limiting his visitation rights with his children Jackie and Jean?

Minutes later, rattled by the thought of Jill actually orchestrating some malicious plan to keep him from ever seeing his children again, Callahan snaps out of his paranoid reverie long enough to realize that the taxi has come to a halt. The cabbie announces the total fare. Callahan slides a ten-dollar bill through the little opening in the Plexiglas partition, and climbs out of the taxi.

The cabbie was not joking. Where Lugosi's had been just a few short weeks before stands the original church. The big steel doors are shut. There are numerous orange stickers stuck on the doors. Callahan wants to get a closer look but the gates on the iron fence that separates the church steps from the street are locked. As he stands there surveying the church, a small group of college kids decked out in black sporting heavy black mascara around their eyes make their way past him.

"Do you guys know what happened to Lugosi's?" Callahan asks as he points at the church.

One of the guys steps up close to Callahan. His long blond hair is a mess of braids and dreadlocks. He pokes Callahan in the shoulder gently.

"Dude," the blond guy says, "are you a ghost?"

Before he can answer, the group continues south along 3rd Street.

Callahan can hear them laughing. He moves north along the street. In front of the Khyber Pass stands a doorman about Callahan's age.

"Hey man," Callahan says.

"Six bucks to get inside," the doorman tells him. "Dollar drafts and two dollar Heinekens."

"Do you know what happened to Lugosi's?"

"Where have you been? Prison?" the doorman asks. "That place shut down like ten years ago."

"I was there a few weeks ago," Callahan informs him. "The bouncers worked me over so badly I ended up in the hospital with a busted leg—"

"Whatever," the doorman cuts him off.

"—until the devil healed me," he concludes.

"Look, man. I don't want any trouble. You want in? Six dollars. Otherwise, take it on the heel and toe."

"You know a girl named Serena?"

"No. Should I?"

Callahan pokes the man in the shoulder. "You are real," he says.

"So is my black belt in Krav Maga," the doorman informs him. "Now, I am asking nicely. Why don't you move it along?"

Callahan fishes six dollars, all singles, out of his pocket and holds them out.

"Do I get a stamp?"

The doorman rubs his fingers over his goatee. He's wearing two rings, one on his middle finger and one on his index finger; both rings are bulky faux silver pieces with the number 11 stamped on each. He takes the money from Callahan and jerks his thumb at the door.

"Enjoy yourself," he tells Callahan.

Callahan's night turns out to be a waste. Everyone in the Khyber Pass is younger than him by at least ten years. After drinking down a few Heinekens he leaves the bar and takes a taxi back to his hotel.

"Good evening, sir," the doorman says after Callahan climbs out of the taxi.

His name tag reads: Billy. Callahan looks him over. Billy is older than the doorman on the previous shift. And he looks like he's no stranger to nefarious activity.

"Billy," says Callahan. "Where can I find a girl?"

"A bookstore," Billy replies. "Or maybe church, sir."

Callahan produces a twenty-dollar bill and hands it to the doorman.

"A girl," he tells him. "Preferably, a redhead."

"What room number?"

"515."

"It won't be long."

By the time Callahan makes it up to his room he doesn't feel much like company. He's hoping that Billy the doorman has just scammed him when the room telephone rings. The caller identifies herself as Honey (not her real name). She's just heard from her friend Billy that Callahan is looking for a late-night massage. Honey announces the rate for one half-hour. Cash or credit. Callahan informs her he prefers to pay cash. Honey assures him that she aims to be discreet. And then she drops the bomb. Cash costs more. Callahan doubts it, understanding that a rate can be quoted over the phone for a credit card charge and the unsuspecting john could be billed at least twice as much. Callahan tells her if the 'massage' is that good, there will be a generous tip.

"You have to pay up front," Honey informs him. Her voice reminds Callahan of the actor Judy Davis, all gravel and grit.

Thirty minutes later, a knock at the door rouses Callahan from a fitful round of sleep in an uncomfortable chair by the window. He rubs his eyes, breathes into his hand, and sniffs. On the way to the door he squeezes toothpaste into his mouth, swishes it around with saliva, and swallows the minty mess before he opens the door.

Honey stands nearly six feet tall in stiletto heels. Her silicone boobs beneath her red tank top shirt are large, but not so outlandish that they might qualify her for a circus sideshow. Her red hair is straight out of a can. Callahan can make out multicolored roots. His attention, however, is drawn to her legs that disappear into a leather miniskirt. Honey steps into the room, brushing Callahan aside. He closes the door. Honey's hand goes into her purse as she sizes him up. Callahan produces a wad of bills and hands it to her. Honey takes the money, counts it, and puts it into her purse.

"So, what do you want to do first?" Honey asks.

Before Callahan can answer she removes her tank top.

"Head?" asks Callahan as if he's ordering a side of French fries.

Honey backs him up to the bed and sits him down. She takes a pillow from the bed, places it on the floor, and kneels on it. Callahan feels uneasy. Chasing a strange woman through Philadelphia and leaving his wife in pursuit of her is one thing; employing the services of a prostitute, he surmises, is something decidedly different. While Callahan experiences these emotions, Honey works his belt free, unfastens his pants, and pulls them down along with his boxer shorts. There's no small talk, none of the subtle playfulness (read: begging) that he had to endure attempting to get his wife to pleasure him orally. Jill had used oral sex like currency. When Callahan was good to her she would reward him. If their relationship had taken a sour turn, Jill withheld such delights, and, unlike real money, the oral sex currency never gained interest. With Honey it was all business. Payment for services rendered. Callahan realizes that the prostitute must be a seasoned pro the way she places a condom over his half-hard prick with her mouth. He doesn't remember her producing one. *Was the rubber in her mouth the whole time?* He wonders.

A minute later, Honey comes up for air.

"If you want," she tells her john, "you can come on my face. That's cool."

That's all Callahan needs to hear. He's on his feet, whipping the rubber off before he unloads. The moment he does a sharp pain racks his head. Undeterred, Callahan maintains eye contact with Honey before she stands up and walks to the bathroom.

When she exits the bathroom Honey removes her leather mini skirt and tosses it aside. She climbs onto the bed. Callahan kicks his legs free of his pants and boxers. It's been a long time since Callahan has made love to a woman. Jill had shunned him for many months on end before he left. Honey shimmies closer to him beneath the covers. Callahan's left hand rubs against her thighs, unable to recall when he and Jill had been intimate. The rule, Honey says, is no kissing. Everything else is fair game. Callahan's left hand moves further up her thighs as he licks her nipples. He pulls down the panties Honey's wearing as he keeps his eyes closed kissing her stomach and making his way down. When he opens his eyes his face is just an inch away from Honey's fat cock.

"What the fuck?" Callahan inquires.

"Are you disappointed?" Honey asks, teasing his hair.

Callahan doesn't know the etiquette for this sort of thing, nor is he aware if ever there was one. He doubts he would get his money back, not all of it since she already blew him.

Honey throws back the covers. She shimmies up the headboard as Callahan lies flat on his back. When Honey's penis tip rubs against his face Callahan decides his fate.

"You want a condom?" Honey asks.

"I have brain cancer," Callahan replies.

"Are you sure?"

Callahan opens his mouth to respond, but the temptation is too great. In no time at all he and Honey are 69ing as they lay on their sides. Honey comes first, and it never seems to stop. A few minutes later, she works Callahan into such a frenzy that he climaxes again. Afterward, they lay side by side like some old married couple.

"Do you want to go again?" Honey asks. "If you do, it will be extra."

"No, I am good," Callahan is just on the verge of sleep when she speaks.

"You want me to come back tomorrow night?"

"Leave me a number."

"You'd be surprised."

"At what?"

"Just how many men want someone like me."

Callahan wipes his face and neck with the bed sheet. Honey gets up to dress. In the half-lit room Callahan understands how some men maintain seemingly normal lives while bedding transsexuals.

"Thanks, buttercup," Honey says as she scribbles her number down on a tablet from the desk.

"Wait," Callahan tells her as she opens the door. "I want to ask you something."

"Oh baby. I got to go. Business, you know?"

"I can pay for another hour."

Honey quotes a different price, far more expensive than the initial negotiation.

"For that," she says, "I'll stay the whole night if you want. But you have to buy me breakfast in bed. That is, if you want."

"I want," Callahan responds.

No sooner than he forks over the additional money he breaks down and starts crying. Callahan expects that Honey will bolt. Instead, she coaxes him back into bed as she undresses. After she slips under the covers beside him Callahan lets it all out, apologizing over and over again for sounding like such a lunatic.

Honey holds him and doesn't let go. It's nearly five in the morning when they go down on one another again. Soon after, Callahan falls asleep.

When he wakes up Honey is gone. Callahan doesn't bother to get up and see if she's made off with his wallet (or the additional money he had stuffed under a seat cushion before he had gone out earlier the previous evening). For an ordinary man it would seem strange putting so much faith and trust in a transsexual prostitute; but, given his circumstances, Callahan is far from ordinary. For he knows that stranger bonds have been made; or so he convinces himself as he drifts back to sleep.

It's already after one in the afternoon when Callahan wakes up. His body hurts, but not half as much as his head.

Downstairs in the lobby he grabs a bagel with cream cheese and a coffee. The bagel tastes like cardboard. After a few sips of the coffee, he's convinced that it is decaffeinated.

"Mr. Callahan?" A bellman approaches him with a folded piece of paper.

"Yes?"

"A message for you, sir."

Callahan gives the guy a dollar and unfolds the message when the bellman hands it to him.

> **Dear Mr. Callahan:**
>
> *I understand that you left yesterday. There was a misunderstanding with Kunda. You were never meant to be charged for the room at The Double Cross. By now, I am sure you have figured out that my mother owns both businesses.*
>
> *Please return to The Double-Cross at your earliest convenience today. Your apartment should be ready within three days.*
>
> *If you have any questions please do not hesitate to call me.*
>
> *Sincerely,*
> *Annabelle Conti*

After the sun goes down Callahan notices the first few scouts from the pending cockroach invasion party as they probe the room for viable holes in the floor where pipes come up to a small sink. As he smashes the cockroaches with his shoe, Callahan second-guesses his move back to The Double Cross. When the cockroaches are all dead, he removes a sock from a dresser drawer and crams it into the hole around the pipe, an attempt at keeping his otherwise dismal room bug-free. Years ago Callahan had read somewhere that roaches leave a scent and that's how others know where to go. Or maybe it was mice. He's not sure. One thing he is sure of is his plummeting sugar levels. Before he exits room 515, he turns on every light.

Roaches do not like light, Callahan reasons. Or maybe he's thinking of mice?

Downstairs in the cramped lobby, a dapper and gunslinger-thin man with dark features dressed in a lightweight tan suit and white shirt sits in an armchair reading a Spanish newspaper. Callahan nods to the man on his way out.

An hour later, Callahan returns to The Double Cross feeling better after a decent meal. The man in the tan suit is still seated in the lobby armchair. Kunda is behind the front desk, offering a wide grin before he wanders into his office.

Up close, the man in the tan suit appears much older than Callahan first took him to be. Despite his advanced age, the man's eyes are what draw Callahan to him; in those eyes are not the sense of invincibility or foolish bravery that plague the young; in the old man's eyes is the look of one who has been the other side, one who has looked into the abyss, fell in, and swam to the far shore. Immediately, Callahan notices a bulge in the coat beneath the old man's left arm. The old man looks out of place with his concealed pistol like some nefarious world-traveling gun-for-hire in a 1940s film noir.

Callahan strikes up a conversation with the old man, sticking to such niceties as the weather and the parade of students that traipse up and down the street going from one bar to the next. It's not long however before such minutiae falls away, and the elderly Latin American tells Callahan his story.

The Condemned Messiah

My name is Pedro Urdermales, and I am one of the disappeared.

I was dreaming of a farm when all hell broke out around the presidential palace. I saw myself as an old man with a huge family living and working the Marxist dream. Until that day I was a member of President Salvador Allende's protection squad. Over the shouts of orders, I heard men screaming; comrades who believed that Allende's Marxism was the answer to Chile's heartbroken prayers.

Tensions escalated that summer over news that the CIA financed strikes by transport workers and shopkeepers in Santiago. At the palace, we knew that one-third of the US Embassy was on the Company's payroll. Still, Allende thought the tide would turn. Even my beloved comrade president didn't see the coming whirlpool in the tide, the very one he helped set into motion. On August 23, 1974, President Allende appointed General Augusto Pinochet the army commander-in-chief, believing that the general would aid him in restoring order against the tide of rising social crisis. My president sincerely believed that his general would remain neutral in the conflict, that he would show allegiance to the cause, and perhaps assist him in ousting foreign influence in Chile. It was such hope that soon hatched the worst despair; the attack on the presidential palace heralded by artillery fire on the ground and the hungry moan of fighter planes overhead.

In the corridor outside my quarters, men scampered in every direction like cockroaches caught in a room flooded with electric light. 'Pedro' they cried, 'grab your gun!' I was trained to protect my president at all costs. And yet that night, amidst the chaos, I froze with panic. Never had I heard such screams, begging General

Pinochet's soldiers to spare them, to let them lay down their arms and surrender. I was thirty years old; some of my comrades were even younger than me; and all of us were stuck in a place without hope.

The smoke and screams in the air were sliced open by bullets that ripped through the palace interior. I made my way down the corridor toward the rear of the palace. Just outside, I saw army soldiers, maybe ten in all, taking turns sticking their bayonets into the belly of a presidential aide. On a small veranda, a female typist suffered a gang rape at the hands of more soldiers. One of the perpetrators drew a large knife from a scabbard on his web gear and slit the woman's throat while another soldier sodomized her.

I slipped past the mayhem there, running as bullets whizzed by and artillery shells blew chunks of stone and concrete into the air. Soon, my eyes and my throat were coated with gunpowder and dust. I ran blindly into the night, waving my pistol into the face of anyone who stood in my way. After I made my way past the Metropolitan Cathedral, heading north, I stopped. From where I stood the flash of bombs lit up the night. Panic spread like a virus. In the short time it took to reach Rio Mapocho there were perhaps two dozen soldiers who chased me. Their bullets buzzed like insects past my ears. A knoll led down to the river. I slipped and fell, sliding to the bank of the River Mapocho. Exhausted, I lay there believing that the soldiers would take target practice at me. A shrill whistle blew in the night. The two dozen silhouettes lining the top of the knoll vanished.

If I believed in God, any god, I would have prayed to him for protection. All around the world, there are stories of simple people seeing the Blessed Virgin Mary, angels, aliens, and the like. I would have hitched a ride by any of them that night. But I was alone, a devout Marxist with no time for superstition. I needed to keep moving. To the east lay the Mapocho Railroad Station which I knew would certainly be watched by Pinochet's devout troops. So, I followed the river in a north westward direction, and headed for the hills of Portillo.

In the hours that followed the coup I feared for my life. I was careful not to get caught. Others were not so lucky. I witnessed Allende supporters being rounded up and taken away. Some offered resistance and were met with instant death by a hail of bullets, or a crazed squad of army grunts brandishing bayonets and machetes. They were the fortunate ones. Those that went along quietly suffered the worst.

By day, I slept. At night, I moved and stole what food I could find. My goal was Buenos Aires. In the early days, however, I was happy just to make it over the border into Argentina. I was not alone. It took me two nights to work up the nerve, but when I crossed the border I saw Chileans everywhere in the back country of Argentina. I kept my distance from them. I knew Pinochet by reputation only, but there were rumors that he had already sent his spies and assassins into other countries. So, I kept moving. I wanted to run until I reached the South Atlantic Ocean clear on the other side of my continent. It was April 1975 by the time I made it to Buenos Aires.

Once there, I heard news of a newly formed secret police, the National Intelligence Directorate, or DINA as they came to be known, whose sole responsibility was creating terror on the home front while organizing the assassination of Allende supporters in all parts of the globe. In those days, I kept a low profile, taking a job as a dishwasher or any other occupation that would keep me from the public's eye. Every stranger I met I considered my enemy.

A year passed. I was still alive. The Chileans I knew who made it to Buenos Aires never let their guard down. Still, like ghosts in the night creeping around unseen by the sleeping masses, DINA struck a blow for Pinochet. On September 30, a former commander in chief, General Carlos Prat, was killed when a bomb blew up his car. Along with the general, his wife Sofia Cuthbert also died. In the hours after the car bombing I realized that I had little chance of survival if I were to remain in South America. If the general and his wife were killed by DINA then what chance did a lowly bodyguard like me have against Pinochet's secret police?

After dark on September 30, 1975, a city bus brought me to the outskirts of Buenos Aires. I stepped out onto a desolate stretch of road. In one direction, the lights of the beautiful Argentinian city; in the other, darkness for as far as I could see.

I walked for a mile or more, heading north, taking care to look back every now and again to make sure I was not being followed.

That's when I spotted something large and dark creeping down the road. The squat silhouette and the low rumble told me that a car was following me, a car with its headlights turned off. Immediately, I called to mind the faces of bus passengers. Did they know me? Did they know I worked for Allende? Would DINA pay them for information? These thoughts clouded my reason as I dashed to the side of the road where I hid behind a thick row of vine-covered trees.

It was unseasonably cold that night. When the car passed I held my breath; afraid, I was, that someone inside the vehicle would see the frost of my breath on the chill air. The car was a black sedan; not unlike the type I drove when I worked for the presidential protection detail. There were four men inside. They passed quickly, leaving me only a moment to glimpse their hard faces behind the side windows. I stayed hidden for an hour or more. When I did move again my legs were cramped. I walked a couple of more miles before the paving ran out and the road turned to dirt. In the air, the smell of burnt petrol. The car was near. Another half-mile and the road I traveled crossed with another one. It was there at that intersection that I saw the black sedan sitting there in the dark.

One of the men sat on the hood of the car. The other three were nowhere to be found. Soon, I heard shouts. I crept behind some trees and watched in horror as the three men hauled an old man and a young woman out of a ramshackle house. Two men took turns raping the girl while the other beat the old man with a tire iron. Then the three men switched up, the two who had raped the girl took turns beating on the old man while the third had his turn with the girl. The three men soon grew bored, and they shot the old man and the girl at point blank range. Afterward, the three men rejoined the fourth who sat on the sedan's hood. The four men got into the vehicle and drove off.

Behind the trees I stood for nearly an hour before I worked up the courage to move. I stepped out into the road, and nearly jumped out of my shoes when I heard keys jingle in the dark. Looking up and down the desolate road, I saw no one. As a boy, I'd heard plenty of stories about spirits trapped in the physical world with no memory of their own death. The old people where I had grown up used to tell me that the soul was given this characteristic by God because He never wanted the soul to lament the lives it had lived. I'd nearly forgotten these tales after I had filled my head with Marxist ideologies.

Somewhere in the dark, the keys jingled again. At the intersection, a dark-clad figure stood. He held a large ring filled with skeletal keys that glinted like silver in the noonday sun. Flight was my first reaction. I think I may have turned around, taking a deep breath, ready to sprint as far away as I could; but something held me in place. A rushing sound filled my ears, like the sound of ocean waves rolling over each other. Suddenly, this magnificent man, this hombre magnífico, stood before me, all dressed in black. His skin was pale, his hair white-blond, long, and matted together in thick rows like a Rastafarian's.

The pale man told me his name was Luno. He revealed secrets to me that night, secrets that you would not believe unless you met him yourself.

We walked along the back road, and the night seemed to permeate from his head; a nimbus of dark matter, casting shadows over everything in its path.

"What are the keys for?" I asked him.

Luno stopped beside a telephone pole. The support cable that ran from a spike in the ground up to the pole, where it was fastened high over our heads, formed a perfect triangle around him. He studied the keys on his ring for several seconds, taking each one between his thumb and index finger, shaking his head as he muttered 'no, no', until at last he picked a key that satisfied him.

I watched in awe as he inserted the key into the empty space before him. The lower half of the skeletal key disappeared inside an invisible lock located in the darkness beside the telephone pole.

"Ready?" he asked.

Behind me I heard the soft hum of the black sedan making its return.

When I looked back, I saw the blacked-out headlights on the engine grill that grinned like a demon in the dark. The four men climbed out of the vehicle with an arrogant nonchalance as if their killing spree were no more important than going out to the market or stopping by some local bar to whet their appetites. Their toothy, sinister grins made their faces look inhuman. I was scared for my life, and for that of Luno's.

A seam split in the dark when the stranger opened the secret door beneath the telephone pole. A glimpse past Luno at the puerta un secreto revealed a dazzling cityscape aglow with electric light so bright I had to shield my eyes.

"Come," Luno said. "We'll go where they cannot touch you."

I hesitated, believing that perhaps my fate lay with the four DINA assassins and not with the magic man holding open a rent in the fabric of space-time. A stolen glance over my left shoulder showed me what the four men had in store for me. The one closest to me held a military issue Colt .45 semi-automatic pistol at arm's length, aiming for my head as he approached. There was a certain satisfaction in knowing that the assassins did not mean to toy with me before they killed me. They might trample my body after I was dead, I thought, but I would go out with dignity.

Luno took me by the arm, shoved me through the secret door, and closed the door behind us. A wave of nausea passed through me as a rushing sound filled my ears. For a moment, I thought I heard in that roaring wind that filled my head the distant report of the assassin's pistol.

I found myself beside Luno on a grassy hill that overlooked a city. To my right, a telephone pole not unlike the one on the empty road where we had stood only seconds ago. To my left, a support cable rose from the ground up over our heads at a forty-five degree angle. Looking up, I saw not the thick cable that kept the telephone pole from toppling over but an abundance of stars that populated alien constellations in the nighttime sky.

"You will meet another," Luno told me, fumbling through his keys again. "He will guide you in the next part of your journey."

"Where am I going?"

"Away from pain," he said, unlocking his secret door, "and toward love."

Shamans, sorcerers, and psychopaths all speak in riddles and allegories. That Luno sounded so cryptic did not faze me. I was just happy to be alive.

"What about the assassins?" I asked.

"They are gone," he replied. "And they cannot follow."
"They followed the general."
"You will end up in a place where they will not get to you," he assured me. *"Go to the Museum of Oddities tomorrow after the sun comes up. I think you will like the main attraction, camarada."*

Nighttime in a strange city can be hell; gray skies in the dark capping tall buildings resemble the cavernous ceilings of the inferno. By the time I reached the strange sprawling city at the foot of the hill it became clear that my journey away from pain would be a long one.

The actions of my first night in that city are of no consequence here; or so I've led myself to believe. After all, when you murder a man in an alternate universe does it count as a sin against you here in this place? It was a matter of self-preservation. By the look in your eye I can tell you want to know more; and so I will tell you.

It happened in the minutes before dawn came and kissed that strange city with its amber light. I found myself in a ghetto for lack of a better word to describe the urban blight that infected that section like a cancer that eats away stone and steel. There were street lights much like our own in this world; only they floated fifteen or twenty feet off the ground. Like the sun that rose later that morning, the artificial light was amber, and it cast a yellow-orange glow everywhere. There were bombed-out buildings from some long-ago struggle. In the shadows, figures stirred; some menacing, and others alluring in shapely female form.

I don't know how long I walked, searching for the city's center, when I came across a young tough with fair hair and pink eyes. He brandished a knife and muttered a threat in a language I did not comprehend. As a protector of my fallen president in Chile, I was well-versed in hand-to-hand combat. The young tough appeared more scared than me. So, I used his fear to my advantage. As we struggled, my memories harkened back to the night of the siege on the presidential palace, to the bombs going off, to the sputtering gunfire, to the cries of my comrades who died defending President Allende. No longer did I see the face of some alien thug; in him I saw me, a coward who ran into the night while others more valiant than me *stayed and met their acrimonious end. Once I had disarmed the young thug he ran down an alley. I could have let him go, but I gave chase and I caught him as he scaled a high wood fence. I drove the knife into his lower back again and again, puncturing his internal organs until they turned into a gelatinous stew. He was dead long before my rage subsided.*

As I made my way out of the alley, two young women done up like whores, girls really with baby fat boobs that peaked out of their low-cut blouses, regarded me with only passing interest. The deadpan stares they rendered sent a chill down my spine. What they had witnessed was not the worst they had seen; nor would it be the last act of savagery enacted in that alley.

By daybreak, I wandered out of the blighted neighborhood and crossed a series of double-decked three lane highways. At last, I made it to the city's center. Odd vehicles were parked everywhere. They resembled the automobiles we know but the vehicles emitted no exhaust. Delivery men made their rounds, dropping off food supplies, linens, newspapers, and all the materials businesses consume during their day-to-day commerce. I felt much more comfortable in that section of the city.

Street signs and business signs over building entrances were all rendered in a script I could not read. The language amongst the people I heard speaking made no sense to me. It resembled nothing I'd heard thus far. So, I walked into one building where a doorman stood outside. Luck was with me as I soon discovered that I had entered a fine hotel. I approached one desk where the young man seated there looked at me like I was from outer space. I asked him in Spanish, and in English, where I might find the Museum of Oddities. He smiled, maintaining his rehearsed professional poise, and spoke slowly and loudly as if I were a child or an invalid.

It was hopeless, or so I thought. I mentioned the museum again but received only a blank stare from the man at the desk. Then I felt a hand clamp down on my left forearm. Turning, ready for another fight, I saw a young girl with big green eyes and long curly red locks that cascaded from her crown down past her shoulders. She wore blue jeans, combat boots with red laces, and a black t-shirt with an image of Bob Marley emblazoned across the front in red, yellow, and black.

"You're from Earth?" the girl asked. "Oh, thank God."

"Miss," I said, "my arm."

"Oh, right."

She let go. "My name's Molly," she told me. "Molly Fitzgerald. I think we're the only ones here that speak English."

"So it appears."

"Where are you going?"

"The Museum of Oddities."

"Me, too. I can't find it."

"You've been looking long?"

"Only since I got here," she said, her voice fraught with frustration. "Where are you from?"

"Chile," I told her.

"Nice country."

"You've been there?"

"A semester abroad in 1999," said Molly. "Something wrong?"

"It's only 1975."

"It's more like 2001."

"How did you get here?"

"That," Molly said, "is a long story."

"Did it have to do with a doorway?"

The color left Molly's face. "Then I'm not dreaming?" she asked.

"Not unless we both are," I told her.

"Thank God."

"I'm not sure He knows about this place."

"Are you hungry?"

"Starving."

Molly took me by the hand. "Come on," she said. "I know where we can steal some food."

The thought of becoming a thief did not appeal to me. Running the risk of getting caught for a petty crime like stealing a cake or a bread loaf also meant someone fingering me for the murder I had committed in the ghetto. I made myself clear to Molly on this last point.

"No shit?" her face went slack for a moment as she stared at me. Then, "that's awesome."

"Hardly," I said.

"No, you don't understand," she said. "I've been a victim of crime, and…"

"And what?"

"Nothing," she told me. "Forget it. Getting robbed in an empty subway pales compared to what happened to you during the coup."

"We could sell this," I showed her the knife I took from the young thug.

Molly spread her arms out wide and spun around. "Do you see any pawn shops around here?" she asked. "No, I like my idea better."

"I won't steal."

"Don't be such a shit."

"Maybe I better do this alone."

"No," she grabbed my arm. "Please, don't leave. I'm sorry. You're not a shit."

"Well," I said, "now that the matter is settled—"

"Not far from here there's a market," said Molly. "You just follow my lead when we get there."

We went back and forth over the pitfalls of attracting the attention of whatever constituted a law enforcement organization. The argument grew heated at times, and Molly's temper was enough to garner a disapproving look from the man at the desk. I knew I could go it alone if I had to, but the idea of knowing that an American, a fellow Earthling, was somewhere in the city as lost as me was bothersome. Besides, she had a sharp wit about her, and she was not unpleasant to look at, even if she dressed like some rock and roll groupie. At the time Molly was nearly my age, and as we bantered back and forth I realized that it had been some time since I'd been with a woman. My head was filled with scenarios involving a late night; both of us weary from our search for the elusive Museum of Oddities, where we would bed down and let nature take its course. My ill-dreamt fantasies never came to fruition, however; in the weeks that followed I came to realize that the worth of Molly's friendship meant more than that.

"Well, then Pedro," she said at last. "Why don't we just trade your damn knife for some food?"

It didn't take long for us to find out that Molly's plan was easier said than done. The marketplace my new friend had told me about *was situated three blocks away from the hotel. Citizens of the amber city moved about, heckling with merchants over the price of food and non-perishables. The merchants and citizens alike bore an uncanny resemblance to the man back at the hotel who looked relieved when we left. True, everyone we saw was fair-featured, with white-blond hair, pale skin, and pink eyes; but the similarity in looks I speak of had more to do with a familial one.*

"You get used to it," Molly said when she detected my astonishment.

"To what?" I asked.

"They all look alike," she answered.

"Like brothers and sisters."

"No," Molly chuckled. "My best guess is that they are all cloned."

"What does that mean?"

"I keep forgetting that you're from the 1970s," she said. "You left in 1974. That's too bad. In 1977, a German scientist named Karl Illmensee claimed to have produced three mice from one parent."

"That's impossible," I said.

"Oh no, it's not," Molly argued. "They were doing it all over the world by the time 2000 rolled around. Some people believe that while it's still against the law the American government has been cloning human hybrid soldiers—"

"Stop," I said. "How do you Americans say it, pulling my leg?"

"Well, in truth," she went on, "no humans have been cloned, or so the media would lead us to believe. But there's been success with a sheep or two, some cows and pigs, and an endangered ox that didn't last too long."

"So, you think..."

"I just call them as I see them."

"They're identical," I said.

"Weird."

"There," I pointed at a stand where a man stood selling various cutleries.

Molly followed me as I made my way through the market toward the cutlery merchant. We stood and watched a dozen different people buy and trade with the man. Then it was my turn. I presented the knife to him, handle first. The merchant looked over the weapon three times before he muttered something and waved his hand at us. An old woman appeared, perhaps his mother, or perhaps his sister, and she shoved a wad of paper currency into my hand.

"Let's see what this is worth," I told Molly.

She led me to a table she knew. The merchant there was a woman about Molly's age. She sold smoked meats, fresh fruit, and various baked breads. I placed a few pieces of the fruit along with some meat and a loaf of bread into a bag. Then I held out the paper money the old woman had given to me. The young woman gave me a dirty look and shouted something in her foreign tongue. A large, bearded man lumbered out from the shade of a tent. He bickered with the woman for several seconds as she pointed to me over and over again, shouting the same word. At last, the man threw up his hands and took the money from me. He peeked into the bag, shrugged his beefy shoulders, and took one bill before he handed the rest back to me. Molly and I turned to walk away. The man shouted something at us as he jingled a few coins in his hand.

"Sorry, sorry," Molly kept saying over and over again as she took the change from the man.

I felt better once we were away from the marketplace. My glee, however, was short-lived. It occurred to me that choosing the doorway may have left me stranded in this bizarre world. There was no doubt I didn't stand a chance against the assassins from DINA, but Luno never guaranteed me that I would survive this place either.

"You look worried," Molly said.

"You're very perceptive," I admitted. "We have no way of telling how long we've been here."

"You've been here a day."

"No," I said, "I meant how much time has passed from where we came."

Molly launched a long, tedious argument, a thesis of sorts, on the nature of time, space, and parallel universes. She told me that the American government possessed the technology to travel between parallel worlds. Her musings bordered on the lunatic fringe. There is nothing as sad as an attractive, young, intelligent woman who falls in for the paranoia spouted by fools. Molly lost me when she started talking about Green I and Green II, alleged known 'alternate earths' that were being explored by clandestine government agencies not just from the United States but around the world.

"While we're searching the skies for UFOs and the Pacific Northwest for Bigfoot," she said, "they've been pulling the wool over our eyes about what's really going on."

Of all the parallel places in all the universes, this paranoid delusional pretty redhead had to walk into mine. Suddenly, as she further expounded her convoluted albeit complicated conspiracy theory, I wondered if living out the rest of my days with Molly might be a fate worse than facing down the DINA assassins on that dark road back in Argentina.

"This is how democracy affects people," I interjected. "Your mind becomes polluted with all sorts of nonsense. Why would your God invent different universes? Were some of them mere sketches? And if so, that would mean that as a Christian, I am assuming that you are one, you must concede that your God does indeed make mistakes which would negate the very basis of—"

"Whoa, whoa, whoa," Molly looked stunned. "What are you?" she asked. "Some sort of Communist?"

"Marxist socialist," I told her. "There is a difference."

"Well, whatever," she countered. "America is the best country in the world."

"From what I've heard," was my reply, "I beg to differ."

"You think I'm making all this shit up?"

"I have to question your sources, yes."

"Dude, get on the internet," said Molly. "You can find all this info for free on the web, man."

"What is this inter-net?"

Molly smacked her forehead. "That's right," she said, "I keep forgetting you're from the past."

She made it sound like it was a communicable disease.

Later, we moved about the city searching for some sign of the Museum of Oddities. The language barrier presented our greatest challenge. Molly, good sport that she was, attempted on numerous occasions to communicate the goal of our search to various passersby; but her intention proved fruitless.

"Jesus," Molly said. "I can't take much more of this."

"Oy!" a voice called out along a crowded street. "English! Over here!"

Turning, I saw a band of young men jumping up and down as they flailed their arms in the air. One of them had a hook for a hand. They were all dressed like pirates from some capitalistic theme park.

"Hey, guys," Molly said as she approached them.

"Aye, she's a fine Irish one," one of the men said.

"I wouldn't mind a crack at that," another said.

Molly hauled off and punched the young man, a boy really, judging by the peach fuzz on his sun-burnt chin. "Pig," she muttered.

"What my mate means, ma'am," another one stepped forward, "Is that he's forgotten his manners. We mean no disrespect. But like you, and your Spanish friend here, we are adrift in this hopeless city locked on all sides by land."

He was tall, broad-shouldered, wearing tan pants, square-toed shoes with a buckle on each, and a dirty white sleep shirt. Around his waist he wore a thick leather belt that held a sword and scabbard.

"Feisty little bitch," the teen said, rubbing his jaw. "Oy! Show us your titties then—"

Molly smiled at him and punted the young man right between his legs, dropping him like a sack of potatoes. For good measure, she smashed her knee into his face. From where I stood, I heard the cartilage crackle as his nose broke. The sound of it made me wince as it did the rest of the pirates. I was still contemplating the pain the young man felt, but his mates had moved on to laughing over the whole matter.

"You'll never learn, Yarborough," one of the men chastised the youth. "You have to woo these Irish women. They love a good yarn whispered into their delectable ear before you take them."

In one fluid motion, Molly reached for the tall man's sword, withdrew it from his scabbard, and held the men at bay.

"Oh, now you did it," the tall man said as he helped his young friend up. Then he pulled a flintlock pistol from his back and leveled it at Molly's face. "That was my father's sword."

The merriment among the men vanished. Suddenly, they all brandished weapons of different sorts, ranging from short clubs to knives.

"Molly," I spoke up as I closed the gap between me and the tall man. "May I have a word with you?"

"Listen at him, boys," the bloody-nosed youth said, rubbing his balls as he stood doubled over.

The tall man looked confused when I snatched the pistol out of his hand. He held his hands up, like a supplicant before Christ's cross. The gesture was not so much a sign of surrender as it was a signal to keep the rest of the men from attacking. There was, after all, only one shot in the pistol. And even if I used the sword Molly held in her trembling hands I doubted we would escape unharmed.

"You are strangers here," the tall man said. "We should get on like mates instead of quarreling in the streets, even if you are a Spaniard and an Irish whore."

The report from the flintlock pistol echoed along the street like thunder when I pulled the trigger. Molly screamed and turned away, dropping the sword at her feet. As the tall man fell down dead, I tossed the pistol aside, swept up the sword, and drove the blade up between the young man's legs. He looked confused, as blood dripped from his broken nose. Holding his hands up in front of his face, he searched frantically for his missing thumbs; unaware, at that moment, that his balls lay in a puddle of blood at his feet.

After that, the fight was on. The training I received as part of President Allende's protective detail paid off well. In all, I killed four men on the street that day. The last two of the half-dozen pirates dropped their knives and knelt down on the ground, pleading for their lives.

"We were prisoners," one of them said. ""Conscripted to serve in Her Majesty's navy under Drake. Please sir, spare me so that I might see my wife and children again."

"Her Majesty's Navy?" Molly asked. "Drake? You mean Francis Drake?"

"Aye," the other man avoided eye contact as he spoke. "We landed at New Albion."

"Molly," I said, "let's go."

"Wait," she told me. Then, "but that's—"

"The year of our Lord 1579," the first one said. "My name is Gillian. Sander Gillian. And this James Forsythe."

"New Albion," it clicked in my head now. "California?"

Gillian stared at me, dumbfounded. Of course, he would have no reference to such a place.

"Drake was sent to find Spaniards," Forsythe informed Molly. He glanced at me only for a moment then focused on the pavement. "We were part of the expeditionary force that Drake led onto the new virgin land."

By now, a curious crowd had gathered to examine the dead bodies. None of them looked concerned; at least no more concerned than someone might if they found a dog struck by an automobile.

"Let's move from this place," I said.

Minutes later, against my better judgment, the two sailors led us to their hideout. A few blocks from the street where I had shot the tall sailor were ramshackle warehouses. In the basement of one building, a drinking establishment that consisted of a few tall tables and chairs, a bar fashioned from unfinished wood, and a few patrons who acted as if we weren't there.

"I never knew this place existed," Molly commented.

Gillian couldn't keep his eyes off her shapely figure. His mate Forsythe appeared mesmerized by Molly's thick red hair, no doubt pining for his home in merry old England. In all, these two were a gangrenous lot, just like their mates who lay dead in the street not four blocks away. There was no telling what contaminants they carried from the 16th century, and there was no way I was about to leave these two alone with Molly.

"Do you have money?" Forsythe asked.

"We do," Molly replied.

Before I could stop her, she sauntered up to the bar, pointed at the taps and held up four fingers. The fat old barkeep backed away, making all kinds of crazy gestures.

"I think I pissed him off," Molly said.

"That's no surprise," a voice came out of a dark corner to my left. "You just told him that his ale tastes like fingers fresh from being stuck up an animal's ass."

In the dim light, it was hard to make out a face that went along with the voice. I took a step toward the stranger, and that's when I heard the hammer cock on his pistol.

"That's close enough, thanks," the man said.

He was a tall, lean shadow draped in a dark suit and a matching dark fedora.

Gillian and Forsythe remained silent. Molly on the other hand was full of questions.

"Who are you?"

"I am who I am," the man replied.

"Cute," she replied. "Quoting the Old Testament."

"Actually," he said, "that would be Ehyeh asher ehyeh. Hebrew for I am that I am."

The glint of blue steel was visible atop the table; likewise, the black glove that held the pistol there. Next to the gloved hand that held the gun, a tall tin the size of a coffee can.

"So how do you order a drink around here?" I asked.

"You have pretty hair," the man in the shadows said to Molly.

"Thanks," she said, adding, "I think."

"And your eyes," he added. "I can see you are searching."

"You don't know me," replied Molly.

"Oh, I know you well enough," the stranger said. "Equal parts spirit made motionless by stupor, eyes that are blind, and ears that are deaf."

Molly looked scared. In the silence that ensued, I lunged at the table. We struggled with the pistol, but his strength seemed that of ten men. He pistol-whipped me and tossed me aside like a rag doll. Glass cut into my back when I landed on the floor. My vision blurred as I got back on my feet, holding the sword Molly had swiped from one of the pirates.

"Idiot," the stranger mumbled.

He shoved the long barrel of his pistol into his belt, closed his suit jacket, snatched up his tin from the table, and receded deeper into shadow. I lunged after him like a wild paramour bent on killing the man who slandered his true love's name; and like an angry, jealous lover made blind by rage, I stabbed into empty air over and over again.

THE ABERRANT LIVES OF DAMIAN CALLAHAN

"You're not lost," the stranger announced, standing several feet away now in the barroom doorway. *"The way is within you."*

I stepped in front of Molly as the man pointed his pistol at us. In the light, the stranger appeared more like a frail old man than a menacing pistol-packing gangster. The long-barreled peacemaker I saw on the table turned out to be a flute which he waved mockingly before he stepped out and vanished from view.

"Did you see that?" Molly asked, placing her hand on my chest.

"Aye," said Gillian. *"He's a warlock."*

"Or worse," Forsythe added.

Gillian and Forsythe bartered with the barkeep for four mugs of ale and waved to me when it was time to pay. After a few rounds, my nerves quitted some even though I insisted on keeping my eye on the door to the establishment. The seating arrangement on our corner booth suited the sailors, leaving them to sit on either side of Molly.

"Have you heard of the Museum of Oddities?" Molly asked.

"Abysmal," Gillian muttered.

"An abomination," Forsythe added.

"Devil's work."

"Perverted and diseased."

"Are we all talking about the same place?" I asked.

Gillian shrugged. *"I guess you'll have to see for yourself, Spaniard,"* he said.

"Then you will take us there?" Molly asked.

The landlocked sailors suddenly looked seasick. They pretended to study their tankards. It was Forsythe who broke the silence.

"We know the entrance," he said. *"But we won't go inside."*

"No," Gillian agreed. *"Never again."*

"A heresy, the place is," Forsythe warned us.

"Heresy indeed," Gillian remarked before he took a long pull from his tankard. He wiped his lips with a dirty sleeve. *"That men should create such places, full of steel and machines—"*

"Aye," his partner cut him off. *"That's enough. Let them see for themselves."*

We drank in silence after that. Molly and I quit drinking when we drained our tankards. Forsythe and Gillian ordered two more each, taking their sweet time to finish, perhaps hoping to avoid going near the Museum of Oddities. When they did at last drain their vessels, both men slammed down their tankards in unison and jumped to their feet.

"Please," Forsythe said, executing a perfect bow, "allow us to show you the gate of Hell on this false Earth."

The gate of Hell turned out to be less impressive than I had first anticipated. An iron door stood in a steel frame set in a drab gray brick façade in the middle of a busy block. The door led to a dank hallway. We followed Forsythe as he walked ahead of us by an arm's length. Once or twice he shivered as if a ghost had passed through him.

The hallway wound toward the right in a long arc; all around us, the hum of unseen machines. The air was hot and thick with humidity. Condensation clung to the brick walls painted dull gray. Here and there lay the remnants of long-dead rodents. We walked the hallway for five minutes before we came to another entrance.

"This is as far as we go," Gillian commented.

"Aye," Forsythe added. "I can feel the death in the place."

"Pardon me?" Molly asked.

"The dead vermin," said Forsythe. "They find their way into this hallway, scurry around in circles like rabid animals until they turn over on their little backs and die."

"It is true," Gillian said. "I've seen it with my own eyes."

"Bullshit," said Molly.

"What's that noise?" I asked.

"That?" he asked, spreading his arms out wide. "That is the devil at work."

Forsythe reached for a latch on the big iron door before him, unhooked it, and swung the door open. He took his place beside Gillian who stood behind Molly and me.

From the doorway I saw winding stone stairs that led down into darkness. A familiar odor reached my nostrils as I stood at the threshold and listened. Suddenly, Molly's cries sounded far away as I was pulled forward by some inexplicable force. My stomach lurched as I somersaulted through the air, spinning head over heels downward in the open space created by the winding stairs. At some point I reached out and took hold of a rail. After I climbed over I traversed the remaining stairs to the very bottom. The walls and the floor around me were illuminated by pale green light. A wave of nausea took me, and I braced myself against the damp wall. Clear, foul-smelling bile shot from my mouth as I vomited. It made a loud splash on the floor, speckling my shoes and trouser legs. I was barely aware that Molly, in no better shape, now appeared behind me.

"Pedro?" was all she managed before she retched all over the wall opposite me.

The vertigo I experienced took several minutes to pass. For Molly, the same.

"What happened?" she asked.

"It is beyond me," I told her.

Molly moved a few feet from the stone stairs. She reached into the air. When her fingertips vanished for a moment, causing a large ripple effect in the scene before us, Molly pulled her hand back and scurried across the floor to take up a position behind me.

"Holy shit," she gasped. "Did you see that?"

"Do it again," I said.

Molly slapped my shoulder. "Are you crazy?" she asked.

"I'll hold you," I offered.

"Pedro," she cooed, "now's not the time."

"So you won't be sucked in," I told her.

Molly took my hand. Next, she reached in front of her and caused the same effect in the air before she dropped her hand to her side.

She let go of my hand, removed a thick belt from around her waist, and took hold of my hand once more. With her free hand, she fashioned a harness that kept our arms and hands locked together.

"Just in case," she said.

The air around her rippled then shimmered. The stone stairs appeared as if beneath clear water. Molly turned to look at me and wink before she crossed through the shimmering air. All but her arm anchored to mine appeared before me. The rest of her vanished.

I felt little resistance or pull on my wrist. Her hand loosened its grip on mine. And then as quickly as she was gone she reappeared with a devilish grin on her face.

"I found it," she said, "I found it. Come with me."

"The museum?" I asked.

"No," she snickered. "Coronado's pieces of eight. Yes, the damned museum. Now, come on."

Stepping through the threshold reminded me of the door I stepped through to escape my would-be assassins. The vertigo and nausea were gone. For as quickly as Molly pulled me through we ended up in what looked like a more modern building; though the same incessant humming reached my ears as soon as we stepped across.

"Take a look at this," Molly said.

She pressed her hand on a slick black slab that hovered shoulder-high with no visible means of support. A frost spread over the slab's dark surface. When it evaporated a long complicated message in alien script glowed against the black smooth stone.

"More mumbo-jumbo," I said. "How are we to make any sense of this place—?"

A sharp exhale from Molly caused the frost to form over the slab again. After it faded from view, the words glowing just beneath the surface of the stone were no longer strange to me.

"Here resides the hope of the world lost," Molly read the words aloud. "To view the fallen Messiah press 'enter'."

The stone slab broke into a million little pieces when she touched the word 'enter' and drifted slowly to the floor. The effect resembled snow falling from pine branches dappled in winter sunlight.

I looked at the floor speckled with the shining dust all over it; barely aware that the walls and ceiling around me shifted and changed shapes.

Moments later, Molly and I stood in a cavernous chamber. Machines of all shapes and sizes whirred, buzzed, and beeped as they emitted a strange green glow from the cracks in their housing. Thick cables led from each machine and ended where they were plugged into a circular metallic base capped with a cylindrical glass vat filled with a milky greenish fluid that emitted its own glow. Upon closer inspection, I saw a man inside the cylinder, spaghetti-thin wires attached to his head, torso, and limbs. Long dark hair floated like a dark halo all around his head, and his face was covered with a thick beard.

Immersed in the lime-colored fluid over the man's head digital images appeared. There were twelve in all, and I recognized them immediately. La Via Dolorosa. The Stations of the Cross. Each image measured a meter high and wide. No one could have painted these images. They looked instead like color photographs taken by some bystander during Christ's last hours: Jesus condemned, Jesus carries his cross, Jesus falls, Jesus meets his mother the blessed virgin Mary, Simon helps the fallen messiah carry his cross, Veronica wipes Jesus' face, Jesus falls the second time, Jesus meets the women, Jesus falls the third time, Jesus is stripped, Jesus is nailed to the cross, Jesus dies.

"Look at this," Molly said, stepping left around the large vat.

A small post stood waist-high. On it, a metallic box with a button and speaker. Molly pressed the button.

"Here, preserved as he was in his last hours," a male voice spoke through the machine, "floats the condemned messiah, condemned by those he came to save because they believed in the man and not the message. Science replaced religion world-wide in the 38th century as the most popular belief system with logic surpassing blind faith for the first time in human history."

The man in the vat convulsed once as he spun in the milky green fluid. Did the pickled messiah dream? I wondered. If so, did he cause children to shriek? These were questions for philosophers and holy men, not for soldiers like me.

A doorway stood twenty meters away, nestled between two great glowing machines. I pulled Molly away from the bearded man in the vat and headed for the door.

Chrono-Reality Timeslip

"On the other side," Pedro concludes his story now, "I stood in a Philadelphia subway not far from here."

"What about Molly?" Callahan asks.

"She's gone, never to return."

"What happened?"

"Poor girl," says Pedro. "She broke free from me at the last moment and closed the door to the machine room after I had exited. It was her choice."

Callahan leaves Pedro in his chair as the old man slips into a light slumber. He heads out of the building. What he hopes to accomplish in this latest jaunt is to come into contact with the elusive siren Serena Moon; only then would there be some semblance of normalcy in his life. He could call home, too; perhaps speak to his children. The night air is warm, and a breeze blows from the south calling to mind a summer not long before Callahan's life unraveled.

It happened one July 4th weekend when both Jackie and Jean were very little. Callahan and his wife had taken the children to Cape May for a vacation. On the way down the Garden State Parkway there had been an accident a few miles before the last exit. As they neared the accident sight Callahan was thankful that both children were asleep in their car seats in the back.

The moment they reached the accident site, a wreck involving a Ford Mustang and an old Chevy pick-up truck, Jill reached for Callahan's arm as he kept both hands on the steering wheel. When she did she turned for a moment to look back at Jackie and Jean. Callahan kept his eyes on the road as a state trooper waved him along.

For the rest of the day, and for many days that had followed the vacation, Callahan recalled the touch of his wife's hand on his arm; how the carnage on the parkway had suddenly seemed so distant. It was after six in the evening when they checked into the hotel. Jill had wanted to stay in a bed and breakfast inn, but none of those establishments were willing to rent rooms to a family with children so young. At the hotel, the Callahans were informed by the front desk clerk that there would be a fireworks show over the beach after dark.

Callahan and his family had dinner at a small eatery along Ocean Drive. Both Jackie and Jean were even-tempered enough through the meal. At home, as both children sought small measures of independence, it was a different story. Jackie could not or would not stay seated at the dining room table for long. And Jean, having recently started walking on his own, wanted to follow his sister's lead and vacate the dining room as well; only, Callahan's youngest was strapped into a booster seat that prevented his escape. Back then Jill and Callahan took turns pursuing Jackie and coaxing her back to the table where, by the time his sister returned, little Jean was in the throes of one of his many episodic fits that often culminated into his inability to draw breath. Whenever this happened Callahan became overwhelmed with a dread feeling that his son was about to die. Jill had always remained calm during these situations. When Callahan was moved to inaction out of fear, his wife would simply blow into their son's face until Jean drew a deep breath and wailed. The breath-stopping fits of crying lasted off and on for only two years. Callahan marveled at how his wife's breath blew against Jean's face, sometimes rustling his downy hair. Only when his son began to wail did Callahan move into action and console him. He knew that little Jean was more afraid of not being able to breathe than he was sad about Jackie's departure from the dinner table. That evening at the eatery all was calm. By the time the Callahans left the restaurant it was already getting dark. They crossed Ocean Drive and walked up the steps to the pier along the beach. It was Jill who spotted the candlelight glow down by the water.

Callahan led his family down to the beach. They watched the procession from the Catholic Church, clergy members and parishioners alike carried candles as they approached the breaking waves. Jackie and Jean couldn't see past the crowd that had gathered to watch the procession. Callahan hoisted his daughter into the air and seated her on his shoulders. Jill picked up Jean and held him in her arms. The priests and the parishioners were too far away for Callahan to hear what was being said. He assumed that it was a blessing of sorts. Jackie gripped her little hands against the sides of her father's head, imploring Callahan not to let her fall. Then, one by one, the candles were extinguished.

A shrill whistle sounded overhead.

A loud boom preceded a shower of white sparks high in the darkening sky; the fireworks had begun, synchronized rockets fired from a barge out at sea.

Jill and Jean stared in wide-wonder at the colorful aerial display. Jackie wrapped her arms around her father's neck as she rested her chin on top of his head. She felt almost weightless now. As for Callahan, he was less interested in the fireworks display. His attention was drawn to the ocean, to the waves that continued to smash into the sand with no remorse.

There was little about the beach that had enticed Callahan when he was a boy. The sun played havoc on his fair skin, and it was always worse whenever it was overcast. Callahan's parents rarely took him to the beach for this reason, but on those odd days during the summer when his father had insisted on packing up and heading for an overnight stay in Ocean City, New Jersey he never looked forward to the beach and the sand. The ocean, however, was another story; there was something about the ocean that had enticed him in his youth.

Callahan was just eleven years old when he had gone to Ocean City with his family. It was a hot and humid July weekend. His father insisted that as soon as they dumped their bags in the motel room they should go to the beach. Callahan's father had always been crazy for the waves and for the seagulls, for the young women in their bikinis, and for cold Budweiser cans he always carried in a Styrofoam cooler. Not long after their arrival, coated in the strongest sunscreen lotion his mother could purchase, young Callahan stood where the sand was wet, and the incoming waves had lost their ferocity by the time they reached that place. He hadn't noticed his mother approaching.

"You look so serious," his mother had told him.

The boy dug into the wet sand with his toes.

"I was thinking that maybe I am standing above the ruins of some long-ago shipwreck," he told his mother. "And when I look out at the ocean I wonder how far it is to England."

His mother laughed.

"A few thousand miles at least," she told him. "But you have to swim around Ireland first."

Callahan made a visor of his right hand over his eyes to peer out toward the horizon.

"How many people do you think have been lost at sea?" he asked.

Callahan's mother rubbed her hand on his head.

"Honest to God, Damian," she told him. "You are eleven years old. Do you have to be so morose?"

That night on the beach with his own family, with the fireworks display exploding high over the water, Callahan closed his eyes for a moment and imagined a horrific sea battle between pirates and Her Majesty's Royal Navy; the kind that he used to read about in library books when he was a boy. After the fireworks had ended, Callahan herded his family up to the promenade where they walked until the children grew tired. He carried Jackie back to the hotel while his wife carried Jean. After the children fell asleep in one bed, Callahan and his wife lay awake in the other bed talking about the accident they had passed on the way into Cape May. *We need to start thinking about life insurance,* Jill had told him. She laid out any number of possible scenarios in which one of them could be taken so easily from the world. Callahan soon fell asleep listening to his wife as if Jill were reciting a doom-laden lullaby.

"Say buddy, head's up."

Presently, Callahan steps aside as a thin college kid skirts past him on a skateboard. Everything on the street looks different. Callahan heads toward University City. He recalls a grocery store there, a family-owned business where he would stop on those rare occasions he had taken the car to work. The grocery store was no longer there. In its place was yet another restaurant; one of those places advertised as 'quaint' which was double-speak for tables pushed too close together. Callahan imagines sitting in the restaurant, feeling the person at the next table breathing on him as he listens to other people chew their food in between inane conversations about pay raises, politics, and medicating their children. They are all now half-asleep dreaming that their lives are somehow perfect, that a good house, a family, and a well-paying job was the endgame for human beings everywhere. Callahan stands with his face just an inch from the big window that affords a panoramic view of the restaurant's interior. Patrons' mouths move as they chew and they talk and they laugh; small traces of red wine remain on the lips of a woman seated by the window, while across the table from her an overweight man is completely unaware that a sliver of shredded lettuce dangles from his beard. The man looks at Callahan for a moment and says something. The woman seated across from him throws her head back and laughs; her teeth are stained dark red like a lion's after a kill. There are some things Callahan will not miss when he's dead.

The image of wine-stained teeth stays with him when he ducks into a bar further down the block. The establishment is small, a nondescript place with low lighting, cheap fixtures, and even cheaper paintings hung from the walls. Callahan reads one of the index cards beneath the painting just inside the door: *Rococo Fuckfest. Oil on Canvas. 24"x36" suitable for framing. $995.* The artwork depicts several men and women, all of them naked, possessed of robust figures, sporting powdered wigs, engaged, as the title suggests, in various acts of sexual intercourse in a lavish English garden of green, purple, blue, and yellow flowers. Further along the wall hangs a triptych. The painting, like its predecessor, depicts more full-figured men and women in the throes of sexual ecstasy in a dark wood with hints of green and subdued sunlight behind the trees; the unimaginative title of the triptych is *Rococo Fuckfest II.*

When Callahan turns away from the triptych the other three walls and the floor appear to inflate from a concave position to their flat normal state as if the room suddenly comes into being. What bothers him is not the sensation of being part of this artificial construct but that the construct, for reasons unknown, might disintegrate and cast him into a void of non-being where even the light of stars are extinguished by tremendous gravitational force.

Turning, he spots a mirror behind the bar that depicts the triptych on the wall behind him. Callahan lets out a yelp when he doesn't see his reflection in the mirror.

"Freaky," says the bartender.

"Can you see me?" Callahan asks.

"It's a copy," the man tells him. "A mirror image of the one behind you. You can't say that my wife does not have a sense of humor."

"Your wife?"

"So she's a little obsessed with fat English people fucking," says the bartender. "Is that a crime?"

"Not at all," Callahan offers.

When he steps closer to the bar Callahan can tell there's something not quite right about the bartender. The man's long face looks ashen enough to make him pass for a corpse. His teeth are stained dark when he smiles.

There are a dozen other patrons in the bar. Seven men and five women. They all have pallid complexions. When Callahan bolts for the door a fat woman grabs him by the arm and laughs. Her breath smells like a wet ashtray. Callahan knocks her aside and bolts through the door he used to enter the bar only moments ago.

Where Callahan ends up is not 20th Street but an alley replete with dumpsters dripping bilge and rats the size of tomcats that double-time past him in columns of two. Callahan swears that one of the rats is calling cadence.

> "Before the day I die,
> there's five things I want to ride:
> bicycle, tricycle, automobile,
> the bartender's wife,
> and a Ferris wheel."

The smell of smoke draws Callahan's attention away from the rats. A dumpster at the other end of the alley is ablaze; spiraling pillars of black smoke snake their way up a brick wall where the alley ends. Callahan follows the rats out of the alley.

What he wants is for the visions to end; what he gets turns out to be worse. For the moment, all Callahan can hear now is the erratic rhythm of his own pulse beating in his ears. When Dr. Stanton had asked about hallucinations, Callahan naturally thought that the good doctor meant such things might occur in time much later. If there's any consolation in the play of events for him so far, it is this: the rats have all gone away. The relief turns out to be short-lived as Callahan, recalling yet again the questions Dr. Stanton had posed to him in the hospital, takes stock of his surroundings.

As if the ghastly patrons in the bar he exited just moments ago were not frightening enough, the setting he's stumbled upon now looks nothing like the neighborhood he knew just thirty minutes beforehand; the storefronts and bars on the street are foreign to him. For starters, every car parked along the street appears to be vintage classics now broken down and rusted; automobile relics neglected long ago and left to the elements' cruel workings. On telephone poles and street lamp posts, in shop windows and doors, presidential election flyers vie for attention.

Keep America Strong with Ike and Dick

Stevenson for President

Great Leadership for America!

Kefauver for Vice-President

A big black car lumbers toward Callahan now. All four occupants are dressed in black suits, white shirts, and black ties. What strikes Callahan as odd is not the crew cuts the men sport or their funeral director attire but the Ray Ban sunglasses the men wear; the dark lenses reflect an eerie pale blue light coming from somewhere within the black car. None of them pay Callahan the slightest attention as the automobile passes along the street.

Callahan turns right and walks against traffic, putting as much distance between him and the strange men in the black car. He comes up to a wrought-iron fence that separates a temple from the sidewalk. A hunched black cat perches himself atop the fence and gingerly steps over the ornamental metal spikes. The feline pauses when Callahan stops; her pink tongue touches her nose as she stares for a moment with her big green eyes. If the spell between them lasts more than a few seconds it is too long. The cat continues her way along the fence a few more steps before she jumps to the sidewalk and skitters beneath a Ford Sunliner parked at the curb. The Sunliner, like the rest of the cars along the street, looks as if it has not been moved in years.

At the end of the block another flier on a telephone pole catches Callahan's eye. The flier boasts a tent revival meeting in North Philadelphia taking place on July 4th.

Chained to a telephone pole he passes farther up the street is a Philadelphia Inquirer newspaper vending machine. The front page of the paper is visible in the wire-reinforced glass display window that faces him. The news displayed on the front page strikes Callahan as even more bizarre than the Ike and Dick posters he spotted just seconds ago.

SAUCERS OVER PHILADELPHIA
CAUSE CITY-WIDE BLACKOUT
Mayor Claims Event
War-time Espionage,
Vows Swift Revenge

HYDROGEN DUD OVER
SOUTH PACIFIC ATOLL
Teller and Ulam to Appear
Before Congress Hearing

JOINT AMERICAN—SOVIET
MILITARY OPS MOON BASE
NEARS FINAL COMPLETION

Callahan leans forward to get a better look at the newspaper date: June 26, 1956. He's read about this sort of alternate universe stuff in science fiction novels. It's a simple chrono-reality timeslip. *But...but...this can't be real,* Callahan tells himself. Seconds later, as he uses the newspaper box to brace himself, the dry heaves set in while his heart races at an irregular beat. To make things even more uncomfortable for Callahan, he suffers a mercifully short-lived bout of hyperventilation, a condition he's not experienced until that night, cut short by the familiar sound of coins rattling around inside an old coffee can.

Callahan runs for all he's worth, mindful of his leg which aches even though the break has healed (the devil, as they say, is in the details). Anchored in the sidewalk and attached to a telephone pole at a forty-five degree angle, a steel support cable stops him in his tracks, clothes-lining him at the neck. The energy of his motion interrupted by this obstacle, propels him forward—except at the neck which acts as a fulcrum lifting his body into the air. When his body is perfectly parallel to the ground, gravity does her thing. Callahan falls to the ground flat on his back. The air in his lungs gushes out upon impact. He's certain his larynx has collapsed or, worse, he's paralyzed. Drawing several deep breaths, he manages to sit up. When he touches his neck he can feel a cut. Blood marks his fingertips. A lumbering shadow passes beneath a street lamp just down the block. Callahan gets up, steadying himself against the telephone pole as he studies the steel cable of his undoing. The cable forms a perfect isosceles triangle with the sidewalk and the telephone pole that is tilted at an odd angle. Callahan ducks beneath the cable and steps into the street.

Vertigo takes hold. A black Humvee nearly runs him over as he continues to study the cockeyed telephone pole. Callahan jumps back onto the curb. Down the street, the lumbering shadow is gone. It's hard to tell now if he's only imagining the sound of coins jingling inside a coffee can. The racket lingers, blending with the familiar sounds of the city. Callahan hugs the telephone pole as he looks around. Everything looks normal. He recognizes the storefronts and bar restaurant signs. Eventually, the vertigo subsides. Callahan eases his way counterclockwise around the telephone pole in order to avoid the steel cable and continues his walk along 20th Street.

Thirty minutes later, Callahan, tired of walking, heads down Lombard Street. Just before 17th Street, he enters The Astral

Plane. Despite the familiarity of the neighborhood outside, once he steps into the Astral Plane something doesn't feel right. The walls and the floors appear to inflate as if the barroom comes into being in that instant. The first order of business is a visit to the restroom. Callahan enters and locks the door. In the dim light he can see the cut on his neck. Dried flakes of blackened blood stick to the wound just below his chin and above his Adam's apple. He soaks a few paper towels in hot water at the sink and pats the wound. Next, a round of paper towels soaked in cold water. The abrasions on his neck do not appear to be deep. A bottle of hand sanitizer serves as disinfectant for the wound. When he applies the alcohol-based gel it stings, but it also stops any new blood from seeping out.

What Callahan wants when he exits the restroom is a stiff drink. As he walks up to the bar he studies the faces of other patrons. None of them resemble the ghoulish ones from the previous establishment earlier that evening. At the bar sits a thin Middle Eastern man reading a NAMBLA Bulletin. Several seats down sit a couple who conduct a heated conversation in whispers.

"What can I get you?" the bartender asks.

Callahan orders a Beck's beer and a shot of Cuervo. As soon as the bartender puts down the shot Callahan downs it and asks for another.

The couple at the end of the bar is still engrossed in their argument. Callahan sits down next to the man with the NAMBLA bulletin. At the end of the bar the woman gets off her bar stool. The man she's with has long blond hair. He's wearing a Nehru jacket. The man waves to Callahan indicating he should join the couple.

As soon as Callahan sits down next to the couple the jukebox kicks in playing an old Joan Jett song. The man in the Nehru jacket introduces himself.

"Uriah?" Callahan shouts at him.

"Uri," he tells him.

"Who's your friend?"

"Not interested," the sad beauty mutters before she saunters off with a sideways gait, John Wayne style, toward the ladies room.

"You will have to forgive Rachael," Uri informs Callahan. "She hasn't been the same since we landed."

"Jet lag?" asks Callahan.

"Acute amnesia. She doesn't remember home."

"And where is home?"

"On the other side."

"Jersey?" Callahan shouts. "I'm from Jersey."

"No," Uri waves his empty glass at the bartender.

Rachael returns a minute later. "I want to leave," she tells Uri.

"Baby," Uri replies, "we just got here. Besides," he jerks his thumb over his shoulder at the Middle Eastern man reading the NAMBLA bulletin, "Massoud is still reading."

Rachael shakes her head. Then she asks Callahan, "are you married?"

"No," he tells her to keep things simple.

"You like women? I only ask because Uri here is on a whole other level where sex is concerned. And that cretin over there, well, he'd like you if you were eleven years old."

"I heard that," Massoud announces without looking up from his man-boy love bulletin.

"Yes," Callahan tells Rachael. "I love women."

"Want to get out of here?"

"And go where?"

"You're the one who's going," she tells him. "I am just here to set things right. You live around here?"

"Not far," he replies. "It's not much. But it's home for now."

Rachael grabs her leather coat off the bar stool, takes hold of Callahan's arm, and ushers him toward the door.

"What should I tell the others?" Uri calls out to her.

"Tell them I found him," Rachael replies as she pulls Callahan out of The Astral Plane.

Once they are on the street Callahan stops. "What was all that about?" he asks.

"Long story," replies Rachael.

"I have time."

"Not really, but I will tell you anyway. Remember when I said Uri wasn't into sex?"

"Sure. Why?"

"He's not supposed to be here," Rachael informs him. "That pervert Massoud conjured him."

By now, Callahan's already lost interest. He fixes his attention on a lone figure standing on the corner less than thirty feet from The Astral Plane. He can't see her face, but the fire-headed siren can be none other than the same one who has caused him to lose sleep.

"Serena!" Callahan calls out.

The siren's name produces waves of exquisite syllables. The syllables roll around in Callahan's head after he shouts it out loud, riotous surf against the wintry shores of his memory.

A traffic light turns from red to green. Serena moves across 20th Street along with a small entourage that includes both men and women. Missing among their numbers is Cockblock.

Rachael tugs on Callahan's hand. "Are you ok?" she asks.

"You know her?"

"Who?"

"Serena Moon."

"What are you talking about?"

He points at the empty street corner. "She's gone now," says Callahan. "We have to find her."

Rachael lets go of his hand. "You don't look so good," she informs him. "Your face—"

The sidewalk and the red brick facades along the street perform a funky little dance.

"—looks slack on one side," Rachael concludes.

Her face, like everything else in Callahan's field of view, joins the dance, shifting from convex to concave in slow motion.

When Rachael opens her mouth to speak again, the light of the world extinguishes, all color and substance collapse. Callahan slips into a deep gloom. Shadows shift from undefined blobs into anthropomorphic shades and vanish. At first, he's aware of his extremities; the terrible ache of limbs in freefall. Far away the faint hint of Rachael's voice, but this too fades along with Callahan until neither the voice nor he exists.

Sages and Crazies, An Interlude

It's the single flaw in the system: the great secret that all the mystics in every era could never figure out; though many a great mind have come close to this secret truth...I am bound by incontrovertible dominion on most things so what I am about to tell you will undoubtedly get me further removed from my post than I care to be; however, in light of Damian Callahan's case, there are a good many issues at stake; for the moment, what I am about to transcribe here is a phenomenon of which whose very description is limited by the languages of humans; in other words, I will do my best. Once I disclose this secret, there will be among my readers those who will scurry to their holy texts of choice and proclaim blasphemy or, worse, confer with psychics and parlor trick whores who will dispute what I am about to say. This much I anticipate; this much I can endure. What is doubtful to one may be bountiful to another. Where was I? Oh yes. The most recent demise of Damian Callahan; the bane of his soon-to-be ex-wife; champion of the odd, tracker of true love, recipient of the devil's own dark miracle (one from which he had, at least for a time, survived to tell). Here's the flaw then, without much further ado.

The system is a vast and complex one, and by challenges presented by language I prefer not to disclose all of its intricate riggings; as such, unlike my brothers and me, humans like Damian Callahan and the rest of you as well, dear reader, live not one life but a myriad of them. The sages and crazies of your present reality will nod in agreement with this quiet affirmation, but they will have missed the mark. Pay careful attention to this next bit of news: there are no past lives. People swear that they have been somewhere else before or experienced some event, calamitous or providential, but they would be, in part, wrong.

The flaw in the system then is that some lives are rewritten; no, perhaps that is not the right word (dare I use the word 'rebooted' in this insular age?), but the truth is that life as an energy is too precious a cargo to allow any human being to go mucking about blindly in the universe; so, to cover our asses, we are afforded for each of our charges a given number of lives which each would conduct; a fail-safe, as it were, in case things go prematurely bad. We do not, incidentally, have asses, per se, which we need to cover. I borrow this phrase to endear myself to you, reader; thus, in the interest of self-preservation, it is important to protect ourselves; for we can be extinguished like everything else in Creation; in a sense, angels like me were the first renewable energy.

With regard to humanity then, when one life is extinguished there is a chance that another will spring up, same identity, same sex, same mind, same etcetera, like so many Whac-A-Moles inside an arcade game. You may experience the faintest taste of this phenomenon in the form of déjà vu. In truth, many signs regarding such elaborate and secret mechanizations are left in full view of intelligent life everywhere. After all, it's not just the devil who is in the details. Alas, I digress. Let's catch up with Damian Callahan and see what's become of him.

Part three: Obliteration

A World Full Of Bastards

Darkness gives over to a sunny day, to green grass, to children's laughter, to a cold beer bottle in hand, to the smell of grilled burgers, hot dogs, and chicken—the accoutrements of a holiday barbeque.

On Callahan's left, someone rambles on ad nauseum about numbers and quotas, the diminishing tenacity of the once-great American salesman. The chatter bores the hell out of Callahan; so many wasted breaths on the stranger's part, an aural pollution that taints the auras of anyone, including the current listener, Callahan, who comes within close proximity. Callahan tunes the man out as best he can, concentrating, instead, on the children dressed in bathing suits who take turns running through the rising and falling water jets of a lawn sprinkler. Among the children is Guglielmo Valero, not the teenaged derelict that Callahan had fought in the woods but a slow-witted, scared boy who appears self-conscious about his abject rolls of body fat. Valero waits in line for his turn. Behind him is Callahan's old friend Jeff from college; only, Jeff is barely four and a half feet tall, a seven year old boy that looks exactly like the one Callahan had seen years ago in a Polaroid Jeff kept tucked in his dormitory desk drawer, the photograph he had shared with Callahan late one night after they had started their affair. A few places behind Jeff is little Lamar Perkins. He looks very much alive compared to the last time Callahan saw him when a twelve-year-old Lamar had been pulled from Ganton Creek after he had drowned. The deal with Ganton Creek was that local adults, even back in the 1970s, complained that the creek carried far too many toxins and therefore did everything in their power to keep boys and girls from swimming there. One summer day, Lamar Perkins had accompanied Callahan and some other boys to the creek. He had never gone swimming a day in his life; that day, however, he was determined to change that. Lamar had moved to the suburbs out of Camden along with his parents and his little sister Rochelle. When he waded out into the creek, a swift current propelled him downstream. By the time Callahan and the other boys were in the water Lamar Perkins had already gone under for good. Callahan is elated to see his boyhood friend again, but Lamar doesn't notice him as he waits in line for his chance to jump through the sprinkler water. What's curious about the sprinkler set up is that none of the other adults, and there are a few dozen milling about in the expansive backyard (the owner of which is unknown to Callahan), seem to be aware of the children; not even when they run and jump through the water only to vanish. When Lamar's turn comes he looks over at Callahan, waves at him, and sprints toward the sprinkler. The moment his body touches the water Lamar vanishes in a brilliant rainbow mist. A few of the other children follow Lamar's exit, including Guglielmo Valero. Callahan notices that young Jeff allows others to go ahead of him, giving up his place in line in order to accommodate the other children. At the end of the long line, Jackie and Jean huddle close together. Callahan calls out to them, but they cannot hear.

Someone taps Callahan on the shoulder. When he turns around Callahan expects to see the face of the blowhard touting the merits of salesmanship. Instead, it's Lamar whose skin in the summer twilight appears a deep shade of indigo. When the boy opens his mouth to speak, Callahan drops his beer bottle on the lawn. Lamar's tongue looks like a piece of rotted meat Callahan and his childhood friends had once discovered on the back porch of an abandoned house. One of the boys noted that it was probably a cow tongue. The question that day had been why anyone would tack a cow tongue, covered in maggots, to the porch of an abandoned house with an old three-inch nail spike. Lamar's tongue, like that of the cow's on that old porch, is covered with maggots as he wags it back and forth inside his open mouth. Callahan doesn't want to look at Lamar for fear that some other ghastly sight awaits him.

"You don't get a turn, Damian," Lamar announces. "Not now."

He takes hold of Callahan's hand and guides him toward a tall wood privacy fence at the edge of the yard. Callahan takes a look around. Jackie and Jean are nowhere in sight. Seven-year-old Jeff, he notices, is still negotiating with other children to go in his place instead.

"Pay attention," Lamar tells him.

The boy's mouth appears normal. He offers a smile as he indicates a gate that wasn't there a moment ago. Lamar unhooks a latch and swings the gate open.

Beyond the gate, Callahan expects to see an alley or a stretch of woods like the one that ran behind his parents' backyard. Instead, there's nothing but a vast dark canopy festooned with stars and nebulae.

"Come with me," Lamar says.

Suddenly, a woman's voice calls out: "Don't you fucking die on me! Breathe, goddamnit! Breathe!"

Lamar tilts his head, rendering an inquisitive look.

"Something wrong?"

"You don't hear that?" Callahan asks.

When he realizes that Callahan doesn't intend to follow him, he looks hurt.

Callahan turns his back on Lamar and starts back across the yard. He runs right into his Uncle Joe, his mother's older brother, the one he never met. Uncle Joe is still dressed in his infantry uniform from World War II. His eyes are missing. His left arm and his left leg appeared badly burned, the fabric of Uncle Joe's uniform sleeve and pant leg torn to ribbons from shrapnel. Callahan runs back toward Lamar, but the boy and the gate are both gone. Light from the setting sun blurs his field of vision. Callahan shuts his eyes for a moment.

"Easy buddy," Rachael tells him when he opens his eyes again.

Callahan starts at the sight of her. "Did you see him?" he asks.

"It's me, Rachael. We just met in The Astral Plane. Do you remember?"

"Friend of Uri? And the other guy. Muhammed."

"Massoud," she replies. "Close enough. You gave me quite a scare."

"I am fine, really," Callahan announces and gets back on his feet.

"All the same. I'd like to buy you something to eat. I think you could use some food. Are you hyperglycemic?"

"No, I am not. Not that I know of. Look, it's been a weird week—"

"I have a cousin who's hyperglycemic," Rachael confides in him. "Whenever she drinks too much there's a fifty-fifty chance she'll black out and become the slut of the universe or Linda Blair from The Exorcist—"

"—and I should just go," Callahan concludes.

"—or worse, she becomes both. Those are the worst nights. There was this one time my cousin ended up with these two guys—"

"I am serious," he tells her. "I have to go."

Rachael takes hold of his arm. "No, wait," she says. "I feel responsible for you now. It's just like with my cousin. She went all ape-shit on these two guys."

Callahan imagines an otherwise innocent young woman who bears a resemblance to Rachael. "Well," he offers, "your cousin should probably not drink."

An awkward silence passes now. For a brief moment, Callahan wonders what his new-found friend might be like in bed. Church bells toll somewhere nearby and quells the sexual liaison Callahan's cooked up in his head that includes oral gratification and, oddly enough, a Phillies game broadcast on a widescreen television. He's sure that there's some sort of psychic interference going on. Callahan doesn't even like television, much less baseball. No, he's certain that he's picking up something from Rachael. Was she some kind of closet Phillies fanatic in her own right? A glutton for seasonal punishment second only to Mets fandom? Dr. Stanton did mention this cross-sharing of psychic imagery as a by-product of the brain lesion. Or maybe the good doctor did not. It's hard to tell with each passing hour what's real and what's false. For good measure, Callahan pokes Rachael in the shoulder.

"She's a mess, all-right," Rachael says in reference to her hyperglycemic cousin. "One time in the Poconos she fell into a depressed funk when her sugar went all out of whack. But you don't want to know the whole story."

In Callahan's experience, anyone who ever offered such a line was, in fact, in desperate need of sharing *the whole story.* Somewhere in time he had been caring enough to listen, and not just listen but empathize as well; these days, carrying around an inoperable cancerous lesion in his brain, everything is different. Callahan's apathy did not start with the diagnosis. He had been building toward it for some time before he ended up in the hospital. Many people didn't possess the intestinal fortitude to admit that they were in the same boat as he was, that despite all of their good intentions; despite all of their talk about social awareness, despite social media postings decrying the injustices of the world such as famine, war, or, even closer to home, class warfare and racism, despite gym memberships and yoga comas, despite giving money to a cause, despite voting for whomever they damn well pleased, despite countless acts of road rage and incidents of sexism (overt, implied, or otherwise), despite secretly hating any number of ethnic and cultural groups (not to mention secretly or even explicitly harboring hate toward their own kind or, if not hate per se, than at least a binding sense of guilt); despite showing up at places of worship every week; most people, in Callahan's eyes, were living the same lie as he; because when all else gets stripped away people are willing to fuck over both friends and family just to get ahead. Callahan considers it a part of evolution: kill or be killed, to the victor go the spoils, and all of that other bullshit.

Rachael goes on about her unfortunate cousin, the hyperglycemia, the near-brushes with unwanted pregnancies, the willingness to leave behind her undergarments in some stranger's bedroom if it meant escaping without waking up the everyman she fell for whenever she fell into one of her states. Everything behind Rachael, the street, the Astral Plane's façade, the other buildings, appears to Callahan as if they are reflections in a funhouse mirror.

With Rachael slightly out of focus now, he notices a nimbus of radiant golden light around her head. It's not the first time Callahan's witness such a vision. Still, he's hard-pressed to make a big deal out of it. The funhouse mirror reflection before him stretches its limits even further, causing its witness to wonder at exactly what point reality will shatter into jagged shards before all of existence gets sucked into a black hole of nothingness. Suddenly, the whole scene appears to exhale; the Astral Plane, the other buildings, the street, and everything else squeeze into concave shapes a moment before resuming their normal appearance.

The gold light around Rachael fades now. Callahan spots Lamar Perkins, the dead boy, seated on the top step leading into The Astral Plane. Other children materialize around him; some are older in their early teens, others no more than toddlers, and like Lamar, they all have indigo-colored skin. A few of the teens are dressed like extras from Fiddler on the Roof. Everyone on the steps accompanying Lamar appears to be in dress from various periods throughout history. One toddler with big emerald eyes fusses with his tunic. He has long curly blond hair which a young Asian girl strokes with her long slender fingers. Callahan blinks, hoping that Lamar and his entourage will disappear. No such luck. The dead boy waves at him. It's an invitation rather than a greeting. Callahan glances at Rachael who appears to be talking in slow motion (no doubt still relating the woeful tale of her hyperglycemic cousin). When he focuses on Lamar and the other children the Astral Plane disintegrates, revealing a vast gray pasture beneath a white sky.

Behind Callahan, the city remains the same: the constant and fixed shadows, the same lights; the same crystalline shards of broken bottles in the street; the smells that call to mind hot tar and shit; countless flyers and stickers affixed to telephone poles, mail boxes, old store windows, newspaper vending machines, the ever-present plywood walls that surround a landmark historical building; a building that spends its golden years in a constant flux of damage and repair; the same voices; the tiresome music that spews forth from various bars as their entrances open and close like the mouths of brick and steel monsters singing some secret song. Yes, the city at Callahan's back remains the same.

What lies ahead is another story, a tale unfolding that he's not quite sure to which Rachael is privy. With each passing day there are more and more rents in the walls of reality. A weakening of actuality that Callahan can appreciate; if only it didn't mean being pulled further and further away from the life he knew; namely, his children: Jackie and Jean.

As he stares at Lamar on the steps of The Astral Plane a longing clutches Callahan. He wants his old life back; perhaps not the marriage (for even now, unbeknownst to Callahan, his ex-wife Jill is quite cozy with her new-found love George Hawthorne; so much so that she's bringing the children down to old Hawthorne's place in Cape May, NJ for a long weekend), but Callahan would like a solid schedule by which he can see Jackie and Jean with some regularity. How then to reconcile the odd miracles and strange synchronicities he's been a party to with fatherhood? Were some men not cut out for raising children? The argument, as Callahan understands it, is that a man shouldn't impregnate a woman if he has no intention of doing what is honorable. How many men and women throughout history have spawned children by accident? Without love in mind? For Callahan, this is the legacy of the human race, that what kept a species alive for millions of years had nothing to do with love and commitment. The world is full of bastards, and some of them have done quite well for themselves. Would Jackie and Jean be among those numbers? And what about resentment? Would his children begrudge having him as a father? Cursing the veritable DNA stamp and all it encompasses that he bestowed upon them? Such questions plague Callahan. Of course, to admit as much to someone else would open him up to ridicule; likewise, telling anyone about the gaps in reality that provide him glimpses of *other places* would mean a one-way ticket to the nut house—brain tumor or not—and there would be no one who would step forward and bail him out, vouch for his sanity, or otherwise validate the purpose of his existence.

The question of existence and purpose remains elusive for most, but the true question that haunts Callahan has nothing to do with purpose or with what role he should play (read: a role deemed necessary or otherwise expected of him in society). That question, one which has advanced to the existential forefront for him, is two-fold: what memories carry the most weight in life, and which of those memories does the soul carry after death? And if one's consciousness continues to exist after death, what benefit is there to hauling all that guilt and doubt into the next place? To consider this tenet one must believe that life in some fashion continues after he dies. Callahan never doubted such a notion. What he got hung up on throughout most of his life was the idea that a supreme being orchestrates everything from beyond the proverbial veil. Well, Callahan has peeked beyond the pall. He's not impressed; nor would others be if they were allowed to see what he has witnessed thus far. It comes back to memories. Do they vanish at the moment of death? Do they fade over whatever constitutes Time in the afterlife? Or are memories stripped from the dead so as not to slow them down? Given the travails of human life, it would be better if only the good memories traveled with the dead; or no memories at all.

As a child Callahan believed in magic; not the card-trick magician-stage-show variety, but real honest-to-goodness magic. Most children do. That time ended for Callahan when he had witnessed Lamar getting pulled out of the creek. It is a memory he'd just as soon forget. In doing so, he might recoup some of the magic he lost over the years. Lately, Callahan's existence has meant little to him and even less to those closest to him. All of the forces at play are converging toward one commonality: the point where Callahan becomes a divorced man whose children, while despising him, invest their love with a different man. This alone serves as the realization Callahan experiences with regard to memory and dying. With a new slate, there cannot possibly be any residual animosity that lingers between souls in the afterlife; otherwise, dying serves no purpose with regard to unburdening the soul from past transgressions.

Presently, Callahan approaches Lamar and his entourage, leaving thoughts of memories, death, and his own children behind for the moment. He can still hear Rachael's voice, but the closer he gets to Lamar and his group the more distorted Rachael's words sound.

The young Asian girl continues to stroke the blond boy's hair. When she sees Callahan she gets up and descends the stairs. Her big brown eyes radiate a peace Callahan imagines Christ or the Buddha may have exuded during their respective times on Earth. The girl takes hold of his hand. Up close, there's something unsettling about the girl. There are two faces she wears, superimposed upon one another; that of a girl perhaps ten years old and another face that belongs to a mature woman.

"I am Hoon," the girl tells him.

Callahan introduces himself. Hoon seems to care less about his name. In her dark eyes exists a secret to be found out, a riddle to solve as if she knows infinitely more at her tender age than Callahan can ever hope to understand.

"We are taking a journey," Hoon informs him. She gestures to the gray wasteland behind the steps of The Astral Plane. "You need to come with us."

The restaurant is gone. The rest of the block fades from view. Callahan looks over his shoulder. Rachael is still talking to him, another Callahan, but the same. *Interesting*, he thinks to himself. Long ago, in a book somewhere, something to do with shamanism, Callahan had read about how one could train himself in the practice of *bilocation*—the ability to be in two places, be it physically or psychically, at one time. The problem is that Callahan is about as versed in the ways of shamanism as he is in astrophysics. A tug on his hand brings him back around.

"Did you hear me?" Hoon asks.

"Sure," says Callahan.

The others leave the steps, led by Lamar, and set off onto the barren gray field. Hoon and Callahan follow close behind. The journey lasts countless steps. Before long, when he looks back, Callahan loses sight of the city altogether. His pant legs are coated with a fine gray dust. By contrast, Hoon's little bare feet appear immaculate as does the simple smock she wears. Even the downy hairs on her bare arms are clean. Lamar and the other children gather no dust either as they trek across the wasteland, kicking up clouds of dust in their wake.

"Where are we going?" Callahan asks.

"To the well," Hoon replies. She keeps a firm grasp on his hand. "It won't be long now."

"What's there?"

Hoon stops walking. With her free hand she brushes her black hair from her face.

"A well, silly," she tells him.

Laughter like crystal chimes clanging in the wind erupts from the other children. The merriment is short-lived. A loud crack reverberates over the wasteland.

"Rent," Lamar whispers.

"There's nowhere to go," the blond boy announces.

Suddenly, a dark chasm forms a few hundred yards ahead of the travelers. An eerie pale blue light seeps from the massive canyon. Objects hurtle out of the canyon, stirring in the strange blue light, and descend in the dark.

"Catastrophe," one of the children says.

"No," Hoon cries. "Serpent men."

She grips Callahan's hand while the blond boy takes hold of his free one. Together, they pull him along, running as fast as they can. Lamar and the others take the lead by several yards. Callahan looks down as he runs with the children; his feet barely touch the ground. Looking up, he realizes that the children mean to run headlong into the swirling chaos of scaly, winged men with hideous faces.

"Jump!" Lamar shouts.

The chasm stretches several hundred yards wide. Pain fills Callahan's legs and abdomen as he sails through the air over the deep canyon. The children land safely on the other side. Callahan stumbles forward, Hoon and the blond boy let go of his hands just as they land. Callahan falls to his knees. The forward momentum sends him into a somersault. He ends up on his back looking up at the dull sky.

"We are safe now," Hoon informs him.

She offers Callahan her slender hand. He takes it, and Hoon struggles to pull him to his feet. The blond boy steps in and steadies Callahan who feels weightless, disoriented.

"Easy," the blond boy tells him. "Just breathe."

"Your life makes you heavy," Hoon informs Callahan. "Over here, it can be a burden."

Lamar and the rest of the children join Hoon, the blond boy, and Callahan. Together, they shepherd Callahan toward a vast tree line along the southern horizon.

The Desert On the Ocean Floor

The forest takes Callahan by surprise—the vibrant green moss, the red trunks of ancient gargantuan trees, the golden underbrush, the purple vines that wind their way around the trees, and the silver mist laced through it all hurt his eyes; accustomed as they were only a short time ago to the dull, barren wasteland.

Callahan's eyesight adjusts quickly to the change in light. He and the children are no longer alone. The branches overhead and the underbrush provide sanctuary for various life forms— most of which can be classified as the mythic variety. Here a griffin nests, keeping guard over her eggs. Over there, cradled by exposed tree roots, a band of pixies sit around the smallest campfire Callahan has ever seen. A chorus of angels hover over a tree stump playing dice with centaurs. Not far from the game, a slender female elf plays a lute for a sleeping ogre.

Further into the woods, rests a rusted heap beneath a tangled mess of vines. Dangling from the mass of metal are broken pistons, ruined circuit boards, and the remains of cracked plastic skin. A red laser light peeks through the weave of vines covering the twisted junk pile. Callahan recognizes the laser eye and the mangled mess that had been a robot; though, for the moment, he cannot recall the robot's name.

"That's Danny," an indigo child remarks. "You don't remember him."

"I do," answers Callahan. "And I don't."

The child shrugs. "It's your life," he tells him.

"Come on," Lamar beckons Callahan now. "We have to keep moving."

As Callahan and the children trek further into the forest, the trace amount of sunlight that penetrates the rich canopy overhead never changes. Callahan wonders if they are all stuck in a single second of the day no matter how far the group moves over ground.

Callahan's thoughts soon turn to the mangled mess of the robot, the one half-buried beneath vines, he had recently encountered. *Danny.* Now it comes back to him. When Callahan was eight years old his parents had given him a toy robot for his birthday. The robot was made of metal and covered in plastic skin colored bright red. It had lights on its shoulders and a single visor-like red plastic eye. Whenever Callahan turned on the robot it whirred, and its eye lit up. The robot also had tiny motors in its lower legs that propelled the wheels built into its feet. One day Callahan was playing with the robot he had named Danny (after a brother who had died shortly after birth, a brother his parents rarely mentioned). Some older kids in the neighborhood walked past his house. One of them Callahan knew only by sight. The boy's name was Hilly. Everyone in town called him Half-face because his face was lopsided. Hilly asked Callahan if he could hold his robot, claiming he'd never seen such a cool toy. The other boys with Hilly snickered. Reluctantly, Callahan handed Danny over to Hilly Half-face. It's heavy, said Hilly. Callahan reached up to take the robot back, but the older boy wasn't through with it yet. He turned his back on Callahan and hurled the robot with all his might at the stretch of woodland across the street. Hilly Half-face and the other boys ran off before Callahan's mother even reached the porch as her boy cried out over the loss of the robot. Minutes later, Callahan and his mother went looking for the robot. They didn't find him. When Callahan's father came home from work that afternoon his mother explained the situation. Young Callahan expected his father to help him search for Danny, but his father had other ideas. Callahan's father read him the riot act over not taking care of expensive toys. *You want to find it,* his father told him, *go on and be my guest. The next time you won't be so trusting with the likes of Hilly Half-face.*

Every day for a week that summer the boy Callahan crossed the street and marched back and forth through the woodland, searching for Danny the Robot; for his efforts, all he ever found were old beer bottles, candy wrappers, cigarette butts, and other refuse worn nearly white by the sun. Callahan thought that he would never forget about the toy robot he named for the brother he never knew. Time and circumstance had other plans. By the time Callahan reached the eighth grade the few acres of woodland had been sold to a builder. The trees were cut down. The roots and stumps were removed. Day in and day out wood chippers shredded the woodland into mulch and dump trucks hauled it away. By the time Callahan reached the tenth grade, there were four new houses built on the lot. The woodland never gave up Danny the Robot.

"Mind your step," a blond girl tells Callahan now.

By the time her warning registers, it's too late. Callahan steps into a mud puddle that gives way. He slips half-way down the proverbial rabbit hole by the time he realizes his predicament. Thick roots slow his descent, becoming more a nuisance than any serious threat. He tastes wet dirt as he continues slipping farther downward until he lands in a heap on soft damp soil. Slugs the size of small cats, filled with luminescent liquid, cling to dirt walls, and illuminate his way as he takes in his new subterranean surroundings.

The rich odor of damp earth smells of fresh rain, an olfactory summoning of a spring day when Callahan was five years old. He had smuggled a stainless steel soup spoon out of the house along with several Hot Wheels cars stuffed into his pockets. Callahan remembers how he had laid out the toy automobiles in a semi-circle in the backyard. He removed grass and dirt with the soup spoon, bending the handle as he did so, until he had excavated a figure-eight track two inches deep for his Hot Wheels. Such an undertaking was not spur of the moment. Young Callahan had to clear permission with his father. *Dig the grass out in clumps*, his father had told him. *Use water when you put them back. And you better hope like hell that grass doesn't die, boy.* His mother worried that the little cars would rust. Little did she know her son had submerged them countless times in the bathtub and the kitchen sink. Callahan's cars had also withstood the might of his Incredible Hulk doll tossing the cars down the basement stairs (the first time The Hulk performed this feat Callahan's father thought a pipe had burst in the cellar); likewise, his toy cars had withstood his father's weight when the old man exited the bedroom one morning to use the bathroom and stepped on seven or eight cars his son had illegally parked in the upstairs hallway the previous night.

Callahan's father, the Great Orator, yawped his way through the dark after having nearly slipped and fallen (*I could have gone over the goddamn railing*), cursing everything that was holy and questioning his familial ties to the boy, denouncing the biological validity of his fatherhood, claiming in a loud voice that woke up both Callahan and his mother that his only son may have been the offspring of some less than intelligent acquaintance his wife had made on the sly. If someone had asked Callahan as an adult what he remembered about his boyhood home he would undoubtedly profess that most of his memories included his father bellowing about some injustice or another.

A few cautious steps now along the subterranean tunnel are followed by Callahan stumbling over a rock. He reaches out to brace himself, accidently palming the slick back of one of the giant slugs, a rather fat specimen colored neon blue. The moment Callahan's hand comes into contact with the giant slug as it clings to the dirt wall the creature's back splits open. Vibrant blue liquid splashes into Callahan's eyes.

Suddenly, Callahan discovers that he's no longer alone. Lamar and the other children swim past him. It takes a moment before he realizes that he's several hundred yards beneath the surface of a vast blue ocean. Callahan assumes the water belongs to an ocean because he tastes salt in his mouth. His gag reflex kicks into overdrive. Lamar and the blond girl, seemingly unaffected by the water, coax Callahan into sitting on the ocean floor until he can come to grips with being underwater and not drowning.

A round yellow submarine with a large window rests not far from Callahan. The window is cracked. A face bobs lifeless into view for a moment. Callahan doesn't recognize the dead man behind the cracked glass, but he feels sorry for him. Right about now another panic attack sets in as Callahan tries to make sense of his ability to survive underwater without any diving apparatus. On the ocean floor there's no life, no seaweed, no coral, no fish, nothing.

"We're almost there," Lamar announces.

Hoon stands over Callahan and offers him her hand. He gladly accepts it.

"This is the ocean of unknowing," Hoon informs him. "You've been here before."

"I don't think so," Callahan replies.

"Before you were born," she tells him. "You wouldn't remember. Not now. They don't let us remember."

"They?"

Hoon giggles as she holds her free hand over her mouth. "Boys are so dumb," she announces. "The archons, of course. They are principalities. They're not angels, but they're not akin to us either."

"I am afraid—"

"Don't be. You're with me."

"—I don't understand," Callahan finishes.

"Oh," Hoon responds. "The living rarely do. You'll find out one day."

"Hoon," Lamar calls out.

"Yes?"

"We're moving."

Hoon tugs on Callahan's hand. Together they follow Lamar and the others along the ocean floor.

"We're almost there," Lamar informs the group.

Callahan scampers along the ocean floor, pretending he's a crab until the ocean waters vanish and he plows face first into hot desert sand. Hoon helps him to his feet again.

"You get used to it," she tells him.

Wind-borne sand stings Callahan's eyes. Hoon and the others appear unaffected. Night falls quickly as a full blue moon looms just above the horizon. Beneath the starry sky marked by unrecognizable constellations, shadowy figures atop the shifting sands shimmer and vanish.

Hoon wraps her arms around Callahan's waist now as he experiences vertigo brought on by the heat and the shifting sands. In Hoon's arms he glides past the towering shimmering shadow figures. Callahan glimpses hints of gold and light, nebulous gases, and newborn stars within what he surmises are the robes of these colossal figures.

"Wings," Hoon whispers.

"What did you say?" Callahan asks.

"They look like robes," she tells him. "But they're wings. It's best not to stare."

Before he can speak, Callahan finds himself with the others standing in front of a pyramid. The structure is no sand-blasted Egyptian ruin. The walls of the pyramid are made from highly polished onyx that reflects the stars overhead. Callahan can see his own reflection faintly as they move along the façade. As for Lamar, Hoon, and the others, they cast no mirror image against the polished stone.

"Come on," Hoon tells him. "One of us is going over."

"To where?" Callahan inquires.

Hoon offers no explanation. As the group shuffles Callahan into the pyramid Lamar looks pensive. The dead boy follows after everyone else is inside. A curved ramp made from the same shining stone as the pyramid's edifice slopes downward into a cavernous room. The ceiling is dome-shaped, and the floor of infinite tiles depicts all twelve zodiac constellations. The room is faintly lit, but Callahan cannot find the source of the light. In the center of the chamber is a stone well; the walls of which are so high that thirteen steps lead to the rim.

"We came this far," Lamar announces from behind. "Everyone goes now."

"All of us?" Hoon asks. "But there are others!"

Callahan holds the girl's hand tightly as they ascend the thirteen steps. The other children fan out around the narrow edge of the rim. The well is filled with a whirling mass of energy and light. One by one, the other children jump into the well and vanish. Lamar pulls Callahan's hand free from Hoon's.

"Go on," Lamar whispers.

Hoon offers a wave to Callahan. She holds her nose as her eyes sparkle. When Hoon tumbles sideways into the well and vanishes, Callahan's chest constricts.

"Not you," Lamar informs him. "It's not your time."

Before Callahan can reply, a little boy with freckles on his cheek and sandy brown hair takes hold of his hand and leads him to the stairs.

"We should bring him back," Lamar tells the little boy.

"You go," the boy replies as he stares into Callahan's eyes. "I will be there after I return him."

Lamar does not argue. He nods at Callahan before making the leap into the well.

"Do you remember the Preacher Man?" the boy asks.

"Should I?" Callahan replies.

"No matter, it's not your fault," he consoles him. "Life can do that to you."

"Do I know you?"

"Pay attention," the boy informs him. "I am going to tell you a story."

The Zoo Oddity, An Interlude

At eleven years old, straddling a banana seat bicycle, I stood on the threshold between existence and oblivion. It was the summer of 1976, the summer I met my killer.

Even now, here in this place between lives, I can still smell the mix of hot road tar and automobile exhaust. While I waited to cross Route 168, a traffic light taunted me with its red eye. Earlier that day I had spent five hours in a school gymnasium along with fifty-six other kids my age whose parents had to work or as was my case, needed a break from raising their own children. That was my mother. She had no job, mind you, but she got restless. That's what my father called it. What my father did not know (and I had discovered earlier that summer) was that my mother worked out many of her so-called anxieties with Tom Benedict, the guy who lived across the street who had come home from the Vietnam War in 1972.

The rumor around the neighborhood was that Benedict was writing a novel about his war experiences. Most mornings, especially during the school year, he did very little writing; instead, he boned my mother for a few hours from mid-morning until shortly before two that afternoon. I only knew this because one time I was sent home from school early because I was sick, and my mother was nowhere to be found. I spent that afternoon sitting in the school nurse's office until the last bell rang. I had a key to the house, but the school principal refused to let me go home alone since I had a fever.

The next day I discovered why my mother could not answer the phone on the day I was sick at school. She was in Tom Benedict's bedroom. I found this out because the next day I pretended that I was going to school, but instead I hid out in the garage of one of the new houses that was built where some woods used to stand directly across the street from where I lived. Benedict's place stood to the right of the new houses being built. From where I hunched in the back of the garage I had a good view of my own home. A little after ten that morning my mother left the house, cut through the lot where the four new houses had been built, and headed straight for Tom Benedict's backyard. Benedict's place was a tiny one-story bungalow. His bedroom was located in the back of the house. I left the garage and followed my mother. There was a hedgerow that bordered Benedict's backyard. I crouched there and watched as my mother tapped at a ground floor window in the back of Benedict's place. The crazy bastard Tom Benedict opened the window from inside and made my mother climb through it. A sheer curtain moved ever so slightly in the open window, brushing back and forth over the sill.

I crept into Benedict's backyard. Lucky for me he didn't have a dog. After spending about five minutes peeking through his bedroom window, I saw all I needed to see. Benedict had picked up some weird practices while he was overseas. He had blindfolded my mother already, tied her up, and when I peeked through the open window he kept his back turned to me as he held a string of beads in one hand. After that morning I never went back to spy on my mother and Benedict. And I never told my father.

Anyway, where was I? Oh, that's right. Fifty-five other losers and I were forced to play inane games inside a school gymnasium at summer camp. There's nothing more pathetic than spending time in a summer camp at the same school you attend from September through June. That morning we started out with fifty-seven kids, including me, but Fat Andy Caldwell had collapsed after he was stung by a bee (he was allergic to bee stings) and could no longer breathe (he was also asthmatic which the allergic reaction to the bee sting only aggravated). Everyone at camp thought Fat Andy was a goner. I wasn't friendly with him. For one, he always smelled like cooked broccoli. Another reason I didn't like Fat Andy was because he was always reading books. Now, some guys loved to read; far be it from me to act like that's a character flaw; only with Fat Andy he lorded it over you like you had some mental defect if you'd rather be out riding a bike in the summertime instead of being cooped up in the house surrounded by books. Then again, I didn't have asthma and I wasn't allergic to bee stings and Christ knows what else. One day after camp (every day after camp, actually), Fat Andy's mother pulled up in the family station wagon just as the camp counselors were letting us out of the school. It was the only time I ever saw Fat Andy run. The moment he exited the building he made a mad dash for the station wagon; all the while his mother stood at the ready with an aerosol can of bug spray. These were the days before epinephrine inhalers and injectors. If someone like Fat Andy got stung by bees, and the reaction was severe enough, there was a good chance that he would not live to see supper. It was quite a spectacle the way he ran headlong toward the station wagon and jumped through the open back seat door. In truth, it was the only time Fat Andy showed any hustle. Sometimes, for good measure, his mother would let loose with the bug spray after she slammed the back door shut, making her way around to the driver's side while creating a cloud of poisonous gas.

If there was one thing I shared in common with fifty-six other summer camp losers (fifty-five not including Fat Andy Caldwell) it was this: all of us would have rather been anywhere than inside the school where we were imprisoned during the school year. Being home and being able to swim in a pool was far better physically, mentally and, spiritually than suffering the inane activities organized by less than enthusiastic hung-over college kids who ran the youth camp in our neighborhood. Of course, not everyone came from families with swimming pools. Only the richies, as we called them, who lived east of Pender Avenue, guys like Fat Andy Caldwell and girls like Tammy Dressler who seemed to live for boys fighting one another over her, had in-ground swimming pools where children swam all day and adults lounged with cocktails in their hands at night. My father used to bitch about people like that all the time as if having more than the next guy was somehow a crime. Conversely, my grandfather used to say that the amount of energy spent crying about one's station in life is directly proportional to the lack of initiative one shows when it comes to making a good living. That was my mother's dad. In our family it was no secret that my grandfather thought my mother could have done better. As for my father, he cursed his father-in-law for being a communist and a cocksucker. He blamed the government, he blamed God, he blamed my mother (who in turn got over it by succumbing to Tom Benedict's desire to insert foreign objects into my mother's orifices), and he often took it out on me as if I were some sieve that sucked all the money out of our house. Luckily, my old man was about as good with a belt as he was with money. On those rare occasions he did beat me, I never suffered for long.

Let me give my old man a rest, for now, and tell you about the day of my undoing.

As I waited to cross Route 168 at the traffic light there was a long line of cars, for as far north as I could see, all of them creeping toward the Atlantic City Expressway and points further south, heading toward various New Jersey shore towns. Hindsight, I later learned, truly is twenty-twenty. If I hadn't been such a nerd about listening to my parents and their endless parochial wisdom (chew with your mouth closed, pay attention in school, wash behind your ears, don't talk to strangers [my father's favorite; if only I had respected his wishes], respect your elders, no swimming until at least one half-hour after you've eaten, no chocolate after spaghetti [yes, my mother was a lunatic in that regard...never mind that the rest of the world used chocolate to curb the acidity caused by tomato sauce], cross a busy road only when the traffic light is green, etc., etc.), my life may have taken a different turn. Who knows? I could have been an astronaut, a doctor, a lawyer, a paleontologist, maybe even a veteran of war who sat at home smoking dope and screwing different neighborhood wives (I was onto Tom Benedict right away...him and his endless parade of mothers from the neighborhood). Instead, the only thing I thought about that morning as I sat on my bike waiting for the traffic light to change was how, within a few weeks, my father would take the three of us on vacation, and my mother, all broken-hearted over her Benedict-withdrawal, would spend hours packing our bags just so before we set off for the Jersey shore where we would join all the other unimaginative mooks who baked in the sun during the day and endured diatribes from their fathers, just like I did mine, about the foolhardiness of throwing away hard-earned money at night on the boardwalk. Might as well flush that cash down the stinking toilet, he told me whenever he had to fork over a buck for pinball or a game of ski ball. Just like the previous summer and each one that preceded it, I was filled with fear over the prospect of my otherwise dull life being turned upside down as we embarked on yet another chaotic family vacation.

For the moment, however, I was content to study the faces inside air-conditioned cars that slowly crept by. It wasn't so long ago, maybe when I was eight years old, that traffic would stop to let a boy like me cross the road. Times change. My father was fond of saying that. He'd read the morning paper before work and grunt his disapproval at the world's state of affairs; never offering the slightest solution. He found it therapeutic to complain about politics the world over and defame those in power. To hear my father habitually carp about things one might think that the Four Horsemen of the Apocalypse were about to come riding out of the west (or east or whatever goddamn direction the bible said they were supposed to come out of) along with mighty Jesus in all of his righteous glory wielding a mighty saber and toppling nations one by one, but what was really going on was that, so far as my untrained eleven-year-old mind could tell, the world had gone and gotten itself dog-tired.

"Apatheosis," my father belched one summer morning as pouring rain pelted the yard outside the kitchen window. "That's what's wrong with this country right now."

"You mean apotheosis," my mother corrected.

Slowly, I took my bowl of Alpha-bits cereal off the table and started for the living room. My parents, thankfully, had become big fans of TV dinner trays, though my mother refused to purchase actual TV dinners at the supermarket. It was my intention to escape the coming storm between my parents and watch my morning cartoons before heading off to summer camp. The TV dinner tray was my salvation. My father had other ideas.

"Sit down, boy," he said. And to my mother, he replied, "You don't think I don't know what that means?"

"I'm not sure," she countered. "You speak in double negatives all the time."

"Do I?"

"The elevation of a person to the rank of a god."

"What?"

"That's what apotheosis means."

"Well, well," my father said, putting down the newspaper. "I'll be damned. Did Tom Benedict teach you that word?"

My father was another in a long string of cuckolds in the neighborhood. Later, I would be afforded occasional glances from Oblivion into the world of the living. I saw that Tom Benedict met his ultimate end not at the hands of some jealous husband, but through an act of his own accord.

"Apatheosis," my father told her. "The degradation of a person to the rank of something less than human through not caring."

"You're an idiot," my mother said.

I put my cereal bowl down on the table. This, I thought, was going to be good.

"I won't divorce you," was my father's reply.

My mother chucked a glass of orange juice at him. My father weaved to his left, avoiding the glass and most of the juice. He picked up his coffee mug, ready to retaliate.

"Father!" I shouted.

He put down the mug. My mother got up and left the kitchen.

"See what I mean?" my father said when we were alone. "Even your mother is infected by apatheosis."

The front door slammed shut. My mother was gone; presumably into the arms of Tom Benedict if he wasn't busy entertaining one of the other mothers.

I said nothing and cleaned up the spilt juice. My father went back to reading the paper.

Forty-five minutes later, my mother returned smelling of cigarettes. Her hair looked messy and tangled. Her shirt and shorts were wrinkled.

"These crazy fads," my father bitched now, rustling the newspaper as if the row between my mother and him had not happened. "Does anybody really think that jogging and disco will make everything better? Says here that both activities promote cocaine use and promiscuity," his gaze lingered on my mother for the moment. "I guess it's just what the therapist ordered for the cracked psyche of post-war America."

"You shouldn't talk about things you know nothing about," my mother remarked.

"Ah," said my father, *"you still pine for the Sixties with all that free love bullshit. The Sixties were a pipe dream. That decade caused more problems than solutions."*

My old man thought he knew everything, excelled at nothing, and credited his miserable existence to being dealt a bad hand. His sole solace was pontificating on current events from the kitchen table. It didn't end at home. That morning he would drive his car to his job in a newly constructed industrial park graced with young saplings and freshly laid sod, and complain to coworkers that industrial parks would one day become a gulag for Americans who would work longer hours and sacrifice family time; to say nothing of how parents would come to rely on television and extra-curricular activities like karate, soccer, music and ballet lessons, and professional learning centers to help mold their children into so-called responsible adults because parenting would no longer be a viable option. The fallout of such practices would be devastating: a whole generation of self-centered assholes who would in turn give birth to another generation that would withdraw into the comfortable confines of cyberspace; the act of playing outside becoming a thing of the past. That morning, however, I knew my father was just getting started. It was true that most of the time the old man didn't know what the hell he was talking about. He was, for better or worse, in love with the sound of his own voice; a simpleton with a split personality whose own musings drew him closer to ruin like the sirens did the sailors passing the Sirenum Scopuli. The way he would go on often drove my mother nuts, but in all of my father's crazy rantings there was some truth. The problem was I didn't want to sift through a ton of bullshit to find even one pearl of wisdom.

The way I felt after summer camp that day I didn't care if the traffic light took forever to change from red to green. As I waited a fat man inside a Country Squire station wagon laden on top with a small mountain of luggage, beach chairs, bicycles, Styrofoam coolers, and other assorted sundries lay on his horn and shook his meaty fist as he shouted, "Goddamn you, Fitzy!" The intended was a skeletal specter of a man who concentrated all his drunken energy on getting across the road with no regard for traffic. The man in the station wagon shook his fist a second time as he honked his horn over and over to the embarrassing detriment of his wife and children. Fitzy, the town drunk, danced to the bleating horns as other cars headed in the opposite direction began beeping at him as well. Fitzy raised his hands in mock surrender; his bare skinny arms were festooned with tattoos.

"Semper Fi!" the fat man in the wagon shouted. "Fitzy, get out of the goddamn road! You'll get yourself killed!"

"Just trying to get to Eddie's," Fitzy said and offered a salute.

Eddie's Bar was notorious for Saturday night parking lot fights and the occasional drug raid. It beckoned Fitzy who looked drunker than usual that day. He was one of those characters I never paid much attention to unless I got stuck in line behind him at Joe's Newsstand or Matt's American Deli. Fitzy had this annoying habit, aside from stinking of alcohol, of mumbling call signs as if he were still in the jungles of Vietnam. The story my father had told me was that Fitzy had gone over to Vietnam early on during the conflict, witnessed enough murder and mayhem to screw him up for the rest of his life, and then returned home. Stateside, he forsook God (Who wasn't really interested in the goings-on in Southeast Asia at the time) and picked up the bottle.

"The Wreck of Edward Fitzgerald," my mother had commented once.

I didn't know anything about war except for old movies I saw on television. In most of those movies when mortar or artillery rounds exploded the actors just pirouetted like ballerinas and fell to the ground. If the main character got shot or suffered injury from shrapnel he just staggered around a bit for dramatic effect. As an eleven-year-old boy in the mid-1970s, I had never heard the real stories; even if someone had told me I doubted that I could get my head around severed limbs, decapitations, and guts pouring out of a guy's ripped open torso.

Fitzy's face with its deep wrinkles and ruddy skin told a long tragic story; one that did not end with a medal or two; not even one that ended with an honorable discharge. Seeing Fitzy on the street, and other men like him, brought the Vietnam War home for many *people in my town. Men like my father, and those of his generation, had been too young to fight in Korea, and they were too old for Vietnam. None of them ever knew the horror of war. My father might have been a bigoted moron at times, but it pleased me to know that he'd never end up looking like Fitzy. As a boy, I never gave much thought to the next war, never thought about how when parents lose their sons in war they could turn into a hollow shell the way Fitzy did. It was only later that I learned a lesson about one's private hell; no one's suffering can be any less legitimate than the next.*

"They're in the trees, man!" Fitzy shouted at the fat man in the station wagon.

There were boys in my neighborhood back then, older than me, who taunted poor Fitzy to no end; especially when he suffered flashbacks. My mother used to tell me to steer clear of madmen. If there had been one person in my life I listened to less than my father, it was my mother. Later that afternoon, the same day Fitzy stood in the middle of the Black Horse Pike screaming about the Cong in the trees, I would learn a valuable lesson about madmen, about how they didn't always come in the form of drunkards screaming about an enemy thousands of miles away from my small New Jersey town.

"Don't worry, Fitzy," the fat man shouted back. "I won't let them get you."

I watched as Fitzy staggered toward the station wagon. He raised his left hand; palm facing up toward God as it shook, looking for a handout.

"Never feed a man's addiction," my father had told me when I was nine years old.

It happened one evening when we were walking home from a little league game. My father and I ran into Fitzy as he sat outside Eddie's Bar and Grill. Fitzy was crying and mumbling to himself. He looked drunker than usual. I felt sorry for him. He asked my father for a couple of bucks just to get him by. My father refused him.

"Broke-dick asshole," Fitzy had called my father before he lumbered off down the pike.

I never knew what he meant by calling my father such a name. Had Fitzy known something about my father that I did not? Did he know about my mother and Tom Benedict? I never found out. That evening I saw my father in a different light. After Fitzy had doled his insult my father shrugged, put his arm around me, and led me up the street to our house. Along the way he had shared his advice about feeding the addictions of others.

"Come on, brother," Fitzy was saying to the fat man in the station wagon. "Help me out."

"Get away from my car, Fitzy," the fat man said. He rolled up the driver's side window and ordered his wife to do the same on the passenger side.

In the back of the station wagon there were four children. Each one bore a similar resemblance to their father: meaty forearms, fat stubby fingers, pudgy faces with thick foreheads. I recognized one of the boys. His name was Eric Carter. He was two years older than me. The previous summer Carter had beat up my friend Chris Fazzi. He spotted me as he looked around from inside the car, flared his nostrils like a wild boar, and flipped me the bird. Traffic started moving again. Carter's fat siblings started cracking up and they followed their brother's lead, each one giving me the middle finger as their father's station wagon lurched forward. No good deed goes unpunished, not even for the Carter kids. Their old man must have glimpsed their obscene gestures in the rearview mirror. Suddenly, the parking lights came on. Mr. Carter climbed out of the car, swung open the back door, and proceeded to slap around all four of his children in the back of the station wagon. In the chaos, one of Eric Carter's little sisters climbed up front with her mother who was screaming up a storm. The parking lights dimmed, and the station wagon lurched forward.

By the time Mr. Carter climbed back into the driver's seat it was too late. The station wagon banged into the rear end of a Philadelphia Evening Bulletin delivery truck. All at once the entire Carter clan started screaming from inside the station wagon. The parking lights on the back of the wagon came on a second time just before I heard the wrench of the emergency brake. Mr. Carter ignored the delivery truck driver who had exited his vehicle to assess the situation. He was too busy swinging wildly at his children as he twisted his large body into a kneeling position in the front seat. Eric

Carter's face smashed against one of the side windows, cracking the glass. Blood spurted from his nose. Seeing the Neanderthal scourge of my middle school in such a state called to mind my third-grade catechism teacher Father Michael McMurphy (another victim of Eric Carter's) and how he described the damned and their wailing and gnashing of teeth for all eternity in Hell. I wished my friend Chris and Father Michael could have been with me that day. The previous spring Eric Carter had jumped the priest one night inside Burke's Five and Dime after Father Michael stepped in his way. It wasn't on purpose. Carter and Father Michael did that awkward 'excuse me' dance as they each attempted to side-step one another in one aisle. After a couple of seconds of this ritual, frustrated and no doubt out to impress his buddies who were elsewhere in the store, Carter grew tired of the game and punched Father Michael in the mouth before pushing him into the plate glass door of a soft drink cooler. The glass broke and Father Michael ended up with stitches on his neck and the left side of his head. To hear my mother tell the story, the priest was lucky he wasn't killed. Eric Carter, despite assaulting a priest, was never arrested. Father Michael, when he came to, refused to press charges. After the incident Eric Carter missed several days of school. When he did return his arm was in a cast, his broken nose was bandaged with white adhesive tape, and he was missing a few teeth. Presently, Mr. Carter quit beating his children and stepped outside of the station wagon to confront the newspaper delivery truck driver. As I waited for the light to change, Eric Carter wiped his bloody nose clean as he stared at me and flipped me the bird a second time.

The damned traffic light remained red. The Carters in their beat-up station wagon rolled further down the pike as traffic started moving again. Heat rose from the cars as they slowly crept forward. At last, the light turned green for me. Just as I put one foot on the pedal to ride my bike across the street a 1968 Chevy Impala, tan except for the various patches of dark body fill, pulled up along the shoulder and blocked my way. The Impala kicked off a wall of heat as it sat there idling. A rosary hung from the rearview mirror. That was the first thing I noticed through the passenger-side window that was rolled all the way down. From inside the car streams of cool lemon-scented air wafted over me. The car stereo played 'Rock and

Roll All Night' from the Kiss Alive album. The driver, a young man close to Tom Benedict's age, sported long blond hair. He wore a handlebar mustache and mirror shades that covered half his face.

"Hey, little man," the driver said, "how's it hanging?"

Despite endless hours of lectures I had endured from my mother on the improbability of coming out unscathed after approaching a stranger's car, I inched my bike forward just a bit. My front wheel was nearly touching the passenger door as the driver lowered the music. He removed his sunglasses and leaned sideways along the front seat to get a better look at me. His eyes reminded me of Father Michael's—pale, blue, and kind.

The first time I met Father Michael was after mass one Sunday morning at St. Mary's. My father waved to a man I did not recognize. Father Michael was dressed in 'civvies' that morning. It was the word my father used as an excuse whenever he ran into someone he didn't recognize out of uniform.

One day we ran into the postman Mr. Baird at the supermarket.

"Sorry, Danny," my father said, "I didn't recognize you in your civvies."

Then there was a waitress from the local diner that time my father and I saw her at Woolworth's in Camden.

"Claire, honey," my father said. "You look so different in your civvies I hardly recognized you."

My father liked Claire; maybe more than he did my mother. The waitress was in her late twenties, attractive and shapely, but my father's fascination with her was strictly platonic. He knew how to play it safe. Getting hurt by another woman besides my mother was too much for him to bear.

"Goddamn Vatican II fallout," my father muttered after he waved to Father Michael.

I didn't know what went on at the Vatican; much less how a meeting of two thousand or more bishops and other church superiors could impact my community. My father was reluctant to change. He liked the old church. He liked to hear mass in Latin. And he disliked any notion of dialogue on the Church's part with the contemporary world.

"What's Vatican II?" I asked as he shuffled me down the sidewalk toward his parked car.

"Never mind," he said.

A few days later, as he thumbed through the latest edition of the Catholic Star Herald, my father became incensed.

"These new priests," he seethed. "Mark my words. From their numbers the Antichrist will come."

My mother looked at me and rolled her eyes. It was one of those rare occasions where she did not seek to confront my father's tomfoolery.

When it came to matters of faith my father was an absolute nut. In another lifetime he was probably a crusader lopping off the heads of Muslims in the name of Jesus throughout the Holy Land. That was the problem with Catholicism. The beginning of the end for an organization in a place of power is the idea that nothing can weaken or destroy it. Sooner or later, something always tips the balance of power. My father saw the Second Vatican Council as another weight to bear on that scale. The withering commitment to old values and traditions, at least for my old man, was the beginning of the end.

How does a kid my age know all of this? When you're dead a whole new world opens up. People on the living plane remember you as an eleven-year-old boy. On the other side, however, there are plenty of powers and principalities with nothing better to do than bring a dead boy up to speed. Sometimes there's a price; other times post-mortem knowledge is shared out of sheer goodness. For many of us it's a matter of gathering positivity about you so that you can move on.

"Hey, dude," the Impala driver said to me. "Do you know how to get to...let's see..."

A map appeared in his hands. Behind the Impala, inside a Ford Galaxy, a nervous-looking thin man blew his horn.

"Wow!" the Impala driver peeked in his rearview mirror. "Welcome to New Jersey!" Another car horn blast masked most of what came next. "...right, already! Jerk off! Go around!"

More car horns drowned out the man after that. His mouth moved a mile a minute, making the same angry shapes my father's did whenever I saw him sitting in his car alone after he came home from work.

"Hey, kid," the man said, "does that dry cleaners have a parking lot?"

"Sure," I told him, "around back."

"Meet me around back," he replied. "I need your help."

"What for?"

Beep, beep, beep!

"Motherfuckers!" the blond man screamed.

The Impala lurched forward and turned right at the corner.

My street was dissected by the highway that ran through the center of town. From where I sat on my bike, I could see my mother hanging white sheets on a clothesline in our backyard. I waved, but she did not see me. Across the street, a shirtless Tom Benedict mowed his lawn. My mother quit her work long enough to wave at the former soldier. Benedict stopped mowing his lawn and waved at my mother. He retrieved his tee shirt off the railing on his front porch and, in a show of false modesty, put the shirt back on. At first, I thought maybe my mother would steal away and join Benedict; but she kept on hanging laundry. I soon lost sight of her as the sheets billowed in the warm wind. It's how I would always remember her: sheets on the clothesline like ship sails that trapped the wind and caused my mother to temporarily vanish before she would appear again.

It troubled me when I saw Tom Benedict leave his mower in the front yard and go inside his house. Was it over between my mother and him? I wondered.

I nearly forgot about the guy who stopped to ask for directions. So I pedaled my bike to the corner and turned right. Mr. Kim, the owner of the dry cleaners, gave me a strange look through the window when I waved to him. I liked the Kims. My father was another story. He always worried that the Kims' dry-cleaning business was some nefarious and clandestine start of something that would grow exponentially across the Garden State and eventually take over every small-town community. For my father it was one thing for 'foreigners' to operate a business; it was something else entirely when a family such as the Kims had a house custom-built on the far side of town, a house that was larger than any other in the community. My father had envisioned foreigners from every country slowly creeping over the once-familiar landscape like stealthy monsters at night, circling the proverbial campfire, and snatching up small business after small business. My father could be a paranoid lunatic that way. Mr. Kim, on the other hand, always treated me with kindness and showed the utmost respect toward my mother. And I liked the way Mr. Kim's daughter Sun-ji smelled whenever I went to the dry-cleaners with my mother to drop off my dad's suits to be cleaned and pressed. Sun-ji always smelled like lilacs; even over the intense aroma of tetrachloroethylene that permeated the shop.

The Impala idled in the parking lot behind Kims' Dry-cleaners. On the automobile's rear end, just below the bumper, there was a Florida license plate. The back door to the dry-cleaning shop was open, the way it always was no matter the season. I could hear Mrs. Kim talking a mile a minute in Korean. Most days she spoke non-stop to her husband. Whenever she spoke to Sun-ji, her daughter always answered her in English. Mrs. Kim wore a painful expression most of the time. I wondered sometimes how often she had second-guessed her family's decision to open up shop and live in our community.

I leaned my bike against the fence that stood between the parking lot and the property next door. Approaching the Impala, I felt like a pint-sized cop making a traffic stop. It was then I spotted the glossy cover of a Swank magazine on the passenger seat beside the driver. The electric window slid down. The driver leaned over the seat to look at me. He made no effort to cover up the nude woman on the cover of the magazine.

"You like the ladies, huh?" he asked.

I felt like a doofus. Suddenly, I remembered something Father Michael had told me about being kind to strangers. For you may entertain angels unaware. Father Michael was always quoting the bible. As for me I thought it was a little spooky that angels might still walk the earth. For an eleven-year-old that was a heavy thing to consider. My friends and I at school never talked about religion. What we didn't know was that the comic books we read, according to

Father Michael, were sort of modern-day tales of angelic intervention.

"There are no more angels," Kevin Baker once said.

Kevin was a catechism classmate of mine, a genuine self-proclaimed expert in all things having to do with the mysteries of the Holy Roman Church and female anatomy. As much as I hate to admit it now, he had been right in that particular proclamation. I am living proof or, to be fair, dead proof of that fact.

"I'm trying to find the Monticello Motor Lodge, kid," the Impala driver said. He grabbed the magazine and tossed it into the backseat. "Do you know where it is?"

"That's in Bellmawr," I told him. "Near the turnpike exit."

"Hey, I got an idea. Why don't you get in and show me where."

"No."

"Come on, kid. I am a pastor. You can trust me."

"A pastor with a porn mag?"

"The Devil's work, to be sure," he replied. "But I am a pastor. Not Jesus. Cut me some slack, kid."

"You're not from around here," I said.

It was too late to take it back. My mother accused my father of being a xenophobe one night after one of his tirades about the Kims and other non-whites who were going into business for themselves. At the time I didn't know what the word meant. Xenophobe. So I looked it up. It was one more attribute of my father's that I hoped I had not inherited.

That summer my father had let up on the Kims to focus his xenophobic energies on a couple that moved in next door to Tom Benedict. The wife, Louisa, was a white woman, blonde and fair-skinned, and her husband Henry was black. Louisa and Henry had two children, a boy that went to the grade school a block from my house and a daughter named Marissa who was my age.

"That's too close for my tastes," my father had said after the moving truck pulled away.

"You're a moron," my mother commented with the aplomb of a woman who was getting it three times a week from a guy who lived across the street.

191

"What?" he cried. "First, the goddamn Chinaman and his family—"

"The Kims?"

"Yes."

"They are Korean, not Chinese," my mother reminded him. "And for your information people are allowed to marry whomever they want these days."

It was no secret by the time I was eleven years old that my father had come from a long line of bigots. But it wasn't until after I was dead that I saw what sort of punishment was doled out for the likes of them. The prejudiced in the afterlife wear the mark of their sin like a big target. For murderers, rapists, and other miscreants, it was another story.

Anyway, back to my father. His sin on earth was ignorance. A few years after my disappearance, my mother ended up leaving him for another man (not Tom Benedict, if you can believe that). My father ended up selling the house and, in some twisted act of remorse coupled with regret, he moved back to the Grays Ferry section of Philadelphia where he had grown up. There he spent the rest of his days hating various ethnic groups that populated his old neighborhood. On a winter night, far into the future I did not live to see, a young man would be chased down and beaten to death on the steps of a church. The police would not respond to calls for help. My father would be killed on the same night, stabbed repeatedly by the husband of a woman my father had accosted earlier that night in a grocery store. My father would die screaming and cursing into the dark as no sirens sounded, not for the young man on the church steps, not for my father who remained bitter to the end.

"Florida," the pastor of porn said from the confines of his Impala.

"What?" I asked.

"You noticed I wasn't from around these parts," the preacher man said.

All I knew of Florida was Disney World and hurricanes. My cousin Rita had gone to Fort Lauderdale for spring break during her freshman year of college. That was the previous year. There was a hurricane, a freak storm out of season. Rita had holed up in a motel along with all of her college cronies. Months later my cousin Rita started to show. Her pregnancy forced her to quit college. Rita gave birth to a healthy baby boy she named Claude (short for Claudius, her favorite Shakespearean character). Of Claude's father, we knew nothing except that he was dark-skinned. My father had a field day with that one. Little Claude had been born with dark skin too.

"You're kidding," my mother had said when my aunt Claire, my father's younger sister, came over to share the news.

They sat together in the backyard on lawn chairs, bed sheets on the clothesline billowing like pirate sails, as they drank Pabst Blue Ribbon from cans and bad-mouthed Rita.

"Please," Aunt Claire told her. "I am completely beside myself. Don't get me wrong. I am not against mixed couples, but you know how my brother feels."

"Now what?" my mother asked.

"Rita tells me she's not sure who the father is," said my aunt.

"I am sure it will be fine."

"How could she be so stupid?"

"Smart women get pregnant too."

That was my mother, all-right. She never knew the right words in times of crisis.

"Hey, little man," the preacher said, bringing me back to the present. "Grab your bike. I'll throw it in the trunk of the car."

A weird grin stretched across his face. He climbed out of the Impala, ready to assist me. On his left arm was a tattoo I hadn't noticed until that moment. It was a crudely etched image in blue ink of Jesus hauling a huge cross.

"Just go back down the pike," I told him. "You'll see it on the right after you drive beneath the turnpike overpass."

"Hey, it's cool," he said.

"It's just that I should get home."

"My friends are staying at the Monticello," the preacher told me. "And I wanted to play a practical joke on them. You like jokes, don't you? Of course, you do. Oh well, not to worry."

"What kind of joke?"

"Here's the thing. My friends are really uptight. Do you know what that means?"

"Sure. My mother says that my father's uptight."

The preacher laughed. Then he said, "Right on, brother. Anyway, my stuffy friends would lose themselves if someone like you just pushed me into the pool at the hotel."

"Sounds stupid," I replied.

"You'd have to know my friends," he said. "They're preachers just like me from down south."

"What are you doing up here?"

"You're a smart kid."

Something flashed in the preacher's eyes; a malice that reminded me of the kind my father expressed whenever he looked across the street at Tom Benedict's house.

"Just go back up to the pike and turn left," I said. "You can't miss it."

"Now, it's daylight," the preacher man said. "And I'd be dressed just like this when we pull the prank."

"My mother's waiting on me."

"What will make it worth your while?"

"It's lunchtime," I said. "And I am late."

"I'll give you twenty dollars," he fished his wallet out of pocket and showed me the bill.

Ever since my cousin Rita had gotten pregnant during spring break, my father maintained that no good could come from Florida. If only he had known how prophetic his suspicion turned out to be.

I tried to picture pushing Father Michael into a pool, but the image in my head was of him dressed in his vestments. There was nothing funny about pushing a man of God into a swimming pool. Catholic priest or traveling preacher from down south, it didn't matter. I was sure to get a time-out in Hell for such a deed. And if the good Lord didn't sentence me to Hell for something like that then I was certain a good stretch in Purgatory was in order. That just goes to show how much I knew about the afterlife. It was nothing like that, nothing like it at all.

"Plus," the preacher man jerked his thumb at the back seat, "I'll throw in a couple of girlie magazines for your trouble."

Nudie magazines equaled coolness among my friends. The life of an eleven-year-old boy, one who was raised Catholic and subjected to all manners of inhibition, was one of secret perversion and vice. No sooner had the preacher mentioned my taking possession of such coveted material my mind raced as I contemplated suitable hiding places for such treasures; namely, a secret and dry place where parents and the elements couldn't make mincemeat out of the glossy color pages.

The next thing I knew the preacher had picked up my bike and stuffed it into the trunk of his Impala. No sooner did we climb into the front seat he reached beneath me, brushing my ass and my balls with his hand, as he swept crumbs from the seat.

"Sorry," he said. "In my line of work you eat on the road."

Less than a minute later, we headed north along Route 168 back toward the Monticello Motor Lodge. The interior of the preacher's car, beneath the lemon air freshener, smelled like musk and stale pot smoke. My parents never smoked weed, but Tom Benedict did. You could smell it sometimes if you walked past his house.

One day my mother had sent me to her lover's house to pick up a brown paper bag. It was awkward. She wouldn't tell me what the item in the bag was. I had seen only a couple of hardcore adult magazines. When I thought about my mother and Tom Benedict locked together in an erotic embrace it made my stomach turn. I didn't want to go to Tom Benedict's house, but I was curious to see what the love shack looked like inside. I had visions of war paraphernalia strewn about the place. It turned out my visions were pure flights of fancy.

Tom Benedict's living room was devoid of furniture in the traditional sense. Instead, the hardwood floor was littered with various beanbag chairs, a hammock strung between walls perpendicular to each other, and numerous images of rock gods cut from posters and magazines and pasted in haphazard fashion on all four walls: Jimi Hendrix, Buddy Holly, The Allman Brothers, Cream, Led Zeppelin, Peter Frampton, Cat Stevens, Creedence Clearwater Revival, Black Sabbath, Van Morrison, Pink Floyd, Santana, Jefferson Airplane, The Rolling Stones, Janis Joplin, and a bunch of other people whose music I never liked, including Country Joe and the Fish, Canned Heat, and the Velvet Underground. In addition to the rock and roll images on the walls, the hammock, and the beanbag chairs, there were a half-dozen hookah bongs and dirty clothes strewn everywhere.

"Wait here," Tom told me that day.

I studied the faces on the wall. The thing about rock and roll stars is that their existence forces young people to call into question their own existence (or lack thereof). Eyeing Robert Plant's image from Madison Square Garden forced me to consider my own dream, even at eleven years old, of getting out of my little town and going somewhere, anywhere. What I did not know then, standing in Tom Benedict's living room, was that the preacher man would help me fulfill my dream of escape, but not the way I had hoped for.

A minute or two later, as I studied the images on the walls, Tom Benedict bounded down the steps from the second floor. He held the brown paper bag my mother had told me about and handed it to me.

"Don't look inside," Benedict told me.

"Yeah, yeah," I said.

"Sorry, kid."

"Cool room," I told him, making a sweeping gesture with my free hand at the rock star images plastered all over the walls. "I love Led Zeppelin. Did you ever see them live?"

"Madison Square Garden," Benedict informed me. "Just last year. What's your favorite song?"

"The Battle of Evermore," the song title escaped my lips before I had time to think.

"Hang on," he said. Benedict fished through a pile of old magazines and paperback books, picked one old book with yellowed pages, and gave it to me. "Here you go."

It was a copy of The Hobbit. I didn't have the heart to tell him that I had already read the book over Christmas break that year. In fact, by Easter I had finished reading the Lord of the Rings trilogy.

Inside the book was an old Mid-Atlantic Bank envelope. If Benedict noticed it was there he didn't say anything. So I tucked the paperback under my arm, along with the bank envelope inside, and bolted for the door.

When I returned home I gave my mother the brown paper bag. I was no longer interested in its contents. What intrigued me was the bank envelope tucked inside the Tolkien novel. I had hoped that there *may have been some money inside of it that Tom Benedict had forgotten about. I went to my bedroom and locked the door. Inside the bank envelope there was no money. Instead, there were five small black and white photographs of Tom Benedict in his army uniform yukking it up with a pretty Vietnamese woman. On the back of each picture, written in blue ink, were the words 'Pham and Me, Saigon, March 1969.' Tom Benedict looked different in the photographs. My mother had told me that our neighbor served in the 101st Airborne Division, that Benedict participated in Operation Apache Snow and that he had been at Hamburger Hill. Whatever that experience had done to him, whatever toll it had taken on him to survive a battle where so many lives were lost, Tom Benedict looked happy in the photographs along with the girl named Pham. Between that year and now something had made him old before his time. My mother said that war did that to men, but with Tom Benedict it was different. Sometimes his eyes appeared like those of a dead man, but only when the light was just right, and he didn't think anyone was looking.*

That evening after dinner I walked across the street and knocked on Tom Benedict's door. He didn't answer. So I slipped the bank envelope containing the black and white photographs through the mail slot on the front door. He never thanked me, but then people didn't have to thank you when you returned things that rightfully belonged to them.

Around the time the preacher man drove his Impala into the parking lot of the Monticello Motor Lodge Tom Benedict had left his lawnmower out in the front yard. It was the last time he ever mowed his lawn. He lay on his hammock, listening to the sounds of insects herald the arrival of night, and held in one hand the photographs of he and Pham. In his other hand he held a .45 Colt semi-automatic pistol. It would be a few more hours before my parents realized that I had not returned home, distracted by the events that would unfold that evening. Having taken one last glance at each of the photographs, Tom Benedict placed them on his chest, put the barrel of the semi-automatic pistol into his mouth, and, as the summer's first fireflies lit up over his half-mowed lawn, pulled the trigger. Days would pass before the police would gain entry to Benedict's home and find Benedict in his hammock, the Colt .45 pistol still in his mouth, the hammock frayed where the bullet along with bone shards from the exit wound at the top rear of his skull had torn through the fabric. On the night the police went into Benedict's home, based on a tip from an anonymous caller, my parents and several neighbors gathered to watch the spectacle. A police officer had told my parents that the former soldier looked peaceful despite the self-inflicted gunshot wound. "Most dead people do," my father was heard to remark that evening.

In the weeks following my disappearance and Tom Benedict's suicide, my mother would suffer a nervous breakdown after telling anyone who would listen to her (her audience did not include my father who had been convinced that Benedict was somehow responsible for my disappearance) that she had experienced a precognitive dream. Two films showed on the screen at once. Tom Benedict and I were abducted by devils of smoke with wings made from shadows. We were both pulled into a deep dark pit.

The next morning Dr. Wayne Braddock, our family physician, came to our house to administer my mother a sedative. Later that day the police stopped by the house to grill my father about Tom Benedict's death. My mother slept through the whole thing. The police were not convinced that the highly decorated ex-soldier had taken his own life. They told my father how they had reason to believe that the decedent carried on a number of affairs with various women in the neighborhood. One of the cops mentioned something about photographic evidence. "Did it ever occur to you that none of those whores measured up for Tom Benedict?" my father asked. One of the younger cops opened his mouth to speak but thought better of it. After four or five hours of going back and forth the police gave up. "Where are those pictures?" my father demanded. "Evidence," was all they told him before they left the house.

You might wonder how I know such things. In death we get to glimpse the present and portions of the past like we are seeing it from a great distance through some spyglass. Most of the time there's too much interference. A thin veil separates the living and the dead. Between us, waves of static camouflage hide the two worlds from one another. If you're lucky, you can peek at intervals where the threads between the dead and the living are strongest; but even this ability goes away over time. Hence, the story I relate here is based on what I remember—both in life and what I had witnessed shortly after my death.

In my last days then, as I rode shotgun with the preacher man, my killer put an 8-track tape into his car stereo. This time it was The Who. As the lyrics from 'The Song is Over' poured forth I thought about my father and how he thought that rock music led to smoking pot. Marijuana, by his estimation, led to less than moral behavior. A natural progression, he believed, was taking place in America. In short, my father blamed weed for all of the country's ills.

"It's why people turned to communism in the first place," my father had speculated one weekend.

My mother looked at me and rolled her eyes. "Here we go," she said.

"Mark my words," he went on. "It will be the end of western civilization."

The civilized west of which my father spoke was no great shakes in 1976. Still, that afternoon I perked up when the old man went on a tirade about how the suburbs would one day be the ghettos of the future, how the rich would move back to the cities and the poor would swallow the picket fence pill as if working two jobs just to pay a mortgage was a privilege rather than a comeuppance. Then, as it went in those days, any semblance of reason derailed if my father spoke for too long.

"Or living on the moon," he concluded.

"Who's going to live on the moon?" my mother asked.

"The rich," said my father. "The space race wasn't about science. It was about real estate prospecting. Why do you think the Russians were so hot to get there first?"

"But the Soviets haven't put a man on the moon," my mother reminded him.

"You're damn right," he replied. "We struck our claim the moment the American flag was planted there."

My mother thought my father was nuts. And no doubt so did Tom Benedict before he took his own life.

"*Planet earth to little dude,*" *the preacher man said presently.* "*Are you there?*"

He pulled into the Monticello Motor Lodge parking lot.

"*If you stop here,*" *I said,* "*I can get my bike out of the trunk and ride home.*"

"*Shoot,*" *he said.* "*Hold on.*"

The Impala rolled slowly through the parking lot. The preacher man bypassed the front office and drove around the back of the motor lodge.

"*I should get going,*" *I told him.*

"*Hold on, son,*" *he said as he drove to the far end of the lot.* "*My friends aren't here yet.*"

"*My mother's expecting me for lunch.*"

"*I got some cold Cokes in the room. You want one while we wait?*"

I didn't say anything.

He parked the car and turned off the ignition. Next, he looked in his rearview mirror like he was expecting someone to sneak up on us. To anyone passing by, we might have been a father and a son stopping off for a rest on a long road trip.

"*Glory be,*" *he said and whistled.* "*I don't know about you, but I am hot. Come on, little man. Let's get a Coke. I got air-conditioning in my room.*"

The preacher man reached into the back seat and grabbed a stack of nudie magazines. He winked at me as he jingled his keys.

"*Is my bike safe?*" *I asked.*

"*It won't get stolen,*" *he said,* "*if that's what you mean. Now do you want that Coke or not?*"

Soda before lunch. My mother never let me imbibe like that. The same went for eating chocolate after dinner, swimming within thirty minutes of consuming any solid foods, and chasing fly balls into old man Renninger's yard. Frank Renninger, a Korean War veteran, looked with disdain upon all the Vietnam vets in our neighborhood. It was not beneath the old man to call out guys like Tom Benedict the way boys at my school did when they were itching for a fistfight. Every now and then I used to play Wiffle ball with friends in my backyard. Old man Renninger lived directly behind us; a low chain-

link fence separated our backyards. Renninger used to have a mean old Doberman pinscher named Mack. It was a glorious day when the police showed up along with a man from the county animal control office. Mack had bitten a number of neighborhood children one summer when I was eight years old; one of Mack's victims, a girl named Tammy Oreland, contracted rabies. That was the end of Mack, but old man Renninger didn't let the dog go without a fight. Renninger fought all three policemen in his driveway, and he might have won the fight had it not been for the animal control officer who knocked the old man on the head with a pipe. After Mack went to doggy heaven (my mother was sure of this despite the sins Renninger's dog had committed on Earth), my old neighbor became even meaner. I made the mistake of retrieving a Wiffle ball that my friend Eddie Wentz had hit into Renninger's yard. The old man shouted obscenities when he saw me. Then he picked up a shovel and chased me back over the fence. After that, any Wiffle ball that left our yard and ended up in Renninger's was off-limits. It was one more thing my mother denied me liked skateboarding in the street, playing with matches, or sledding down Suicide Hill after a blizzard for fear that I would break every bone in my body. I did my best to honor my mother's wishes, but I didn't think a Coke before noon would be such a grave sin.

"Are you sure my bike is safe?" I asked.

"Your bike?" the preacher man replied. "Sure."

I let him walk ahead of me. After a few steps, I stopped.

"I should go," I told him.

"Nonsense, little man. My friends will be here any minute."

"I told my mother—"

"My name is Steve, by the way."

I told him my name. He went on ahead, giving me no indication that he would get my bike out of the trunk of his car. The preacher man stopped in front of a door and unlocked it. He motioned me to follow him inside.

"Come on, man," he said. "We're wasting air-conditioning."

There was one window in the room that faced the parking lot. The heavy curtains were drawn, and the room was dark. Steve the preacher man turned on a lamp beside the bed. Then he proceeded to the bathroom. A minute later, I heard the shower running.

On the bed were the magazines Steve had taken from the back seat of the Impala. They lay atop other magazines scattered across the bedspread. On the nightstand, beneath an ashtray that contained three half-smoked joints, was a copy of Swank. A Hustler magazine with dog-eared pages lay on the floor next to the bed. On the bed near where I stood there was a Playboy magazine. I picked it up. Beneath the Playboy there were other magazines; glossy color mags with men on the covers; on one cover two men stood arm in arm wearing cowboy hats and nothing else; on another cover there was a man standing over a guy who couldn't have been more than sixteen years old, judging from his zits, whose skinny arms were bound with black electrical tape.

It wasn't the first time I'd seen magazines similar to that. In the local news shop near my house there was a shelf in the magazine section where 'adults only' mags and books were kept. A boy in my school, Barry Holmes, an eighth grader, brought one of the 'man-on-man' magazines to school. The magazine fell into the hands of some ruthless eighth graders. After that, Barry Holmes became Barry Homo.

On any given school day there was a gang of older boys who chased Frankie into the woods behind the school. Ordinarily the gang's intent was to beat him up, but Frankie had what my mother called the gift for the gab. He could talk his way out of any predicament. It was rumored that Frankie gave two eighth graders a handjob each in the boys room just prior to the magazine scandal. He named the two boys he had serviced, one of which was among the group that had threatened him. It wasn't long before all hell broke loose, and Frankie escaped unscathed.

Frankie's other saving grace was that he hung out with at least a dozen different pretty girls at school. At lunch they sat at a table together talking about clothing, soaps, shampoos, and conditioners. One of the girls, Paula Edison, had a mean streak in her. She had coaxed Frankie into hanging a sheet in his basement with a hole in it. Paula thought it would be a hoot to dupe some of the older boys into Frankie's basement under the pretense of sex with her; only instead of Paula doing the work on the other side of the sheet it would be Frankie. One Saturday night a few boys came by with Paula while Frankie waited behind the curtain. Paula would make out with a boy, getting him all excited, and then she would go behind the sheet. All it took was for the boy to see Paula's slender fingers beckoning the boy through the hole in the sheet. Frankie gave blowjobs to two boys that night. Afterward they left with Paula. A half-hour later she returned with a crazy eighth grader named Brick Markham who fell for the bait almost immediately, but soon after he put his dick through the hole in the sheet he knew something wasn't right. He punched the sheet and ended up striking Frankie who yelped. Crazy Brick Markham did not want to entertain Frankie's gift for the gab that night. Despite Paula screaming for help and trying to pull Brick off him, Frankie was beaten unconscious, lost seven teeth, and nearly lost his eye by the time Brick was done with him. Frankie's mother came home from work to find her only child alone in the basement. In the end Brick Markham went away to a juvenile detention facility for six months (it seemed he had a habit of nearly killing any boy he beat up). Frankie Holmes and his mother moved to another town the summer after the eighth grade ended.

I was thinking about Frankie when Steve exited the bathroom. He wore a towel around his waist as he marched across the floor to the front door and closed it. He opened a cooler at the foot of the bed, pulled two bottles of Coke out, removed the caps, and handed one to me.

"Come sit down," he beckoned me as he slid most of the magazines off the bed. He lay down with his back against the headboard, a man-on-man magazine in his lap. "I want to show you something."

"I better get going," I told him.

Steve tossed the magazine aside. He unfastened his towel from his waist and exposed himself. His dick looked like a fat pink snake that reached his belly button.

I bolted for the door. He could keep my bike. Steve caught me before I could open the door and put one hand around my face as he came up behind me, covering my mouth as I tried to shout. Through the back of my shorts I felt his hardness press against me. I tried to turn around and knee him in the balls, but he was too strong. He forced me faced down on the bed as he kept his hand over my mouth. I managed to bite his hand which made him angry enough to punch me with his free hand as he lay on top of me. The pain in my head caused me to nearly black out. Steve the preacher man pulled my shorts down as he grunted into my ear. That time he did not penetrate me; instead, he rubbed himself between my buttocks for a minute or so until he came on my lower back. Afterward, he pulled me off the bed, stuffed a washrag into my mouth and pressed a strip of duct tape over my lips before he handcuffed me to his bed. I tried to kick him, but it was no use. Steve swatted my legs each time I did like it was a big game to him. Then he held my legs down and lowered his mouth onto me.

Afterward he said, "You ever scream or shout the way you did earlier, I will kill you."

Later, when he came at me a second time, he stood over me masturbating before he pulled the tape off my lips. He reached past me for the dresser, opened a drawer there, and pulled out a shiny pistol. He held the gun to my head as he removed the washrag from my mouth. The preacher man told me to keep my mouth open. When I refused he cocked the hammer back on the pistol.

"You want to see your mother and dad again?" he asked.

I thought of my mother and my father. I wasn't ready to die. I wanted to see them again. I wanted to believe that Steve would let me go. When I opened my mouth I shut my eyes, but the preacher man wanted me to look at him as he straddled me and rubbed himself on my face a moment before he pressed the head of his penis into my mouth. My life as the preacher man's thrill toy had only just begun.

From that day forward Steve subjected me to several levels of pain. At first, the physical pain involved in rape takes over the mind; only later does the mental anguish, the guilt over wondering what I did wrong to end up in such a predicament. After that there was the pain of loneliness. I imagined that all captives felt this way; in my case, however, I was, at least in the beginning, just mere miles from my home.

By nightfall on that first day any designs I may have had about escaping my monster were dashed when Steve tied me to the bed and crammed the sock back into my mouth. Next he applied a strip of duct tape over my lips to keep me from spitting the sock out. In my mind I saw myself hitting him with anything I could get my hands on the next time he untied me.

The preacher man went back into the bathroom. A few minutes later he emerged dressed, carrying a small black satchel. He unzipped the satchel and removed a syringe. That night he gave me a tranquilizer shot. I struggled against the ropes that bound me. Before long, I drifted off to sleep.

When I opened my eyes again I felt like I had slept only a few hours. I was no longer in the motel room where the preacher man had raped me. My mouth was no longer covered with duct tape and the sock was gone. The ropes that bound me to the motel bed had been replaced by handcuffs and chains. The room where I lay now was little more than a small cabin. Dark oblong stains marked the wood floor. Upon waking up I had detected an odor that I smelled only once before in my life. It was the stench of a dead dog rotting in the noonday sun on a trail near Suicide Hill. I was riding my bike that day along with two friends. Flies buzzed over the dead dog as maggots ringed the dog's empty eye sockets. Somewhere nearby the cabin there had to be a dead animal. That's what I told myself rather than contemplate the alternative: something was rotting away directly beneath the wood floor. The ramshackle two-room abode had one bedroom, in which I remained chained to a metal bed frame, and it contained a common area with a small kitchen that I could see through the bedroom door that had been left ajar. It didn't occur to me that such a structure might have a basement. That much I would discover soon enough; just as I did why the threadbare room where I lay chained reeked to high heaven of rotting flesh. The preacher man, when that time came, would assure me that he would not make the same mistake again.

"You killed someone in this room," I said.

"Teddy Roscoe," the preacher man replied. "That was his name. I buried him in the basement, but the smell got to me. So I dug him up and buried him elsewhere. There's a fresh grave next to the one where he's buried now."

The preacher man turned out the light and shut the door. The bedroom's sole window had been boarded up from the inside. I screamed bloody murder, as my mother used to say. The door swung open. Steve turned on the light and removed the belt he was wearing. The belt had a big metal buckle. Without saying a word he began to whip me across the legs. When he was done he tossed the belt aside.

"No one can hear you," he told me as he lay down on the bed next to me. His hard calloused hand came to rest between my legs. "It's just the two of us, buddy. There's no one but you and me now."

He left the bed and exited the room. A minute later he returned bearing his little black satchel. He removed the syringe and a small plastic bag with brown powder in it. Then he took out a small water vial, a lighter and a teaspoon with a bent stem. It took no time at all to cook up the heroin before he injected me with it.

The first time he gave me heroin I became ill. For three days after that there was always another dose. I could no longer tell if it was night or day. The preacher man would lay on the bed with me and maneuver my body into various positions; sometimes I dreamed he did this, but after a week I could no longer tell what was real and what was imagined.

After a few weeks, with the preacher man forcing me to eat when I wasn't high, I came to crave heroin. One day, Steve unchained me and led me to a small bathroom where he told me to bathe. I did as I was told. He sat on the floor and watched me. When I finished he toweled me off and told me to wait in the bathroom. He closed the door and locked it. There was a window, but it had been boarded up like the one in the bedroom. The preacher man came back to the bathroom and escorted me to the bedroom where he gave me yet another injection.

On the night the first of the men came to the shack, I was high enough that I didn't put up much of a fight. Since that first night it went like this: sometimes I heard an automobile pull up; other times the bedroom door opened, and Steve stood there with some stranger. They conversed in hushed tones. One man told me he had come all the way from California. Others came from as far away as Canada, Germany, France, and one all the way from Africa. I never saw them exchange money with the preacher man. All of the men grunted and whispered horrible things as they sodomized me. Ordinarily it was just one man. Then came the night when Steve allowed four men into the room at the same time.

I became an animal, a zoo oddity and my keeper charged grown men, perverted monsters all of them, to come to the shack in the middle of nowhere and have their way with me. I was allowed to eat and sleep during the day, but the nights belonged to the preacher man and his sordid congregation. Then one day, as I was coming out of a junk sickness, the preacher man came to the room, got me on my feet, and dragged me out of the house. It was night and it was cold. Not far from the shack was an old barn.

"Keep your mouth shut and do what you're told," he told me.

A few lanterns inside the barn cast a low, pale light. I saw shapes shuffling in the shadows. There were maybe twelve men in all. Though I could not see their faces, their eyes were visible and full of anticipation. Something snorted in the dark. One by one the men forked over huge wads of cash to the preacher man. Toward the back of the barn there was a black horse fitted inside a harness contraption that suspended the stallion a couple of feet off the ground. The preacher man dragged me toward the horse. There was a pail filled with cooking grease. The preacher man pretended to dip his hands into the gelatinous mess and rub his hands together.

"Do it right," the preacher man whispered, "and the stud will come quick."

To show me he wasn't playing around, he drew a buck knife out of his coat pocket.

That night I did as I was told. My arms tired quickly. It felt like I was rubbing down a baseball bat wrapped in slick cowhide.

"Get your face under there," the preacher man instructed me.

Flashbulbs lit up the dark barn. When it was over I ran out of the barn, fell to my knees, and puked my guts out.

The horse show went on for a year, once a month every month. The rest of my nights were filled with heroin dreams or the company of strange men. One morning I awoke to the sound of someone whimpering. My body ached. Chained to the floor at the foot of the bed was another boy. He looked to be a couple of years younger than me. His mouth was duct-taped, and his clothes were missing.

A few minutes later, the preacher man entered the room. He took hold of me by the scruff of my neck and marched me out of the cabin. I asked him what I had done wrong, but he remained silent as he took me into the barn. It was dark out and I expected to see more men gathered for the horse show. There were no lanterns lit inside the barn. The preacher man pushed me hard in the back. I stumbled and fell onto my hands and knees. He stomped on my back, once, twice, three times before I lay flat on the ground. Pressing his knee into my back, he wrenched my head backward by pulling my hair.

"I don't need two boys," he said in the dark.

The preacher man cut my throat open with all the precision of a butcher slaughtering a pig.

Somewhere a boy screamed.

With my eyes closed I pictured my backyard at home.

A tall black man with dreadlocks stood behind bed sheets on a clothesline that billowed like sails. My mother was there, but she did not see him. The man had a curious grin on his face. He beckoned me to join him. The moment I did so, I ceased to be.

The Court Of Amenhotep

The boy cocks his head now as he stands on the rim of the well.

"After the preacher man killed me I thought the only way to unknow anything was to die," says the boy. "But even in death there are no guarantees. Here though I get to begin again."

"Do I know you?" Callahan asks.

"Does anyone ever know themselves?" the boy replies and leaps into the well.

The moment the boy is gone, everything changes for Callahan. Water from the well splashes him from head to toe, drenching him.

The first thing that hints at the end of this dreamland tour is the odor. The night air stinks of hot tar, barbeque smoke, and a hot mix of piss and beer. Callahan pats his face, expecting to feel wetness there; but his skin is dry.

Callahan can't focus just yet. So when a face looms into view he becomes startled. The woman appears familiar; but, when she reaches out to him, he crab-walks backward away from her.

"Wait," Rachael cries out.

That's her name. Callahan remembers now. *A biblical name. Surely, it must mean something.*

He's up on his feet after that, stumbling down the street and trying to forget the tale the boy at the well just shared. Callahan pictures his own children—Jackie and Jean. Are they safe? Sadness takes over him. He wonders if he thinks about them hard enough that he might be able to conjure them right there on the street.

Are my children even real? Callahan wonders. *Was anything in my life ever tangible?*

As Callahan continues down the street, he can feel Rachael following close behind. Suddenly, he's convinced that she's been sent here by some otherworldly presence; perhaps not the Coffee Can Man, but one of his agents.

There's no time for answers. A large man, equal parts muscle, tattoos, piercings, and drunkenness, materializes out of the dark and pushes Callahan into a heap of garbage along the curb. A woman's laughter drowns out the Neanderthal's threat. Callahan rolls over. His head aches, as if the cancerous growth within seeks a way out. A slender Asian woman steps into view dressed in worn-out combat boots, a short leather skirt, and a black half-shirt that reads *Going Down*. She renders a sympathetic look. Callahan, spurred by the combat-boot-wearing young woman, grabs a trash bag filled with garbage and windmills it just as the tattooed hulk turns his back. The trash bag hits the big man on his head, rips open, and spills fish guts, chicken bones, and assorted organic filth all over the Neanderthal's head.

"I will kill you!" the muscled monkey announces as he turns on his opponent with clenched fists.

"I am already dying," Callahan informs him.

The big man cocks his right fist, ready to deliver a knockout blow. Callahan kicks him in the balls once—closing the gap to grab his larger opponent by his shirt—and for good measure he kicks the guy between the legs twice more. As the giant's knees buckle, Callahan sidesteps him and kicks him in the head. The big man goes down.

"Enough," Rachael grabs Callahan's arm and hurries him across the street.

A taxi cab skids to a halt, barely missing them both. The driver steps out. He's dark-skinned, cadaverous in build, and when he shakes his fist at Rachael and Callahan he swears at them in Tamil. A police car pulls up behind the taxi cab with its lights on.

Rachael shuffles Callahan toward an alley. Their shoes sink into stagnant puddles. Callahan feels a little like Frankenstein's monster as he lumbers down the alley. His right foot throbs from kicking the tattooed goon in the face. When he looks down there's an oily rainbow-colored claw that comes straight out of one puddle, attempting to pull him down into the puddle's depths. *Daddy!* If Rachael hears Callahan's daughter's voice she doesn't let on. She keeps moving forward. Callahan trails closely behind and spots Jackie and Jean at the end of the alley. He bolts forward, hobbling along on his injured foot. Rachael's voice becomes a distant echo; as if she's calling down into a well. *We're going now*, Jackie tells his father. Callahan calls out their names. His children are but faint shadows by the time he stands before them. Jean's face appears nearly transparent. When Callahan reaches out to touch his son's face Jean vanishes. Jackie turns into a plume of mist and collapses into a puddle at Callahan's feet. In the air there's a faint trace of ozone. Nausea stirs Callahan's stomach. He bends at the waist, reaching out to steady himself against a dumpster, and vomits. Callahan collapses just as Rachael reaches him. She wipes his mouth with a cocktail napkin from the Astral Plane. Callahan peers over his shoulder as Rachael attends him. Anthropomorphic shapes of shadow, light, and steam beckon Callahan to join them.

Escape this life. The voice belongs to Callahan's father.

"Dad?" Callahan calls out.

"Shush," Rachael tells him. "There's no one here." She helps Callahan to his feet. "It's time for you to meet someone who can help."

When they exit the alley at the other end they turn right. Rachael holds him around the waist with one arm as she helps Callahan cross the street. There stands a brownstone building with white marble steps and tall wood doors that remind Callahan of a cathedral entrance.

"Where am I?" Callahan wants to know.

"Almost home," she tells him.

Side by side, they traverse the seven marble steps that lead to the tall double doors. Callahan's headache abates some. With each step he takes ascending the marble stairs the pain in his right foot fades.

As Rachael fumbles for a key on a large ring she wears at her waist, Callahan reaches out and takes hold of the ring. There are easily a hundred or more keys on the ring.

"Where did you get this?" Callahan asks.

Rachael doesn't answer.

When Callahan turns to his right he spots a hulking shadow lurking near a basement window.

"Uh...Rachael?" Callahan starts to speak.

"Just a second," she cuts him off.

The shadow on the pavement creeps toward the curb. It squeezes itself between two parked cars. Within the dark between the cars brilliant sparks of light shine and fade. The creature becomes visible each time the sparks shine. It chitters at Callahan from beneath one of the cars now.

At last Rachael slides a key into the door lock. The dark mass creeps out from beneath the car and approaches the marble steps.

"Beat it, Jezzy," Rachael calls over her shoulder.

She opens the door, making room for Callahan to step inside first.

"Can you see that thing?" he asks.

Rachael wrinkles her nose at him. "It's a cat," she tells him.

Callahan's gaze follows the length of Rachael's arm down to her slender finger pointing at a black alley cat at the foot of the stairs.

"Are you going to make it?" Rachael asks.

"Sure," Callahan replies.

"I doubt it," the cat counters.

"Are you talking to me?"

"It won't be long now."

"Until what?"

"The Can Man's coming," the cat announces. "Escape from this life."

"Jezzy," Rachael calls to the cat. "That's enough. Now go away."

"You heard that cat talking to me?" Callahan asks.

"Jezebeth? Sure."

"I think I need to sit down."

"If you stay out here too long," Rachael warns, "Jezebeth will just put you back where you started."

"Who's Jezebeth? Some kind of spirit?"

"A demon of falsehoods. What we call a scavenger," Rachael informs him. "Now, please step inside."

A cone of light illuminates a grand stairwell just inside the main doors. The walls, made from a polished dark wood, appear moist. The carpeted floor, dark green in color, gives off a rank odor. Rachael steps forward looking like the patron saint of dilapidated buildings as she waits at the foot of the stairwell.

Callahan follows Rachael as she leads him up the stairs to the fourth floor. He doesn't notice any doors on the floors leading up, suspecting that Rachael may be the sole tenant in the building.

"Where are you taking me?" he asks.

"I want you to meet Mr. Vollmer," she replies.

"Who's he?"

"He's an asset."

Half-way down the hall on the fourth floor Rachael stops in front of a door. She raises her fist to knock.

"Isn't it late?" Callahan inquires.

"Mr. Vollmer is a night owl," Rachael informs him.

The light wrap of her knuckles on the door ends any further discussion. She offers him a beatific smile; the kind that adorn the faces of angels and madmen alike.

"Wadhdas University is no longer accepting applications," a deep drawn-out voice sounds from behind the door. "Please try again in another lifetime."

"Mr. Vollmer. It's me, Rachael."

Locks disengage behind the door. Each one sounds like a round being chambered in a bolt-action rifle. The door cracks open only a few inches. A yellow eye, encased in a face as pale as bone, peeks out.

"Who's the stiff?" Vollmer's eyeball focuses on Callahan.

"A friend," Rachael replies. "A friend who is lost."

The door swings open. Vollmer is dressed head to toe in black.

"Rainer Ulysses Vollmer," he extends a slender hand to Callahan. "At your service."

"Damian Callahan," he replies as he takes the old man's hand in his.

"You will excuse my dis-ease," the words drip from Vollmer's mouth as he savors the sound of them. "There were agents in the building tonight. Security is not what it used to be."

"Did you know Jezebeth is hanging around outside?" Rachael asks.

"That bottom-feeding whore," the old man winks at Callahan as he speaks.

"It's safe now, Mr. Vollmer."

"Believe nothing of what you hear," he tells Callahan, "and less of what you see. The third eye was the first eye before we came out of the ocean's dark depths, young man. You remember that. Now, forgive me. I have forgotten my manners. Won't you please come inside?"

The apartment is impeccably neat. Bookshelves line all four walls from floor to ceiling. There are no windows. A large desk takes up one corner. Atop the desk there's an old Remington electric typewriter. To the left of the typewriter sits several reams of blank paper. On the right, there's a manuscript stacked six inches high.

"A chronicle of this life," Vollmer announces as Callahan eyes the manuscript.

"Mr. Vollmer's had several lives," Rachael announces.

"It's true," the old man tells Callahan. "Once I served in the court of Amenhotep. The next life I remember is the one in which I was slain on the pilgrims' road to Jerusalem. I was to attend the Council of Nablus, but things got a little...dicey."

"I don't believe in past lives," says Callahan.

"Who said anything about *past* lives?"

"Mr. Vollmer possesses acute occult powers," Rachael interrupts now. "But sometimes he doesn't know when to keep his mouth shut. Isn't that right, Mr. Vollmer?"

"The first death is nothing to be ashamed of," the old man says. He takes a seat in an armchair draped in shadow. "Read the Qur'an."

Callahan looks down at the manuscript on the desk. The title page reads: *Many Lives, Many Deaths: An Existential Inquiry into Immortality.*

"You're a philosopher?" Callahan asks.

Vollmer guffaws and crosses one thin leg over the other.

"Let me tell you about philosophy, son. It's no more than man's attempt," Vollmer leans forward now, "to ward off the shadows cast by the light of true knowledge."

"What about your book?" Callahan asks.

"Don't look for it in bookstores," he replies. Nodding at Rachael, he adds, "A hazard of the trade, I suppose. I signed that non-disclosure agreement several thousand years ago."

"You know the rules, Mr. Vollmer," Rachael reminds him.

Vollmer waves a dismissive hand at her.

"Young man," he says. "I can see your aura."

"What color is it?" Callahan asks.

"Black. Say, angel. Where did you pick up this Qliphoth anyway?"

"Mr. Vollmer," Rachael begins.

"Save it," the old man cuts her off. "You're here for my help. I understand. It would be much easier if your kind would just explain to our kind what's expected."

"That's not how it works."

"So you keep telling me," replies Vollmer. "Say, Callahan. Have you ever heard of the deadlands?"

"No," he tells him. "I have not."

"Well, judging from the looks of you we don't have much time. So I will spare you the details. How about the Que?"

Callahan scratches his head. "Is that an underground train station in London?"

"The Que is the place where the dead wait to be born again," Vollmer informs him. "A diarrheal river of madness and despair. Do you know the origin of despair?"

"Desire?"

"You're lost, son," the old man answers as he points a bony finger at Rachael. "That's why she brought you to me. But my soul has a bounty on it. So, I will gracefully decline acting as your guide."

"Perhaps you will be kind enough to inform Damian of what to expect," Rachael suggests. When Vollmer fidgets in his seat, she tells him, "He needs to hear it from you."

Vollmer spreads his hands out in supplication as he lowers his head.

"As you wish, angel," the old man whispers. He looks up at Callahan and tells him, "Pull up a chair, young man. We've quite a bit to discuss."

The Last Doorway Or, An Epilogue

The last leg of Callahan's journey is one he must make by himself. After we leave Vollmer's apartment, we part ways. I remain, as always, faithful to my charge; only there is no reason to remain in my Rachael form anymore. I mentioned at the start of this tale that Damian Callahan was already dead when I intervened on his behalf. This much is true. It happened the night he collapsed outside The Astral Plane restaurant. When a human life gets rebooted there are preparations to be made; only I did not know at the time that Callahan would so desperately cling to all the lives that came before this one; likewise, the many off-shoots of his life in parallel times and places, the many possibilities of lives he had led until I had pleaded my case, each of these lives were as true as the next. The unwillingness to let go presents specific problems, but none that cannot be overcome; for in all this there remains the variable of hope.

For Callahan, then, Vollmer's tale made perfect sense. You need to peel away your current life one layer at a time, the old man had said, to free yourself up for the next one. I know my charge resists doing so. The importance of going through the last doorway on one's own remains beyond explanation. As for my kind, we do not know birth and death and rebirth. And even if we did we would possess no recollection of those past lives; as it is above, so it is below.

It is early in the morning. Alone, Callahan walks close to the buildings. He moves at a quick pace. Black metal doors spot the sidewalk along the way. Callahan jumps on each one, the way he used to when he was a child, creating an awful racket. With each bang the memory of me in my Rachael disguise and Vollmer both fade along with the old man's confusing diatribe concerning his numerous lives he could recall in full detail. As Callahan jumps from cellar door to cellar door, the noise reverberates off the buildings across the street. All around him now are strange kaleidoscope colors that could be a product of his cancer-riddled brain or, perhaps, the remnant light of angels who hurry on ahead to prepare the way for him down by the waterfront. There are many memories to shed during the walk; each one falls away like leaves from a tree in late autumn; remembrances no more than red, brown, gold, and yellow before they snap off and drift slowly to the ground, stirring in the phantasmagoric winds. Here's the face of a strange man who speaks with a southern twang; there a girl and a boy Callahan should know though both children appear foreign to him; even their names taste funny in his mouth as he mutters them each one last time. Another memory stirs in which Callahan meets two childhood friends in a supermarket back when he was in his late twenties, their names, like those of his own two children, are stripped away; likewise, the bully who had nearly drowned him in a deep puddle over four quarters that was meant to be Callahan's lunch money; the dreamer from his fifth grade class, the girl whom he had thought was so pretty, the one who harbored some secret that made her think she was ugly through and through; the guy in the ninth grade, tall, lanky, bespectacled, the one who read the Pennystock News each day during lunch period, the very same guy whom everyone laughed at, including Callahan, who went on to form his own shipping company, made millions, and went all the way to Vietnam to find a bride, a young woman who once lived in a refugee camp where she gave handjobs to guards for cigarettes, the bride of the shipping magnate who was all tricked out with collagen lips, fake hips, fake ass, and fake boobs the last time Callahan had seen them both at a high school reunion, the bride of the successful businessman who still wakes up in the middle of the night after all this time wondering where her next meal will come from; during this purge Callahan's mind speeds up the emptier it becomes; a long line of automobiles simmering in the summer heat along Route 168, the shore-bound vacationers whose station wagons resemble the Joads' truck making its way through The Dust Bowl; the residue of a life unexamined stripped from the deepest recesses; ahead of him now only the inevitability of the end; blessed be the convergence point where all pain will cease; blessed be the angels that will taxi his weary soul from this world; blessed be the end of this life and the promise of another; the infinite cycle of rebirth without end, amen.

Across the street there's an old man walking a few dogs. Callahan quits pouncing on the cellar doors to get a closer look. It's not a group of dogs the man walks; it's one dog with three heads. The old man wears a long skeletal key on a thick cord around his neck. He stops beneath a street lamp where someone has tied a clothesline. The other end of the rope is fastened to a wrought-iron railing of a second-story apartment balcony. The old man removes the key from his neck. He inserts the key into nothingness and unlocks a passageway. When the old man beckons Callahan the dying man follows him. Once he crosses to the other side the old man and his dog part ways with Callahan. There's a tune the key-holder whistles as he departs; a song familiar to Callahan that helps him recall the summer scent of a girl's neck on a summer evening after a rainstorm, the aroma of freshly cut grass on all the lawns in Callahan's old neighborhood in springtime, chasing the ice cream truck—that's it! The old man's whistling song was the same as the canned music the ice cream truck played.

The other side looks the same as the former to Callahan; if anything, the streets appear cleaner and the city stench he's become so accustomed to is gone. He walks all the way down Spruce Street, crossing Front Street, until he reaches Christopher Columbus Boulevard. The sun has yet to rise over Camden across the river. And there's a fog colored like mustard gas coming in from the Delaware River. A chill creeps into Callahan's body. As he nears the waterfront another memory departs now, the one in which a Jehovah's Witness had visited Callahan's parents' home when he was teen. His mother and his father were both out. Callahan the teenager invited the woman inside just so he could stare at her luscious mouth and watch her breasts move beneath her blouse as she breathed. The woman was older than his parents, but beneath all the God talk there was something primal about her. He took a fistful of brochures from her, promising to pass them out to his friends, and asked her question after question about their beliefs compared to that of the Catholic Church.

Young Callahan had no interest in converting, of course; his ruse was simply to keep the woman in his living room for as long as he could. After half an hour the woman announced that she had to go. When she was gone Callahan buried his face into the sofa cushion where she sat and took several deep breaths of the perfume trace she had left behind.

The chill digs deeper the further into the fog Callahan wanders. And like so many other memories he's shed during his walk from Vollmer's to the waterfront he's afforded one last recollection of the Jehovah's Witness, her sensual mouth, her large breasts beneath her blouse, and the trace of perfume she left behind on the sofa. In the fog there are half-formed shapes that appear and vanish; among them are mere mockeries of Callahan's discarded memories. Something in the fog taunts him.

They will do their best to keep you in this present life, Vollmer had told him. There are malevolent forces at work that will keep you down if you let them. Be aware and be prepared. That's my motto. Remember: if you can reach the water they cannot touch you on the other side.

The yellow fog darkens, turning a pale orange hue. Callahan can hardly see anything in front of him. He's not surprised when the fog turns from a gaseous state into a viscous fluid that drowns out the early morning noise of the city and lifts him off his feet; something tells him he's been this way before.

When his feet come to rest on terra firma once more Callahan stands before the dirty wide river. The orange fog remains. Stairs lead down to a narrow dock where a man in a hooded sweatshirt stands at the rear of his motorboat. The engine idles as the man removes the hood from his head.

"Are you Callahan?" the man asks.

"That's me," he replies.

"I am supposed to take you to the other side," the man informs him. "But I'll need a couple of bucks for fuel."

Callahan fishes out a fistful of bills—tens, fives, and a few ones, and hands it to the ferryman. He descends the steps to the narrow dock and boards the boat. The ferryman bids him to sit in the forward seat.

"Better to see where you are going," the ferryman tells him, "rather than watch what falls away."

Out on the dark waters of the Delaware, Callahan's earliest memories are the first to vanish. Their weight has slowed his journey until now. The orange fog thickens and dissipates and thickens once more. A sound plays in his ears now—metal against concrete. There is no one else on the water. A hollow drumbeat accompanies the metallic scraping sound now. These random sounds accompany the stripping of so many memories, turning into a cacophonous purge. The trip across the water is slow. The daylight never changes. It remains stuck in the minutes before sunrise as the orange mist drifts all around him. Now the metal against concrete noise sounds in Callahan's ears again. There will be one memory that will take root and not want to go, Vollmer had warned him. As the boat drifts aimlessly across the water, it's the olfactory portion that comes back first; the smell of moldy carpet, dirt, and dried cum on coarse bed sheets; a dozen devils that had followed the preacher man into the barn. Suddenly, Callahan senses this memory pulled out by the root. The ferryman's boat sits higher on the water now, and the vessel picks up speed. Somewhere in the orange fog someone whistles. Callahan feels the ground beneath his feet as the boat and the ferryman and the orange fog all vanish without a trace. An unseen hand grasps Callahan's neck, a comforting hand as this new guide leads him away from the river on the Camden side.

To Callahan's left and slightly behind is The One. The tall man's rags hang from his shoulders like wings; his dreadlocks a nimbus fit for a cosmic trickster, a forgotten god just trying to get by until the end of time. There's a lid on the coffee can The One carries. He exhibits the grin of Christ as he gestures to a park bench near the riverside. Callahan sits down. The One joins him on the bench and places his coffee can between them.

"It's time," says The One.

He removes the lid and tilts the coffee can so Callahan can get a better look; inside the can, a whirling mix of nebulous gases, stars being born, and angels orchestrating everything with diligent precision. The last of the doorways you will know by its splendor, Vollmer had told Callahan just a few hours ago.

Callahan leans over to study the can's contents, and invisible hands, gentle yet strong, pull him into the whirling mass. As Callahan swims through such vibrant creation, he understands that he's not the old Callahan anymore.

Falling.

No more memories.

Falling.

No more pain.

Something reaches up between young Callahan's legs as his hands grip handle bars. He's a boy again, eleven years old, sitting on his bicycle in front of Kim's Dry Cleaners. A large Impala idles in front of young Callahan. The driver leans across the front seat to peer out the passenger side window.

"Hey, little man," the driver calls out. "Do you know how to get to the Monticello Motor Lodge?"

The traffic light changes from red to green. Callahan the boy gets off his bike and walks it around behind the back of the Impala which blocks the crosswalk. On the other side of the Black Horse Pike the boy turns to get one last look at the man in his car; only the sun is so bright that everything blends into a vibrant bright orange haze. Car horns blare despite the summer shore traffic creeping along slower than a snail's pace.

The boy turns his back on the sun and gets on his bike. He rides up the street past a few houses until he reaches his own. Callahan's mother spots him from the backyard and waves. The boy waves back as he jumps off his bike before he comes to a full stop, a stunt that his mother warned him about time and again. He takes a step forward and his right foot connects with something on the sidewalk. It's an old coffee can. Callahan uses his left hand to make a visor over his eyes and looks back toward the Black Horse Pike. There's a man seated at the bus stop. His back faces the boy, but he can see the man's long, matted gray and black hair. A bus pulls to a stop as young Callahan looks on. The man approaches the bus door when it springs open. It may be a trick of the sunlight, but the boy swears that the old man tucks a large black wing under his raincoat.

THE ABERRANT LIVES OF DAMIAN CALLAHAN

"West Indians," Callahan's father announces from the front yard. "Goddamn Jamaicans. Bad enough we must deal with the Kims. What's this neighborhood coming to?"

Callahan's father looks agitated, but the moment his wife approaches him and touches his arm he relaxes. His father kisses her on her forehead.

The heat of the summer day bears down on the boy's back. His father opens the gate. He takes the bicycle from his son as his mother drapes one arm over her son's shoulder. Together, the Callahans ascend the porch steps and head for the front door.

Inside the house it's cool. It's just after twelve noon, according to the clock on the kitchen wall.

"Summer camp ended at eleven," says Callahan's father. "Where have you been?"

"Nowhere," the boy replies.

About The Author

Richard J. O'Brien Lives in New Jersey. He attended Rutgers University, and he holds an MFA in Creative Writing from Fairleigh Dickinson University. His novels include *The People's Republic of New Arkaim*, *Rejoice for the Dead*, *The Accidental Hero of the City of Brotherly Love*, *To Dream the Blackbane*, *Under the Bronze Moon*, and *The Garden of Fragile Things*.

Readers can follow Richard on Twitter @obrienwriter or at his website: https://obrienwriter.com.